LADY RECKLESS

NOTORIOUS LADIES OF LONDON BOOK 3

SCARLETT SCOTT

HAPPILY EVER AFTER BOOKS

Lady Reckless
Notorious Ladies of London Book 3

For Steve and our girls. I couldn't do this without you guys.

CHAPTER 1

LONDON, 1885

There remain those who question the wisdom of women being accorded Parliamentary franchise. One must wonder at the reasoning for their desire to perpetuate injustice. We must not stop until we are afforded the same privileges as men, as is only fair and right.
—*From* Lady's Suffrage Society Times

*S*he was not going to go through with it.

Huntingdon checked his pocket watch for at least the tenth time since his arrival, relief sliding through him. One quarter-hour late for the appointed assignation. Lady Helena must have seen the error of her reckless decision.

Thank merciful heavens.

His heart, which had been pounding with pained expectation ever since his arrival at the nondescript rooms where she had arranged to meet—and lose her virtue—to Lord Algernon Forsyte, eased to a normal rhythm at last. The

1

notion of the innocent sister of his best friend so sullying herself had been appalling. Horrifying, in fact. He had scarcely been able to believe it when Lord Algernon had revealed the plan to him the night before.

Over a game of cards.

The swine had been *laughing*.

And then he had dared to include Lady Helena's maiden-head in his wager. As if she were a trollop so accustomed to being ill-used that anyone's prick would do. Huntingdon had been disgusted and outraged. He had also made certain he had won the game and that Lord Algernon would never again bandy about Lady Helena's name without fear of losing his teeth.

Huntingdon's sense of honor had prevented him from going directly to Lady Helena's father. The Marquess of Northampton was an unforgiving, draconian clod, and Gabe had no doubt that the repercussions for Lady Helena would have been drastic. It had been his cursed compassion, along with his decade-long friendship with Lady Helena's brother Shelbourne, which had brought him here this morning to save her from ruin himself.

Huntingdon paced the stained carpets, trying to tamp down his impatience. He would wait for a full half hour just to make certain she had not been somehow waylaid. As distasteful as he found it to be cloistered in Lord Algernon's appallingly unkempt rooms, he had only—he checked his timepiece once more—ten minutes remaining until he could flee and forget all about this dreadful imposition upon his day.

A sudden noise drew him to a halt.

Surely it was not a knock?

He listened, and there it was again. A hesitant report. Once, twice, thrice.

His heart began to pound once more and the heavy weight of dread sank in his gut.

She had come.

He stalked to the door and hauled it open. There, on the threshold, stood a lady, her face obscured by a veil. There could be no doubt as to her identity. Huntingdon grasped her forearm and pulled her into the room before anyone happened upon them. The fewer witnesses to her folly, the better.

She gasped at the suddenness of his actions, stumbling forward and tripping over the hem of her skirts. There was nowhere for her to go but into his arms. Huntingdon was scarcely able to throw the door closed at her back before he had warm, feminine curves pressed against him.

The scent of bergamot and lemon oil, undeniably welcome in these shabby rooms badly in wont of cleaning and dusting, washed over him. Her hat fell from her head as she was jostled into him, revealing her face. He found himself looking down into the astonished emerald eyes of Lady Helena Davenport.

He had a moment to note her breasts were ample and full, crushed against his chest, and her lips were wider than he remembered. She had the most entrancing dusting of freckles on the bridge of her nose, her pale-blonde hair coming free of her coiffure in silken wisps.

She looked like a Renaissance Madonna.

But she had come to this cesspit to be thoroughly ruined.

The part of him which could never be entirely governed by reason and honor suddenly rose to rude prominence in his trousers. He was seized by a crushing urge to taste her lips. To slam his mouth on hers and give her a punishing kiss.

Would she kiss him back?

Would she be scandalized?

He inhaled sharply, shocked at himself, at the cursed

weakness he could never seem to overcome no matter how hard he tried. *This is wrong.* He exhaled. *Think of Lady Beatrice.* Inhaled again. A mistake, as it turned out. All he could smell was Helena.

She clutched at his shoulders as if he were a lifeline. "Huntingdon! What are you doing here?"

He settled her on her feet and released her, stepping back, recalling his outrage. This was his friend's sister. Shelbourne would be devastated if he knew what she was about. And as Shelbourne's friend, he was duty-bound to act as another brother to her.

"I am saving you from the greatest mistake of your life, my lady," he told her grimly, trying to forget the way her body had molded to his. "What in heaven's name were you thinking, arranging an assignation with a disgusting scoundrel like Lord Algernon Forsyte?"

"I was thinking my reputation would be destroyed," she snapped, irritation edging her voice now that she had regained her balance.

She was angry with him, he realized, astounded. She ought to have been awash in gratitude, thanking him for his generosity of spirit. Instead, her lips had thinned, and her jaw was clenched. Her brilliant green eyes glittered with irritation.

He blinked. "You *wanted* to be ruined?"

Surely he could not have heard her correctly. He had expected her to say Lord Algernon had wooed her with pretty words of love and coerced her into meeting him here. He had imagined she would tearfully thank him and then promise to never again do anything so rash and dangerous.

"Of course. Why else do you suppose I would have arranged to meet him at his private rooms?" she asked.

What the devil?

Huntingdon struggled to make sense of this bloody mire. "You do not fancy yourself in love with him, then."

"No."

"You know a man such as he will never marry you," he pressed.

"I would not marry him, either."

He frowned at her. "Then I fail to understand the meaning of this horrible folly, Lady Helena."

"The meaning is freedom." Lady Helena's chin tipped up in defiance. "Mine."

Freedom. The word was strangely alluring, the notion foreign. Huntingdon had been trapped by duty from the time he had been a lad in leading strings.

"Freedom," he repeated, as if the word tasted bitter on his tongue.

Because it did.

He had been born into an acrimonious union marked by selfishness and mutual enmity. What had once begun as a love match had deteriorated into a state of perpetual hatred and misery for everyone involved, including Huntingdon and his sister, who had paid the ultimate price for their parents' many sins. His grandfather had impressed upon him at an early age the need to uphold his honor and duty. Grandfather was gone, but the heavy weights of obligation which the former earl had set, rather like tombstones, had not left this earth with his mortal soul.

"Freedom, yes," said those full, wicked lips.

Lips he had previously had occasion to notice were quite inviting. Lips he had promptly forced himself to forget. Lady Beatrice was the bride Grandfather had settled upon, the betrothal contract struck just before his death. Huntingdon had promised he would follow through, and his strict code of honor forbade him from courting his friend's sister.

"You do not know what you are saying," he said, as much to himself as to Lady Helena.

Curse it, even the small gap between her front teeth was entrancing. Her scent curled about him like some witch's spell.

He had to force her to see reason. To send her on her way.

Only sternness would do.

Huntingdon braced himself for a battle.

* * *

Helena made a habit of offering prayers each evening before bed and every morning when she rose.

As she faced the man she had always loved—the man who would forever be lost to her—she said her prayers again.

Thank you, Lord, for sending me Hungtingdon in place of the odious Lord Algernon.

Hmm. That was rather poorly done of her, was it not? One ought not to cast aspersions upon the characters of others in prayer.

She hastily amended.

Thank you, Lord, for sending me Hungtingdon in place of Lord Algernon.

Even if his presence boded ill for her plan—which it decidedly did, since paragons did not ruin ladies for sport—she could not help but to be filled with a giddy sense of relief that Lord Algernon had failed to arrive.

And that, instead, Huntingdon was here.

Where she was meant to have been all along. Where she had planned to be. In the precise spot she had chosen—albeit in desperation—to escape the loathsome marriage her father was intent upon forcing her into. A woman without means had precious few choices, and Helena had settled upon ruination to procure her liberty since Father refused to see reason.

She could do anything, commit any sin, if only it meant she could escape a grim future as the wife of Lord Hamish White. She was running out of time. Father had informed her the betrothal's formal announcement would come within the next fortnight. Desperation edged her every action.

"You do not know what you are saying," Huntingdon was telling her, breaking through her tumultuous thoughts.

Drat him for his handsome face. For his debonair, gentlemanly air. For his dark hair and sparkling blue eyes. Drat him for refusing to see her as anything more than his friend's sister. For never showing a hint of interest in her—because surely her father would have settled upon an earl before he would have decided she must wed his political crony, Lord Hamish.

Drat him, drat him, drat him.

"I know what I am saying," she corrected the arrogant, beautiful earl who owned her heart.

And who was betrothed to the irritatingly perfect Lady Beatrice Knightbridge.

Drat Lady Beatrice, too.

"No," Huntingdon countered. "You cannot. This is madness, Lady Helena. Sheer and utter lunacy. The risks you have taken with your reputation…freedom is not what will come of such a foolish action. Of that, I can assure you."

How certain he was.

How sure he knew better than she.

Resentment stung her. "How do you suppose you know better than I do, my lord? Do you think me an imbecile?"

She loved him, but Huntingdon was *Huntingdon.* Proper and frigid and exuding an overall aura of untouchability that both attracted and repelled her. She longed to kiss his jaw

7

and muss up his hair every time she saw him. To undo his necktie and slide her hands inside his coat. To break down his icy walls.

But in this moment, Helena could not resist the urge to challenge him in a different manner. Part of her was currently rejoicing he had saved her from an untenable fate. But the other part of her railed against his highhandedness. Moreover, he had just dashed her plans.

How *dare* he?

His countenance—almost too pretty to belong to a man, it was true—reflected his shock at her outrage. "I have always prized your intellect, Lady Helena. However, there is only one deduction I can make from the lack of sound reasoning and logic you exhibit in this disastrous attempt at being the architect of your own ruin."

Huntingdon could have been an orator.

His voice was deep and smooth and melodious, rather like silk to the senses. And even his speech was impeccable, his words eloquent without being flowery, his charismatic charm ineffably persuasive. Too bad it was all wasted upon her at the moment.

"Are you being forced into an untenable marriage?" she demanded.

His lips parted. With surprise at her rancor, no doubt.

Forget about how delicious his mouth is, Helena. You will never have the opportunity to kiss it.

Much to her everlasting disappointment.

She rushed on without bothering to wait for his response. "Of course you are not. You are a *man*. How could you possibly understand what it is like to be pressured and coerced into accepting a marriage that will drain your soul? A union so despicable you would sooner give your inno-cence to the nearest available scoundrel than submit yourself to the yoke? And this, to say nothing of the laws which remain in his favor to keep me pinned beneath his hated thumb."

Although there had been laws introduced to aid the plight of women in marriage, they had not provided complete protection. In truth, there were not sufficient laws in existence to govern a marriage with Lord Hamish.

"I did not come here to argue the laws of the land," Huntingdon said, his tone taking on a curt note.

"Why did you come here then, Lord Huntingdon?" she asked him, begging the question that had been nagging at her from the moment she had crossed the threshold to find him here.

There was something undeniably agreeable about the earl's strength. He excelled at athleticism and it showed. He was an estimable rower and swimmer, with the broad shoulders and musculature of a man who did not dally on dance floors or aimlessly haunt his clubs.

Of course he was the epitome of masculinity.

The Earl of Huntingdon was *perfection*.

Full stop.

And that was the problem with him. Also, likely, the problem with Helena. She was far from perfection. Unapologetically imperfect, that was what she was. Too loud, too bold, too opinionated. Hair too light, laughter too brash, teeth unevenly spaced. Her father had hoped for a dedicated daughter who would meekly cower to his whims and accept his matrimonial guidance. But she was doing everything in her power to thwart him.

"Why did I come here?" he asked, repeating her query, a note of disbelief edging his baritone now. "By God, my lady, do you even dare to ask such a question of me? It is plain as the sun's rays that men such as Lord Algernon Forsyte are not to be trusted. The scoundrel was letting it be known to everyone within earshot what he intended to do with the incomparable Lady Helena Davenport. What else was I to do, hmm? Find my oldest friend and inform him that his lady sister was about to forfeit her innocence to a villain like Forsyte?"

Dismay washed over her.

"Lord Algernon was obviously the wrong man for the task," she said. "Next time, I will choose better."

He caught her arm again—her elbow, to be precise, his touch like a brand—and pulled her nearer. Almost imperceptibly. A gentle tug, nothing more. The Earl of Huntingdon would never deign to importune a lady. No matter how vexed he was with her.

And as she eyed his visage, Helena was willing to wager her entire dowry that Huntingdon was indeed quite vexed. Mayhap outraged would be a more effective descriptor...

"What the..." Huntingdon paused and seemed to gather himself before continuing. "No, my lady. Whatever nonsense is rotting your mind, I implore you, steer yourself in a more beneficial direction."

A more beneficial direction being marriage.

To Lord Hamish.

No cursed thank you, my lord.

She pulled her elbow from the earl's grasp. Reluctantly, of course, because she did so enjoy his touch, and she could not deny it. But he was acting the elder brother to her now. Pretending he knew better of her future than she could possibly comprehend.

As if a man such as he—an earl who had possessed endless independence from the moment of his birth—could possibly understand.

"I will steer myself in the course I choose," she informed him coolly. "In the course that is the best for me. Lord Hamish is not my future. I would sooner throw myself from a roof."

"Your melodrama is tiresome, my lady." He offered her his arm. "Come. I will see you safely escorted home."

Of all the men her stupid heart could have chosen to love. Why this one? He was maddening.

Helena ignored his arm, her frustration and desperation superseding all other feelings. "I will see myself home, Lord Huntingdon."

He frowned. "Of course you will not. Shelbourne would have my hide if I allowed anything ill to befall you."

The mention of her brother had Helena's back stiffening. It was like a dagger's sharpened edge, the reminder that Huntingdon was only here out of a misplaced sense of duty to his friend. Not because he cared about Helena. He had Lady Beatrice.

"If Shelbourne cared about me, he would stand up to my father and insist he cease pressuring me into an unwanted marriage," she countered.

Instead, her brother had attempted to dissuade Father before ultimately siding with him, telling her she must honor their father's wishes. Her objections she wanted a love match had met with disapproval. Love, he had told her cuttingly, had nothing to do with one's happiness or one's future.

"Shelbourne is right in encouraging you to do your duty," Huntingdon said then.

Duty.

A hated word, especially in connection to Lord Hamish.

But Helena was tired of arguing. Now that Huntingdon had spoiled her chances of ruination, she needed to ponder her next move.

She bent to retrieve her fallen hat, then placed it upon her head, rearranging her veil. "I have no wish to continue quarreling with you, my lord. I must go home before my absence is noted."

It was imperative that her father not discover what she

had been about. She could not take the risk he would hasten her marriage to Lord Hamish if he feared she would jeopardize the nuptials. She needed all the time she could get to arrange for a scandal.

"Lady Helena," he said, a warning in his voice.

She ignored him and swept past. "Good day, my lord."

Out the door she went.

She had arrived by hired hack, and she would leave the same way. Just let him try to stop her.

CHAPTER 2

For a woman to truly possess her freedom, she must be allowed the rights she deserves.
—*From* Lady's Suffrage Society Times

The stubborn chit refused to listen to reason.

Huntingdon had no choice but to follow her. He could not, in good conscience, allow her to disappear into some hired hack. Lord knew how she had arrived. He slammed out of Lord Algernon's dingy rooms and followed a swirl of silken skirts. Fortunately, he was long-limbed. He reached her on the street. By a stroke of fortune, she was near his own waiting carriage.

His efficient groom saw him and opened the carriage door.

Huntingdon struck with haste, sliding an arm around Lady Helena's waist and hauling her to the carriage. She put up a fight, as expected.

"What in heaven's name do you think you are doing?" she

demanded, attempting to wrest herself from his grasp to no avail. "Huntingdon, I insist you release me."

She could insist all she liked, but the cursed woman had caused him enough trouble today. He was not about to allow her to make more.

"I am seeing you home safely, my lady, and that is that," he told her calmly, even as he stuffed her and all her flounces into his carriage.

"Cease manhandling me, you ogre," she charged. "This is abduction!"

His groom's expression remained carefully blank, as if it were an everyday occurrence for Huntingdon to shove a squawking female into his personal conveyance. Thankfully, such instances were rare. This was the first time he had ever had cause to rescue Shelbourne's sister from the gaping maws of ruination.

But he had a grim feeling it would not be the last.

"Change of plans," he said calmly. "My companion will need to be discreetly delivered to Curzon Street."

Huntingdon joined his unwilling occupant, climbing into the carriage and halting her from attempting further escape by seizing her waist once more and settling her upon the leather bench. Her hat was again knocked from her head as the carriage door closed. The warmth of her curves seemed to burn his hands even through her silk, and he wished he did not take note of the charming flush staining her elegant cheekbones as a result of her exertions.

Lady Helena was beautiful and wild and everything he dared not covet. He well understood her father's desire to see her properly married.

"Cease struggling, my lady," he told her, nettled by the huskiness of his voice.

He should stop touching her. And he would, just as soon as the carriage went into motion and he could be assured she would not tear open the door and throw herself into the streets.

By God, he did not feel any boning at all. Was she not wearing a corset? If he slid his hands higher, would he be able to... *No*. He must not think that.

"You are an overbearing oaf," she accused, still sounding as outraged as a hive of bees which had just been overturned.

Her scent was invading his senses again. He breathed through his mouth to keep from inhaling bergamot and fresh lemons and *her*. "I will happily play the overbearing oaf to your shrew."

He was irritated with himself as much as with Lady Helena.

The carriage lurched into motion, and he released her as if she were made of flame, settling on the bench opposite her with a surge of relief. What the devil was coming over him? He had seen, spoken with, danced with lovely women before. Why was this troublesome one driving him to distraction?

He called Lady Beatrice's brunette beauty to mind and pinched the bridge of his nose.

"I was going to take a hack," Lady Helena huffed.

She was gorgeous in her dudgeon.

He wanted to kiss the pout from her lips. This was why he kept his polite distance from her as often as possible. Why he had never once danced with her at a ball. Why he had not touched her before today. Mayhap that was where the problem lay.

He had felt the supple softness of her breasts pressed against his chest. That ought to have been his first inclination she had not donned proper undergarments. He wondered if she was even wearing drawers beneath that gown of hers.

Self-loathing buffeted him like the gales of a storm.

"I am seeing you safely home," he snapped. "It is my—"

"If you say duty, I shall stomp on your foot," she interrupted, quite rudely.

He knew Lady Helena was a hoyden from the stories carried to him by her brother. If he had required more proof, he need look no further. She was laying all bare to him on a silver salver.

Now that was a thought, Lady Helena bare...

No, Gabe. Stop that.

"Obligation," he said simply, reminding them both of what he had been about to say. "As is extracting from you the promise that you will refrain from doing something so foolish again."

"That word is hardly any better." Her eyes were so damned verdant, burning into his, searing him. "And I will not make you any promises of that sort, Lord Huntingdon."

Stubborn creature. Never mind. He was made of sterner stuff than she.

"Yes, you will."

Up went her chin again, in that defiant slant he had come to recognize. "No, I most certainly will not. I owe you nothing."

"You owe me your gratitude for saving you from a wretched fate," he countered, frustrated with her anew. "Forsyte is a rotter. You have no notion of what awaited you in those filthy rooms."

The mere thought of her acting with such reckless disregard for her welfare infuriated him. How could she possibly believe debasing herself with a scoundrel such as Lord Algernon would be preferable to a marriage? Lord Hamish White was a rather loathsome fellow, and that could not be denied. But as Lord Hamish's wife, she would want for nothing, and she would maintain her respectability. Then again, the notion of her becoming Lord Hamish's wife also filled him with a maddening disquiet.

"I most certainly will not thank you for your unwanted meddling," Lady Helena said, as august as any princess. "Nor for your high-handed manner of forcing me into your carriage. How am I going to return home without notice when I arrive in the Earl of Huntingdon's carriage?"

"How indeed?" he challenged her. "Perhaps I will deliver you to the doorstep myself and have an audience with Lord Northampton."

The color fled her cheeks. "You would not dare to do something so cruel."

"It is the honorable thing to do," he pressed. "You cannot carry on in such a reckless fashion, Lady Helena. If I had not been there to keep you from making the greatest mistake of your life, you would be on your way to a life of penury and heartache."

That was the truth. She could not possibly expect her father to blithely accept her ruination and suddenly bend to her whims, allowing her to marry as she chose or run wild as any hellion. Society would turn its collective back upon her. No man would wed her. And Northampton…he would no doubt be enraged by her actions.

"I can and will carry on as I must," she insisted, stubborn to the last. "I refuse to marry a man who believes women should not have a voice in the governing of England. Lord Hamish thinks all women are intellectually inferior to men. Can you credit it?"

No, he could not.

But nor could he change the opinions of such a man. He did, however, have a chance at forcing Lady Helena to see reason and promise that she would never again take such drastic measures to free herself from her unwanted betrothal.

"I am not here to debate Lord Hamish's political persuasions and hopelessly wrongheaded notions," he said. "I am here to save you from destroying your reputation. Have you thought of what would happen to you if you were to be ruined? What if there had been issue from your liaison? Where would you have gone if your father had turned you out?"

Thoughts of Lisbeth, never far from his mind, returned to him and he balled his fists. He could not afford to suffer one of his attacks now. He focused instead on Lady Helena.

Her lips tightened, and a small furrow appeared in her brow, both of which suggested she had not considered the ramifications of her actions so thoroughly. "I have been reading a great deal on the subject. I am not as foolish as you believe me, my lord."

"Reading," he repeated, sure he was misunderstanding her once more. "On the subject?"

"There are journals to be had which describe the act of lovemaking in excellent detail," the minx had the daring to reply.

The word *lovemaking* uttered in her pleasant contralto had more unwanted effects upon him. His damned cock twitched to life. Why was it so bloody hot in this carriage? When the devil had she grown so bold?

"How in heaven's name did a lady find herself in possession of such filth?" he asked, outraged at his reaction.

Outraged at her, too.

She shrugged. "I found them in Shelbourne's library. So you see, Huntingdon? I did a great deal of research when I decided upon my course of action."

Research.

He swallowed against a rush of lust. Base, horrible, unbecoming lust. For his friend's innocent sister. Then again, just how innocent was she?

You have a betrothed, Gabe.

And yet, Lady Beatrice could not be further from his mind at the moment.

"Reading bawdy books is hardly sufficient preparation for destroying the rest of your life, Lady Helena." He was gratified at the sangfroid he was able to somehow muster.

One would scarcely guess his trousers were as snug as the breeches of a Georgian dandy.

He disgusted himself.

She twitched her skirts in annoyance, revealing a flash of stockinged ankle in the process. "That is where we differ, my lord. I am not seeking to destroy the rest of my life, but to save it."

That ankle of hers was not helping matters.

Gabe pinched his nose again, wondering why the hell it was taking so long to get to Curzon Street.

* * *

This was the longest carriage ride of her life.

At least, that was how it felt to Helena, who had been miserably lodged within the equipage with Huntingdon for far too long. Train journeys to the country passed with more speed than this small journey home from Lord Algernon's rooms had.

She had been miserably torn between the urge to kiss the earl senseless and throw one of her boots at him ever since he had unceremoniously shoved her inside his conveyance.

He pinched his nose and glared at her now as if he found her horridly offensive. And still, her stupid heart loved him.

Her life was a study in misery.

"I suppose we shall have to accept we are at a stalemate," he said.

Had his gaze just slipped to her lips?

She dashed the fledgling hope.

Also stupid. Infinitely more stupid than mere stupidity. Utterly ludicrous.

"Yes, I suppose we shall," she agreed, not without a touch of bitterness.

"No more of this foolishness," he commanded, as if he had a right to make demands of her. "You will cease all future attempts to debase yourself."

"You cannot dictate what I do, Huntingdon," she told him, injecting some frost into her voice.

His countenance turned grim. "Yes, I can."

Even with the mien of a man attending a funeral, he was beautiful. Why had her brother chosen to become friends with the Earl of Huntingdon during their school days? Why could he not have chosen someone who was bald-pated and overly fond of cakes?

"No," she argued, "you cannot."

Huntingdon was imperious and austere, but surely he had to realize he possessed no true sovereignty over her. He was neither her brother nor her father. And he most certainly was not her betrothed.

If he had been, she would not be doing everything in her power to flee the entanglement. Instead, she would have prepared her trousseau and requested a hasty wedding.

His nostrils flared in displeasure. It was a habit of his she had taken note of long ago. Helena studied him at dinner parties and balls and at every opportunity. For an entire season, she had hoped he would not honor his long-standing engagement with Lady Beatrice, and she had made every excuse to arrange chance encounters with him. But the earl had always been preoccupied with making his escape, and he had always paid attention to everyone but her. The most she had ever managed was a striking connection of gazes on a handful of occasions.

"If you do not promise me to put this nonsensical notion of yours to rest, I will have no choice but to approach Shelbourne and Lord Northampton with my discovery," he said. "Indeed, I would not be surprised if they had already been made aware by another. Lord Algernon was making no secret of his intentions."

His assertion gave her pause. What a henwit she was for failing to realize Lord Algernon's inability to keep from shamelessly boasting about himself every sentence would extend to mentioning her. How she would like to box his ears for the muck he had made of her excellent plans.

"You may as well resign yourself to the notion you are not my Sir Galahad," she told Huntingdon. "I will do as I wish, without your further interference."

He gritted his teeth. "You will most certainly not."

Her patience wore thin. "And how do you propose to stop me, my lord? If you go to my father and brother with tales, I will have no choice but to tell them you are the man who ruined me. That I went there expecting to meet Lord Algernon, but found you instead. I will tell them you took me in your arms and kissed me passionately, and then you raised my skirts and undid the fall of your trousers and released your…"

Here, the lewd word for his manhood she had read in one of her brother's naughty books escaped her, and she allowed her words to trail off as her mind frantically sought the correct term.

"Damn it, Helena," Huntingdon ground out. "That is the outside of enough."

She had shocked him sufficiently with her outrageous claim—all of it a bluff fashioned loosely of material from Shelbourne's wicked literature. But because the word chose that moment to worm its way back into her mind, she said it aloud.

"*Prick*," she stated, fire licking over her cheeks. Even her ears went hot, but she carried on. Because to the devil with him, that was why. "I shall swear that you took your prick and—"

"Not another bloody word!"

His infuriated growl rapped through the carriage like the report of a pistol at dawn. Helena blinked, all the filthy things she had been about to say vanishing from her mind in the face of his unmitigated fury. Well, mayhap she had gone too far. On an ordinary day, she would never dream of repeating aloud the lewdness she had only read about. But this was not an ordinary day, and each passing hour, minute, second, dragged her mercilessly closer to the day she would marry Lord Hamish and lose her freedom forever.

She had no doubt Huntingdon would think her a madcap jade after he had caught her attempting to ruin herself, and then she had done her utmost to scandalize him. But a perverse part of her rather enjoyed the expression on his countenance at the moment.

The carriage slowed at last.

"I hope I did not shock you with my candor, my lord," she said lightly, as if she were paying a social call.

When in fact she had just crudely informed him she would tell her brother and father he had taken her virtue himself. And in the most vulgar fashion she could manage.

"Where did you hear such language?" he asked.

The smile she gave him was equal parts regretful and sincere. "I read it."

She peered out the carriage window, gratified to discover they had stopped on the wrong side of the street, several houses down. Thank heavens this endless carriage ride was over at last. She scooped up her forgotten hat and arranged her veils. Rising, she opened the carriage door herself.

"Do enjoy the rest of your day, my lord." With that, she clasped her skirts in her hands and leapt to the street.

Her landing was effortless and flawless. Not even a side step. *There.* He could take all his good intentions and cast them straight to the devil where they belonged. She would not marry Lord Hamish, and she would not be diverted from the path she had chosen.

Ruination *would* be hers. And after that, liberty.

"You neglected to give me your promise, my lady," Huntingdon called after her, sounding aggrieved.

She turned back, allowing herself one last moment to drink in the sight of him. "You will not be getting a promise from me. It would only be a lie."

He pinned her with a glare.

She pretended not to care and spun away, making good on her escape.

It was only later, when she returned home, that she realized her favorite necklace—pearl strands accompanied by an emerald pendant—was missing. She must have lost it somewhere in the madness of her dash to and from Lord Algernon's rooms.

She may have lost her necklace, but she still had her ambitions of freedom. Those could not be lost or stolen. Indeed, they were all she had left.

CHAPTER 3

Our struggle, I am sad to say, is not a new one. Woman's suffrage has been brought before parliament ceaselessly since 1867. Some nearly twenty years later, we fight on.
–From Lady's Suffrage Society Times

"The female constitution is frail and delicate, prone to hysteria. Imagine the ruinous danger to our society were we to enable such wild creatures to have a vote in matters of grievous national import."

Helena looked at the polished silver knife on the table before her and envisioned curling her fingers around it, taking it from the snowy linens, and launching it directly at the pompous Lord Hamish White.

He had a face, she thought unkindly, like a dish: wide and round, with a sagging jowl. He also possessed thinning blond hair, with the shiny evidence of his greasy pate gleaming beneath the chandeliers. His nose was a pronounced beak, and when he stood, there was no denying the paunch which slumped over his trousers and swelled his waistcoat seams.

He was an altogether unattractive man.

But not one whit of his unfortunate outer appearance could hold a candle to the hideousness which spewed forth each time he opened his mouth to speak.

She looked around the table—a small gathering consisting of Mama, Father, Lord Hamish, and Lord Hamish's mother, Lady Falkland. In celebration of the looming betrothal announcement she was doing everything in her power to avoid. None of them seemed prepared to gainsay Lord Hamish's deeply insulting assertion.

"The women cannot have the vote," her father agreed. "Men are, by our nature, stronger and rational and far more intelligent than the fairer sex. It cannot be disputed. A woman's place is at her husband's side, and she must look to him for guidance, trusting he will make the right governing decisions on her behalf when she cannot."

Helena ground her jaw. She was more than familiar with her father's views of her sex. He believed they were intellectually inferior to men. If he had an inkling she spent her time at the Lady's Suffrage Society instead of paying social calls as she claimed—thank heavens for a lady's maid she could trust —he would have an apoplectic fit.

And Mama—well, Mama was quiet. Marriage to Father had crushed her spirit, and now Father had found a man fashioned in his mold to be Helena's own husband.

"Precisely," said Lord Hamish, a small morsel of his dinner flying from his mouth as he spoke. "Suffrage would be too great a burden for ladies to bear. They must turn instead to the far more rewarding sphere of home and hearth. Tending to one's husband and children, that is the true meaning of a lady."

Mayhap she could launch a boat of béchamel sauce in his direction.

Plant poison in his fish course?

Was it too much to hope Mama would at least be the voice of reason? She cast a glare in her mother's direction, but she was too busy sipping her wine to take note.

"It would be perilous indeed should such a travesty ever be enacted," Father said. "Our government would weaken and decline, as a matter of course. I cannot countenance the lords who are vouching for this utter tripe. Coerced by their wives, I have no doubt."

Helena fumed some more, stabbing at the contents of her plate with more force than necessary.

All the eyes around the table settled upon her.

She could hold her tongue no longer. "Has it not occurred to any of you that the government would instead strengthen if all voices were to possess an equal share in the decisions which affect our lives?"

Lord Hamish's lip curled. "Sentiments such as those are unbecoming in a lady, my dear."

A peal of laughter rose in her throat. Bitter laughter. Irate laughter. She released it. Her hands trembled with the violence of her reaction. "Of course you would hold such a position in the matter, my lord. You, like all other men, are well pleased to keep women silenced. To decide laws that affect us deeply, without consulting us, without allowing us to offer our opinions, to cast our votes accordingly. Why should a woman be deprived of her own sovereignty merely by the circumstance of her birth?"

Lady Falkland's shocked gasp echoed in the sudden silence of the dining room.

Her mother frowned at her. Her father was scowling. Later, she would suffer his wrath, she had no doubt.

"While your passion for your subject is commendable, I

am afraid you are all wrong, my dear," said Lord Hamish in the same tone she imagined he might reserve for small children.

It was dismissive and insulting, much like the man himself.

Once again, she could not keep herself from responding. "It is you who is wrong, my lord. Your view of women is inherently flawed. What logic have you to support the supposition that a woman is frail and delicate and incapable of deciding matters of import?"

"Lady Helena, that is enough," Father intervened, his voice dripping in disapproval. "You are consorting with the wrong set if this is the sort of nonsense filling your head. Apologize to Lord Hamish at once."

Apologize to him?

Helena would sooner toss the remnants of her wine in his supercilious face.

She lifted her chin. "I will not apologize for my opinion. Neither for the possession of it nor the expression."

The fish course arrived, shattering the charge of the moment. Grilled salmon with accompanying boats of *sauce verte froide*. Helena bit her lip to keep from speaking further and could not help but to feel as if the fates were encouraging her to have her revenge upon the odious Lord Hamish. Here was a sauce boat and the fish course. She could brain him first and lace his salmon with poison second.

"I heard the most intriguing *on dit* about those dreadful American catfish being introduced to our English waters," said her mother, in an obviously desperate bid at changing the subject and avoiding further embarrassment at her outspoken daughter.

"Horrible shame that would be," Lord Hamish chimed in, happily taking up new cudgels. "I read in *The Times* that they are inedible. Possessed of mighty, fearsome teeth, and they feed on offal. Despicable things, really."

Oh, the irony. Mayhap Lord Hamish recognized his own kind.

Helena forked up a bit of her fish and plotted her next move.

* * *

In the heart of the Duke and Duchess of Bainbridge's ballroom, Huntingdon twirled with Lady Beatrice in a quadrille, his least favorite form of dance. Not that he enjoyed any dancing. It was an art that was lost on him. Overhead, hundreds of electric lamps blazed. He ought to be taking note of the sparkle in her blue eyes. Of the way her mahogany locks gleamed beneath the glow of the chandeliers. Of the pale beauty she made in her pink silken ballgown, demure and perfect. He should be admiring her elegance and grace, both of which could not be denied.

He ought not to be thinking of the last time his hands had been upon a lady's waist.

Ought not to be thinking of golden curls, emerald eyes, and a saucy mouth.

Ought not to be thinking about how much he preferred Lady Helena's scent to Lady Beatrice's strikingly floral perfume.

Or the way Lady Helena's breasts had felt, pressed against his chest.

Duty, Gabe. If you do not have your honor, you have nothing, as Grandfather always said.

But still, she was like an infection in his blood. In the

week since he had last seen her, all defiant beauty on the pavements, he had been able to think of little else.

"Do you not find it so, my lord?" Lady Beatrice asked as they whirled and performed the proper steps.

Damnation, he had not heard the beginning of her query, so lost had he been in his own thoughts.

"Forgive me, Lady Beatrice," he said ruefully. "I fear I was distracted."

"I was merely observing the ball is a crush," she said, and if his distraction perturbed her, there was no hint of it in her countenance. "And that the air is quite stifling. After this dance, I do believe I shall need some punch to refresh myself."

The ball was indeed an undisputed success. Not that he cared for the social whirl. He preferred to occupy himself with more worthy matters which affected his lands and his people. He took his responsibility as the Earl of Huntingdon seriously. He had every intention of doing his grandfather proud.

"It is warm," he agreed, inwardly taking himself to task once more for his failure to pay proper attention to his betrothed. "Would you care for a turn on the terrace?"

They spun about once more. The notion of escorting her to a darkened corner filled him with apathy. Theirs would be a passionless, loveless union based on mutual respect, nothing like his parents' disastrous marriage.

"I do not think we should dare," Lady Beatrice said, ever the height of propriety.

Although there would be nothing amiss with him escorting her for some fresh air, particularly since they were engaged, he was not surprised at her objection. Instead, he was relieved. There was only one lady he wanted to kiss beneath the moonlight, and it was not the woman in his arms.

He cleared his throat. "Very prudent of you, my dear. This close to our nuptials, there is hardly reason to court scandal, is there?"

Three months.

Three months until she was his bride. Grandfather would have been pleased that a date had at last been settled upon. Although Huntingdon had long had an understanding with Lady Beatrice, they had not made their betrothal formal until recently. In the wake of his grandfather's death, sorting out estate matters, along with the suitable period of mourning, a wedding had hardly been a concern for Huntingdon.

The dance finished. He bowed. Lady Beatrice dipped into a perfectly executed curtsy.

"Thank you for the dance, my lord," she said softly.

She was so soft-spoken he almost could not hear her over the chattering of their fellow revelers and the subsequent orchestral hum of a waltz as it struck up. He offered her his arm and escorted her back to her waiting mother.

Another interminable round of conversation, and his duty was done.

A turn on the terrace alone, a bit of fresh air, would be just the thing.

Huntingdon excused himself from his future countess and mother-in-law and made his way to the opened doors leading to the night. And that was when his eye was inevitably caught by a flash of golden hair.

He knew instinctively, though her back was to him, that it was *her*.

She was in attendance, but the crush was so immense, he had yet to cross paths with her since she had been announced. But there was no mistaking the silhouette—tall, statuesque, curved. Or the way she carried herself. She moved with a natural confidence that most ladies could never affect, let alone possess. Her gown also gave her away

—ivory trimmed with yellow flowers, matching yellow flowers in her hair. Daffodil was a color Helena favored.

But before he could reach her, she was moving. Escaping through the same doors he had intended to flee to himself. Except, she was not alone. Lord Dessington was accompanying her. She was smiling at him. Laughing at a quip he made. Clinging to his arm.

Everyone knew Dessington was a rakehell of the worst order. Huntingdon had to wonder how the scoundrel had even managed to obtain an invitation. Realization hit him.

No.

Surely Helena was not going to use Dessington to ruin herself.

Bloody hell.

His strides lengthened. Huntingdon bustled into a frowning dowager in his attempt to reach the couple before they disappeared into the darkness. He mumbled an apology and carried on. She had warned him she would not stop with her nonsensical plans.

He ought to have spoken with Shelbourne. Taken him aside, as a friend, and explained the looming disaster. What had stopped him? His disgust at his own reaction to her?

It little mattered, for now, Helena was about to ruin herself with Dessington. Yet another scoundrel who did not deserve to touch even the dirt on her slipper.

And Huntingdon was honor bound to stop her.

By the time he descended from the terrace and reached the gardens, Helena and Dessington had disappeared down one of the darkened gravel paths. He heard the crunch of footfalls and a rustle of silk, and his gut clenched. If only Shelbourne were here this evening, looking after his sister instead of drinking himself to oblivion. Something had long been eating at his old friend and Huntingdon could not fathom what.

But that was neither here nor there. In his friend's absence, Huntingdon would act the part of protector.

Except you do not want to protect her. You want to ruin her yourself.

He banished the taunting voice. Because it was right. But he had honor, damn it, and a duty to uphold. He would not dare to dishonor Lady Beatrice in such a careless fashion. Nor could he bear to lose Shelbourne as his friend.

He possessed icy restraint. Which was more than could be said for Dessington, who was already holding Helena in his arms when Huntingdon rounded a set of hedges and came upon his quarry at last. The sight of another man holding her, about to kiss her, filled him with so much fury, he acted without thought.

On a low growl, he seized Dessington and hauled him across the gravel. Perhaps with more force than necessary. The viscount was taken by surprise and tripped on his own feet, landing on his arse.

Helena let out a shocked gasp. "Huntingdon! What do you think you are doing?"

"Keeping you from folly," he said grimly.

"Devil take you, Huntingdon, I was only having a spot of fun," complained Dessington as he rose from the gravel and dusted himself off. "I ought to plant you a facer for that."

"I ought to plant *you* a facer," he countered, his fists balled at his sides. He was tempted. So tempted. "Keep your distance from Lady Helena."

"What do you care whom I kiss in the gardens, old chap?" Dessington asked, sounding smug.

Curse the rotter. How dare he taste those lips when Huntingdon had not?

The ability to control himself fled entirely. One moment he was standing there on the gravel walk as calmly as any gentleman taking the air. The next, his fist was connecting with Dessington's jaw.

There was a satisfying snap of the man's head.

And another outraged sound from Helena. "Huntingdon, are you mad?"

Dessington rubbed his jaw. "If you want her for yourself, you need only have said. I do not fight over petticoats. They aren't worth it."

And then the blighter promptly took himself off, hastening back to the ballroom like the scurrying rat he was. His words echoed in a whole new taunt after he had gone. *If you want her for yourself...*

Huntingdon shook his hand. His knuckles throbbed from the connection with Dessington's jaw. He had not punched anyone since his school days.

"What in heaven's name is wrong with you?" Helena demanded, simultaneously *sotto voce* and furious.

He was asking himself the same question, and there was only one reasonable answer he could settle upon. *She* was what was wrong with him.

"I am the one who ought to be posing that question, madam," he said sternly. "You are once more acting rashly. A rotter like Dessington? He has bedded half London for sport. If anyone would have come upon you in his embrace—"

"I would have been ruined, yes," she hissed, interrupting him again. "That was what I was aiming for, until some fool arrived before I could even manage so much as a kiss."

Relief he had no right to feel washed over him.

She had not kissed Dessington, then.

Thank God.

He dashed the thoughts. "You leave me with no choice but to inform your father and brother of your attempts at sabotaging not only your betrothal, but your reputation and good name as well. You cannot believe Shelbourne or

Northampton would be pleased to discover you have been cavorting in moonlit gardens with conscienceless rakehells."

In the silver light of the moon he could see all too well those lush lips of hers forming a pout. "I have only managed to do so just this once, and you quite spoiled it, my lord."

"You are welcome," he growled, reaching for her. "Now come back to the ball."

But Helena eluded his grasp, dancing backward, deeper into the garden path. "I will return to the ballroom when I am good and ready, and not a moment sooner."

Damn the minx, he had no doubt if he left her here to her own devices, she would simply find the next ne'er-do-well mingling in the moonlight and ask him to kiss her instead. Huntingdon had two choices: he could abandon her and return to the ball himself, or he could follow her, potentially opening the door for his own scandal.

The crunch of gravel mocked him. As did her golden hair, disappearing around a wall of boxwoods. His legs were moving once more, because now that he thought upon it, he had no choice at all, had he?

"Helena," he called, careful to keep his voice low. "You are gambling with your reputation each second you remain out here."

In her heavy skirts, weighed down by the pronounced tournure that gave them their lush fullness, she was no match for him. He caught her in a trice, taking her elbow and spinning her to face him.

"Curse you, Helena," he said, and then lost his ability for further speech.

The ethereal light of the night bathed her lovely face. Her bosom, pale and full, was a temptation he had not previously noted in the haste of his altercation with Dessington and her subsequent retreat.

"You are remarkably obtuse for a man who is otherwise possessed of an estimable intellect," she snapped.

Her ire ought to have ruined the effect, but he still felt as if he were a drunkard with his favorite vice laid before him. He wanted to consume her. Drown in her. He wanted to do all the things he had never dared to do.

With her.

Only her.

Why did he have to be afflicted thus, with a weakness for a woman he could never have? Even if his honor did not demand he keep a respectable distance from his friend's sister, he had promised Grandfather he would marry Lady Beatrice, a woman who could not be more opposite to the fiery, scandal-courting siren facing him now. Lady Beatrice would make him an ideal countess, and their marriage would be perfectly polite, bereft of ruinous passion or emotion. It was what was best for him.

"What you are doing is wrong," he said, hating the huskiness in his voice. Despising himself for the snugness of his trousers. A gentle breeze blew, bringing with it the scent of bergamot and citrus. He forced himself to continue. "You will only hurt yourself and your family if you carry on in this vein."

"Why should you care?" she asked.

Excellent question.

He was beginning to wonder the same.

He clenched his jaw. "Because I am an honorable man. Because I am friends with Shelbourne, and I owe it to him to look after you as I would my own sister."

She tugged at her elbow, but he held firm. "I am not your sister, Huntingdon."

No one knew that better than he did.

A certain portion of his anatomy was painfully, rigidly familiar with that fact.

"Nonetheless, I consider you my sister in name, if not in truth," he insisted, which was a loathsome lie. There was nothing brotherly about the way he felt whenever he was within Lady Helena Davenport's presence.

And that was why he had always done his utmost to avoid her.

Why he ought to be avoiding her now.

If only she would see reason.

"Would that you *did* have a sister so you could go chasing her about in gardens," Helena said.

And just like that, her words brought all the hated past rushing back to him. Lisbeth's face, contorted in death. For a moment, he could not breathe. When he finally did, his lungs burned with the effort, as if he were beneath water. The crushing weight that had never been far from his chest in the early days of what had befallen her returned.

Panic assailed him. He could do nothing but double over, drawing the thick night air into his lungs with painstaking precision.

He must have released his hold on Helena, but she had not fled. Gradually, he became aware of a slow, steady caress on his back. Of a sweet voice, melodious, piercing him through the fogs of agony.

"I am so sorry, Huntingdon. I was not thinking when I spoke," Helena was saying. "Please forgive me. I was angry with you and said something I should not have."

The weight receded. He could breathe again. The anxiety lessened, bit by bit. These attacks were reminders of why he was a man of duty and honor. He must never forget.

His heart yet thumped in rapid beats, but he felt more himself. Was it wrong that he remained as he was for a moment longer than necessary, absorbing those tender caresses he had no business receiving?

Yes, it was.

And yet, Helena was touching him. Soothing him. He liked her hand upon him far too much. It made him feel as if she cared. For a fleeting heartbeat of a second, he could almost pretend she did.

But that was a greater foolishness than her campaign of ruination. Futile, too.

He straightened, gathering himself, chasing the old fears and pain, the anxiety. "You are forgiven, my lady. But if you truly wish to make amends, you will return to the ballroom and cease this recklessness."

His hopes that she would put some much-needed distance between them were dashed when she remained where she was, perilously near, and her chin went up in that familiar show of rebelliousness. "My actions have nothing to do with you. I absolve you of any misplaced responsibility troubling you. Go back to the ballroom and your betrothed."

Curse his undeserving hide, he had forgotten all about Lady Beatrice. His thoughts, much to his shame, had been completely owned by Helena for the last few minutes. But still, he could not go. Would not leave her in the gardens, alone and determined to ruin herself with whomever she could.

"I will escort you to the edges of the garden," he countered, "and watch from the shadows as you re-enter the ballroom."

She sighed. "You are a ridiculous man."

"On the contrary. I am a logical one." For reasons he refused to contemplate, he knew he would remain here in the gardens with her, guarding her like a dog. "I will not be dissuaded from my course."

"And nor will I."

They faced each other as he imagined duelers of old would have, waiting and watching the first to make a move.

"Stalemate once more, it seems," he observed.

"I will stay here all evening if I must," she replied.

They stared each other down some more. When stubborn met determined, what could be done, really? Until, at last, Mother Nature intervened in the form of a drop falling from the sky. First one, then another. A breeze kicked up the fauna in the garden, making branches rustle as clouds passed over the moon.

The scent of rain was suddenly in the air, mingling with lemon and bergamot.

"It would seem the fates have a different idea," he said wryly. "If we do not return to the ballroom, I dare say we will be caught in a deluge."

More rain fell, deciding their course for them.

"Oh, very well." Helena gathered up her voluminous skirts. "I shall return first and you may follow. But do not suppose for a moment this means you have won, Huntingdon."

He watched her flounce past him down the darkened path. There was no winning in this particular battle.

CHAPTER 4

We cannot stop fighting to right the injustices perpetrated upon our sex. The denial of equal representation in the matters which affect our daily lives must come to an end, one way or another. Let us hope it is with reason and sound intellect prevailing.
—*From* Lady's Suffrage Society Times

*H*elena had been thwarted by Huntingdon on two occasions.

But today was a new day, and her plan was a new plan, and the ball being held by Lord and Lady Cholmondeley presented the perfect opportunity for her third attempt at courting scandal. The Marquess of Dorset had already agreed to slip away from the fête and meet her in the library at the appointed hour.

The hour was now.

Helena was early because balls were dreadfully boring affairs, and she could not be bothered to feign her enjoyment when Lord Hamish was in attendance as well. Which he was. Already, she had suffered a Viennese waltz with him. He had stepped on her hem thrice. And his breath had smelled of fish and whisky. His hand had been far too familiar with her person. The entire affair had left her feeling as if she ought to take a good, comforting soak in the nearest bath.

But instead she was here, in the cavernous library, which had been lit so lowly with a lone gas lamp that the shadows on the walls resembled monsters. The chamber smelled of old leather, mildew, and tobacco. Hardly an auspicious setting, but Helena told herself she did not care.

Dorset was a legendary seducer. He was handsome, as was to be expected for a man of his reputation. Dark haired, much like Huntingdon. Broad of shoulders, lean of hip, long-limbed and tall, with a commanding presence and dark eyes which seemed to be shadowed with sadness. Common fame had it that his heart had been broken by Lady Anna Harcastle, who had gone on to become Marchioness of Huntly.

He was debonair. He was broken. He had danced with her and flirted shamelessly. When she had coyly suggested a meeting, he had not hesitated to accept.

In short, she was certain she had found the man who would be her savior. A few well-placed whispers of gossip, and she was equally sure Lady Clementine Hammond—who had never made any secret of her disdain for Helena, nor shied at the opportunity to bring her low—would be entering the library within the next half hour.

The timing was impeccable and essential. Helena had realized, partly because of the Earl of Huntingdon's cool reprimands, and partly because of her own conscience, that she could not bear to endure a true deflowering. Kisses, embraces, mayhap a raised hem—she would suffer it in the name of her freedom from Lord Hamish. But this evening's scandal had been planned, down to the minute. No more than one quarter-hour alone with Dorset before Lady Clementine appeared.

Lady Clementine would be shocked. And secretly pleased. And she would carry her tale to every available ear in London. Helena would feign horror and rebuff any obligatory offers of marriage the marquess might offer. She had it all planned, down to what she would say, down to her affectation of surprise.

Yes, this time, victory—and ultimately, freedom—would be hers.

No one, not even the Earl of Huntingdon, could stop her.

The door to the library opened.

She spun about, and her heart sank.

There, crossing the threshold and closing the portal at his back, was none other than the one man who had been plaguing her for the last fortnight. The man she loved.

If only she could stop loving him.

And if only he would cease his relentless determination to thwart her plotting at every turn.

"Huntingdon!" she said his name as if it were a curse, and indeed, in this instance, it was. "Why are you here?"

He strode toward her. She told herself to ignore the effect he had on her in his evening wear. To ignore his neck cloth, waistcoat, and trousers cut to perfection, the way he made her breath catch. And above all, to ignore his face, so beautiful her heart ached at the mere sight of him, even as fury at his high-handedness rattled through her.

"Need I answer that question?" he asked, as effortlessly as if they discussed something of scant import.

The weather, for instance.

Or the Serpentine.

The rising and falling tides.

The number of guests in attendance. Another crush—surely two hundred. She had sworn he was not a guest this evening. How was he here? Oh, it hardly mattered, did it? For he was before her, tall, handsome...

Infuriating.

"Yes," she gritted. "You do need to answer that question, my lord."

"Saving you," he said solemnly. "That is why I am here."

Helena twitched her skirts in agitation, then stalked several paces away to put some distance between them once more. "I do not require saving!"

And if she did need saving, it was decidedly not of the form he was offering. She had yet to forgive him for the humiliation of their last encounter, during which he had informed her he viewed her as a sister.

A. Sister.

She still longed to rail at him for such a stinging insult, and likely she would have done at the time had not she made the error of mentioning his dead sister. She could kick herself for her thoughtless words; seeing the way he had reacted still haunted her.

Still, she could not help wondering. How could he feel nothing for her when she felt *everything* for him? Helena vowed she would never understand it.

Silly, ignominious heart.

"I would suggest that your presence in this library conveys the direct opposite of what you are saying," he said smoothly.

Her heart thudded, and that same liquid heat that pooled in her belly whenever he was near returned. If only she could control herself. If only she could stop loving him. If only she could keep from longing to throw herself into his arms and banish that frown with her lips.

What would kissing him be like?

She would never know. Because he was betrothed to

42

another and he thought of her as a sister who required him to storm to the rescue like a gallant knight of old.

"Dorset is joining me here at any moment," she informed him, bumping into a wall of books at her back in an effort to keep him as far away from her as possible.

There was nowhere else to escape to.

Huntingdon reached her, those impossibly blue eyes sparkling with an emotion she could not read. "Dorset is not coming."

Not again.

Oh, drat him. Drat him for his meddling. Drat him for crowding her, for trapping her between the bookshelves and his powerful body. Drat him for his scent, taunting her now, musky and delicious.

"How do you presume to know what Dorset is doing and what he is not doing?" she asked, though she was afraid she already knew the answer.

Huntingdon smiled grimly. "We had a discussion, he and I. I persuaded him it would not be in his favor to dally with you."

Would he never cease plaguing her?

Frustration and irritation blossomed, making her bold. She settled her hands on his chest and shoved. "Your concern is misplaced, Huntingdon. Direct it toward your betrothed and leave me to do as I wish."

Touching him was a mistake.

Because she liked it far too much. The texture of his coat was smooth seduction. Heat radiated from him, seeping into her palms, making her weak. Making her want him. Her gaze dipped to his lips. One kiss. She had been doing everything in her power to ruin herself, and all she wanted was this man. His mouth on hers.

"My sense of honor forbids me from leaving you to your

own wayward actions," he growled, flattening his palms on the bookshelf at either side of her head, trapping her there.

A fruitless action. At the moment, she had no desire to go anywhere, though she knew all too well she should.

"I do not need your sense of honor," she protested, despising herself for the breathlessness in her tone. For her inability to guard her heart against him. For the longing that washed over her, when she knew he could not ever be hers.

"On the contrary, my dear." His voice was forbidding. "You very much do. If it were not for me, you should be on the cusp of making the greatest mistake of your life. You will thank me later. The Marquess of Dorset is not worthy of touching your hems."

Was it her imagination, or had Huntingdon's head lowered?

Of course it was her imagination. He thought of her as a sister.

"Whether or not Dorset touches my hems is for me to decide. Not you." But as she issued her stern warning, her hands moved, sliding up his broad, firm chest. Settling upon his shoulders.

"This was your final chance, Helena. I have no choice but to go to Shelbourne now."

* * *

Gabe stared down at Helena's upturned face. She was a tall woman, but his uncommon height meant she was the perfect fit for him. All he needed to do was lower his head, and her lips could be his.

But that would be wrong, he reminded himself.

So very wrong.

"You are bluffing," the spirited minx told him. "If you were going to go to Shelbourne, you would have already done so by now."

She was right, damn her. He did not want to go to her brother with this. And if he bothered to examine the reason why, he would have to admit it was because he enjoyed chasing after her. Watching over her gave him an excuse to be in her presence. To be near. So near, her massive skirts billowed into his trousers. So near, he could ravish her pouting mouth to his content.

"I was hoping you would see reason." His gaze strayed to those pink, lush lips, and he swallowed against a staggering rush of need he had no right to feel. "But you have proven again and again that you are incapable of knowing what is best for you."

That much was the truth. It aggrieved him to no end, thinking of the rogues and scoundrels she would have given herself to, without thought, all in a desperate—and foolish—bid to escape marriage. First Lord Algernon. Then Dessington. Now Dorset. None of them deserved her.

"How like Lord Hamish you are," she said, dragging him from his thoughts. "Believing you know better what I need than I do. You may think I am acting recklessly, but I can assure you that I have weighed my options with care. I am running out of time to save myself. Now kindly go away so I can carry on with what I set about doing."

She thought him comparable to an arse like Lord Hamish White? That rather nettled. Huntingdon knew he should back away from her. That he should put some necessary space between them. But the light touch of her hands on his shoulders was filling his head with fire.

"I understand that you think ruining yourself is the only means of avoiding your match with Lord Hamish," he allowed. "But you must see there are other ways, better ways. Have you spoken with your father about your wishes?"

Her golden eyebrows raised. "You must think me an imbecile. Of course I have spoken with my father. He does not take my concerns seriously. I have also spoken at length with my mother and my brother. No one seems inclined to aid me. Do you suppose I would throw myself into the arms of any man I could find as a first choice?"

Her question stung, and only partially because she was right—he had underestimated her. But also because the thought of her in any other man's arms made him want to tear all the books in the room from their shelves.

"You ought not to be throwing yourself into anyone's arms, damn you," he ground out, itching to touch her. One pass of his fingers over her silken jaw. That was all.

Damn it, Gabe. Stop this madness. Step away.

And yet he could not leave.

"Says the man who considers me a sister," she snapped, an edge to her voice he could not mistake. "Just because you see me as a burden rather than a woman does not mean I am yours to command."

No, she could never be his.

She was forbidden.

But that did not stop him from lowering his head, falling into her emerald eyes. "I do not think you a burden."

He thought her the loveliest, most tempting woman he had ever known. He also wished, briefly, that he was a scruples-lacking scoundrel like Dorset.

"Of course you do." Her chin quivered. "Please, Huntingdon. Leave me alone. Stop following me. Stuff your sense of honor and duty."

Her eyes glistened. Tears, he realized, and the sight of them did something to him. His restraint snapped. He touched her at last, brushing the backs of his fingers over her cheek in a tender stroke. A mistake, as it happened. Her skin was a revelation. She was a mystery and a temptation, everything he wanted and yet could never dare to have, knowing where it would eventually lead.

"Do not weep, Helena," he said, his voice a low rasp.

Her eyelashes fluttered, and a tiny bead of moisture clung to them. He had upset her, and he hated it. Hated it more than what she was doing to herself.

"Go," she told him, but as she voiced the directive, her fingers curled in his coat. "Let me do what I must to save myself."

He told himself he should stop touching her. But a tear tracked down her cheek, and he caught it on his thumb. He told himself to step away, but his head lowered. Her mouth was close to his. So close, her breath feathered over his lips. So close, he could not resist settling his mouth over hers.

He was aware of a gasp. Perhaps hers, mayhap his. He did not know. Because in the next moment, her soft lips moved, clinging to his. The fire in his head roared through his blood, overtaking him.

The gentleness in his kiss fled. He kissed her harder, with all the pent-up desperation he had spent the last few years tamping down and ignoring. Kissed her as he had longed to.

Kissed her as if she were his.

Wanted her to be his.

And when her mouth responded, he could not help but to feel she *was* his. That this moment, this woman in his arms, was meant to be. He teased her parted lips with his tongue. She tasted sweet and tart, like champagne. Huntingdon could not seem to have enough of her now.

One word rushed through his mind, repeating itself to the pounding beat of his heart. *More. More. More.*

He cupped her face, angled her head to allow him to ravish her mouth properly, as he wanted. Her tongue moved against his, tentatively at first. She kissed like an innocent and not like a wanton who had been throwing herself into the arms of scoundrels.

Gabe groaned as he sucked on her lower lip before catching it between his teeth and tugging. Her fingers sank into his hair, raking over his scalp and leaving sparks in their wake. Flames licked down his spine. Spread over his skin. He was ablaze for her.

He kissed her as if she were his life source, as if he would never again have the opportunity to know her mouth beneath his.

Because he could not.

This is wrong, Gabe. Think of your duty, your honor. Stop this madness at once, before it is too late.

There was the voice of reason which had been eluding him, arriving far too late to keep him from madness. He raised his head against his will, ending the connection, staring down at her flushed cheeks, her kiss-bruised mouth. Her eyes were wide, fringed with tear-stained lashes. Glazed with passion.

Scalding shame hit him, joining the perilous heat of his ardor. What had he done?

A second word hammered its way through his thick skull then.

"Huntingdon." Helena blinked, as if she were dazed, her hands returning to his chest and pushing.

Her tongue ran over her lower lip, almost earning another groan from him. He was harder than he had ever been, rigid and ready in his trousers.

What had he been thinking? That he would take her against the wall of books?

Dear God, he hated himself. He had not thought of Lady Beatrice or the consequences of his actions once. Not until now. Not until he had already gone too far. Grandfather was surely rolling in his grave. Mayhap he was no better than his mother and father had been. Cut from the same disastrous, selfish, sinful cloth.

"Huntingdon, you must go," Helena was saying, dragging him from the depths of self-loathing.

Shaking him from his thoughts.

What had he done?

"Forgive me," he said stiffly, before realizing he was still cupping her face.

Instantly, he released her, stepping back in retreat.

"We have not much time." Helena smoothed the fall of her skirts and raised a hand to her hair, tucking an errant tendril back into place. "Lady Clementine Hammond is expected within minutes."

All the fire in his blood turned to ice. "Lady Clementine Hammond?"

Though he need not ask. He knew well enough who and what she was. A notorious gossip with a reputation as a lady who had forced more than her fair share of marriages after catching couples in alcove embraces and moonlit kisses.

Helena nodded. "She was to have happened upon Dorset and myself... Oh, dash it all. We haven't time to tarry, Huntingdon. You must go, now, or risk being caught in a compromising position with me. What will Lady Beatrice think?"

Likely what he thought of himself. That he was an abysmal rogue.

Still, whilst he knew he needed to put as much distance between himself and temptation as possible, he felt the need to explain himself. Not that he could.

"I will go, then. But first, I must apologize for acting in such a dishonorable fashion." He paused, attempting to gather a proper excuse when there was none to be had, save that she hopelessly enthralled him although she was the last woman who should. "I cannot think what came over me. You are like a sister to me, and I was so overcome by my need to comfort you that I acted irrationally. I should never have been so familiar, and I can promise you, such a loathsome, unworthy action will not occur ever again betwixt the two of us."

He heard himself and inwardly winced at how bloodless he sounded. How cruel and cutting. It was a brutal lie to suggest he had kissed her for any reason other than that he had wanted to feel her lips beneath his more than he had wanted his next breath. But he could never admit as much to her.

Hell, he could not admit it to himself.

The truth was terrifying, and better left buried. But as he railed against himself for what he had done, for giving in to this desperate, terrible weakness he possessed for her, he noticed she had gone pale, all the color leaching from her expressive face.

"You are forgiven, of course, Lord Huntingdon," she said coolly. "Naturally, I would never expect such a *loathsome*, *unworthy* moment to happen again. And mayhap I, too, should ask for your forgiveness. I never meant to force my attentions upon you, and I assure you it is not my intention to entrap you into scandal. Which is why it is imperative that you go before Lady Clementine arrives."

Damn it, he had mucked that up, had he not? He had somehow managed to act the cad and then insult Helena as well in his attempt to make amends for his lack of control. Gabe would go, because what other choice had he?

He bowed, feeling like the world's greatest ass. "I shall take my leave."

With that, he hastened from the library, hating himself more than he ever had before.

CHAPTER 5

One need only look to the territory of Wyoming, where women have enjoyed the right to vote since 1869, for an example of how women's suffrage benefits the community.
—From Lady's Suffrage Society Times

Helena's closest, dearest, oldest friend, Lady Juliana Somerset, had finally returned from abroad. The much-awaited reunion had thrilled her when she had first received word of Julianna's arrival in London. She had thrown every other social obligation out the window for the opportunity to see her friend once more.

Now that the day had arrived, she should have been overjoyed. Instead, Helena was fraught with agitation as she awaited Julianna for afternoon tea.

All because Huntingdon had *kissed* her.

Because his lips had been hot and firm and insistent upon hers.

Because his tongue had been inside her mouth.

The moment in the library had been electric, and she had relived it at least a thousand times—possibly more—in the hours since.

But then, he had promptly taken the best moment of her life and ground it beneath his heel by calling their kisses *loathsome* and *unworthy* and by claiming he only viewed her as a sister.

Yet again.

A lady could only sustain so many blows to her hope and pride.

She paced the length of the salon, consulting the ormolu mantelpiece with each pass. Julianna was not due to arrive for another ten minutes. With a sigh, she turned back toward the open door. A shadow in the shape of her brother passed.

"Shelbourne!" she called, eager for distraction. And the opportunity to sway her brother in her favor.

Thus far, he had remained immovable as a stone, insisting she should accept a marriage of convenience and that love matches were the stuff of fiction and fantasy.

The shadow retraced its steps and paused on the threshold.

Her brother's appearance shocked her. He had the Davenport height and their father's dark hair, coupled with an aura of perpetual brooding. But this afternoon, he was still dressed in his rumpled evening wear—presumably from the day before, with purple crescents bruising the skin beneath his green eyes. His countenance was pale as well.

She wondered if he had slept.

For the past two years, her brother had become increasingly reckless. She could not understand the change, which had been sudden rather than gradual.

He bowed. "Hellie. You are looking well this morning."

She dipped into a brief curtsy, mimicking his formality,

so at odds with his pet name for her. "It is afternoon, Shelbourne."

His brow furrowed. "Ahem, yes. So it is. Forgive me for misspeaking. Shall I join you for tea, then?"

"You may," she said, "if you wish to listen to feminine chatter."

He grimaced. "One of your Suffrage Society ladies joining you, then? I do believe I shall pass. I support your cause, but I am hardly in the mood for entertaining just now."

Shelbourne, for all that he was in their father's uncompromising mold, was also beloved to her. She confided in him. Not everything, of course. Certainly not her inconvenient and unrequited love for his friend the Earl of Huntingdon, for instance. It was one of the reasons his refusal to take her side in the matter of her betrothal to Lord Hamish was such a betrayal.

"Not a member of the Lady's Suffrage Society yet, as it happens," she answered him lightly, doing her utmost to cast all thoughts of Huntingdon—and his kisses—from her mind. "However, I do have hopes she will join us in our efforts soon. Rather, it is an old, dear friend of mine, Lady Julianna Somerset. She is newly returned from abroad. You do recall Lady Julianna, do you not?"

If possible, her brother's skin turned a shade nearer to pale, milky white. His jaw tightened, his entire bearing changing. Stiffening. "I do not think I remember her. I will leave you to your chat. Father has demanded an audience, and I was just on my way to him when you stayed me."

There was something suspicious about his reaction, about his manner. Helena could not quite determine what. Or why. She did not think Julianna and Shelbourne had ever had cause for much interaction. She and Julianna were quite a few years younger than Shelbourne, and Julianna had gone to America just after her comeout to live with her mother.

Although her friend had written dozens of letters during her absence, she had never explicitly explained—at least, not to Helena's satisfaction—the reason for her abrupt departure from London. However, for today, Helena would simply focus upon the happy event of her friend's return.

"Will you not remain for a moment?" she asked her brother, when he seemed almost itchy to flee. "I was hoping we could speak."

Shelbourne tugged at his necktie as if it had suddenly fashioned itself into a noose. "I dare not keep Father waiting."

"A minute here or there shan't make a difference," Helena tried, although it was hardly the truth when it came to Father.

He despised tardiness. But she needed her brother's help.

"Hellie, I haven't the time for this," he bit out, his voice possessing the lash of a whip.

She was taken aback by his vehemence. "Just a moment, please. I am begging you to help my cause and plead with him on my behalf. I cannot bear to marry Lord Hamish, and the announcement of our betrothal is imminent."

"I do hope you are not persisting in your wrongheaded notion of marrying for love." Her brother's lip curled in distaste.

Of course she was not. The man she loved was marrying another. But she could not say that. Not to Shelbourne. Not to anyone. Loving Huntingdon was her carefully guarded secret.

"It has nothing to do with love and everything to do with Lord Hamish being an odious boor who believes women are empty-headed ninnies who require men to make all the decisions for them." Frustration surged anew within her. "Have you ever spoken to him?"

Shelbourne inclined his head. "I will own that he possesses a shortsighted understanding of the fairer sex, and that he shares some of Father's antiquated and thoroughly wrong views. However, Lord Hamish is a gentleman. He respects you and holds you in high esteem and will never cause you shame. You will want for nothing as his wife. Father wishes to secure your future. I want that for you also."

She wanted a secure future as well. But not with Lord dratted Hamish White! Why could no one see reason?

"Shelbourne, please," she began.

"What would you wish instead of the marriage Father has found for you?" he snapped. "To go gadding about New York City, courting ruin in the fashion of Lady Julianna Somerset?"

"She had the approval of her family. I have already pleaded my case to Father and he has remained stalwart. As a woman without means of her own, what else am I to do but hope my family will not force me into a hated union?" She paused, something new occurring to her. "I thought you said you did not remember Lady Julianna."

"My memory has restored itself." His tone was cold. "A scandalous baggage, that one. I am surprised Father allows her to pay you a call."

Not Shelbourne as well. It seemed he was shaping more to their father's mold with each passing day. She was about to correct him when their butler arrived to announce Lady Julianna.

Shelbourne cut a quick bow, excused himself, and fled the room as if the seat of his trousers were aflame. So much for his help with Father. Why did he persist in believing love was a fiction and marriages were best made in duty?

Helena was still frowning over her brother's odd behavior when Julianna crossed the threshold. But she promptly dashed her misgivings away as her beloved friend hurried across the salon to her.

"Helena! I have missed you, my dearest friend." With her

brilliant red hair and decidedly Parisian gown in shades of *aubergine*, Lady Julianna Somerset cut a striking figure.

Helena embraced her dear friend tightly, thinking she had scarcely changed at all in the years she had spent away. "I can scarcely believe you are here, returned at last!"

"Nor can I." Julianna stepped back, her smile somewhat tremulous, an undeniable glitter of emotion in her blue eyes. "It is so good to see you. You must tell me everything I have missed in my absence."

Where to begin? There was much to tell. So much. Her concern over her impending betrothal to Lord Hamish had not made its way into her letters, as she had done her best to keep from straying to upsetting subjects. As Mother always said, bad news does not travel well.

But now, her friend was here, just when she needed her guidance and support most.

"Have a seat and I shall ring for tea," Helena said grimly, for she had quite a story to tell, and she suspected Julianna did as well.

This distraction was just what she needed to keep her mind from returning to ruinous thoughts, like the way Huntingdon's lips had molded to hers. Or how desperately she wanted him to kiss her again.

* * *

The day after he had courted ruin by kissing Helena senseless in the library at the Cholmondeley affair, Huntingdon had come to the bitter realization that he needed to engage in two thoroughly unwanted calls. He was presently undertaking the first, and the second would necessarily follow.

Lady Beatrice held his arm as he took her for a turn in the small gardens at her father's Mayfair townhome. The day was unseasonably warm, and beneath his coat, he was perspiring, the fine fabric of his shirt sticking to his skin. He wished he could appreciate the manner in which the sunshine caught the hints of copper in his betrothed's dark hair. However, all he could see was Helena after he had kissed her.

That sultry mouth so dark red and inviting.

"Your call this afternoon is an unexpected pleasure, my lord," Lady Beatrice said softly.

She had been at her needlework when he arrived, and he had regretted the interruption of her day and the potential disruption of her emotions as well. But it was necessary to unburden himself. His sense of honor would allow no less.

He wondered where the devil to begin. What a godawful muddle. "Forgive me for not sending word, but I needed to see you as soon as possible."

Because he was a scoundrel.

Because he could not control himself.

Ah, bloody hell. The temptation of Helena in his arms, her body curled to his, had been too much for him. He tried to cast all thoughts of her from his mind—she had no place there. And she most certainly did not belong in this moment of solemnity between himself and the lady he had wronged.

But she would not go. Helena remained. For a moment, he swore he could detect her scent on the breeze. His heart squeezed in his chest.

"I am flattered you were so eager to see me," Lady Beatrice said, a hint of flirtation in her voice. "It has only been a few days since you were in my company."

Guilt lodged inside him with the violence of a swinging pickaxe.

"I am always eager to see you, my lady," he forced out. "You know that. No other lady can compare."

What a hideous liar he was. Helena very much compared. She outshone Lady Beatrice in every way. But Helena was a wild hellion, his friend's sister, altogether forbidden to him. Lady Beatrice was the woman Grandfather had chosen to become the next Countess of Huntingdon. For all the right reasons.

His betrothed smiled at him, and her loveliness could not be denied. Nor could his distinct lack of reaction to her. Not a twitch of his prick. Not the slightest hint of heat in his belly or a sense of awareness.

Apathy was excellent, he reminded himself. Respect the foundation for a sound marriage, the sort of union he wanted for himself. He would not be doomed to repeat the sins of his parents.

"You flatter me, my lord." She turned her head to admire a clump of fat, blooming roses. "I am not worthy of your high regard."

"You are worthy of my highest regard," he said solemnly, "and for that reason, I must confess that I come to you today with an apology, Lady Beatrice."

She stiffened, her gaze flying back to his, and yet, her countenance remained oddly emotionless. "I am certain you have done nothing which requires my forgiveness, Lord Huntingdon."

He hated himself. "While I appreciate your high opinion of me, I fear it is misguided in this instance. I acted in an inappropriate and far too familiar fashion with a female acquaintance yesterday. I remain deeply ashamed of my actions, and I felt the only honorable path was to be honest with you at once. Naturally, if you decide you cannot proceed with our marriage, given my lapse of judgment, I will understand."

They paused on the path. Her mother watched from the salon windows, but they were out of earshot. It was enough for a spot of privacy, but not enough to be an affront to propriety.

"Of course I would never dream of judging you so harshly, my lord," Lady Beatrice said calmly. "Gentlemen will have their moments of temptation. My place as your wife will be to offer my sincere affection and support however I may."

Her response left him stunned. He had imagined a host of reactions from his betrothed on his carriage ride here, and none of them had been complacency and acceptance.

He cleared his throat. "Your understanding is much appreciated, my dear. However, I wish to reassure you I will never again allow myself to act with such dishonor again."

"You need not fear I will object to your keeping a mistress, Lord Huntingdon," she said briskly, as if she were speaking of something as simple as the rose bushes in bloom. "Indeed, I am more than prepared to encourage you to do so."

Helena was hardly his mistress. The wickedest part of him contemplated the notion of her, naked in his bed. Of making love to her.

No, Gabe. You are better than this. Cling to your honor...

He did not dare reveal the identity of the lady in question. He had been spending the last few weeks doing his utmost to keep Helena from ruining herself, damn it. Confiding in Lady Beatrice would only undermine that purpose, to say nothing of the other problems it would create.

"I will not be keeping a mistress," he said stiffly, the use of the word, spoken to his future countess, feeling shameful and wrong. "I intend to be a faithful husband."

Indeed, faithfulness was one of the most important tenets which should guide a marriage. Neither of his parents had been faithful to each other. And look at what had become of them, of Lisbeth.

"Forgive me for being so forward with my wishes, but I do believe it for the best if you are to keep a mistress, Lord Huntingdon," his betrothed returned then, leaving him further shocked. "It is expected and, in many ways, natural. If you should wish to pursue more with this...female acquaintance of yours, I would not object."

This was not what he wished to hear. Suspicion rose within him. Was she encouraging him to take a mistress so she, too, could pursue another? Because the last thing he wanted was to bind himself in a marriage like the one his parents had shared.

"Mayhap this is a conversation we should have had before, Lady Beatrice. I will not accept infidelity within the bonds of marriage."

She smiled brightly. "You need not fear on that account, my lord. I will be more than happy to be a faithful wife and provide you with the necessary heirs, while you are free to pursue whatever you wish. I wholeheartedly appreciate your candor, and now, I do think it best we returned inside as we have tarried quite a bit in the gardens."

"Of course, my lady." Bemused, he turned and guided them back into the house.

After a few minutes of polite inquiries between himself and his hostesses, Huntingdon was once more in his carriage. He needed to speak with Shelbourne. Unfortunately for him, a call at his friend's bachelor's residence revealed he was not at home.

Feeling grimmer than he had upon waking that morning, Huntingdon returned home and promptly took up a bottle of whisky, hiding in his study. Even more unfortunately for Huntingdon, he was an infrequent imbiber.

Which meant that in no time at all, he was desperately bosky.

And which also meant that in no time at all, he was once more finding himself desperately in trouble.

With the wrong woman.

Again.

CHAPTER 6

*As for anyone who argues the granting of woman's suffrage would
be a mistake, I challenge them to provide sound, logical reasons
why. Of course, they can be in possession of none.*
—*From* Lady's Suffrage Society Times

The Earl of Huntingdon was soused.

Impossible as it seemed—for she had never witnessed the paragon overindulge—there was no denying the truth of it.

Helena's first indication was when he arrived for dinner at the Marquess and Marchioness of Hartstock's townhome and entered the dining hall swaying like a tree caught in a maelstrom. The second indication was when he spoke too loudly at dinner and laughed overly long at one of his own jokes. To be fair, the fact that he had told a sally at all was yet another troubling indicator. The third was the manner in which he quaffed his wine over the many courses, also quite unlike himself.

And the fourth was when he followed Helena into the lady's withdrawing room, stuffing her inside and crowding her with his presence much as he had in the library.

She had not heard him follow her, and as she eyed him warily, heart hammering, she could not help but to wonder how. He was so large. He could not have trod silently, especially after the amount of wine he had drained over the course of the evening.

Regardless of his unusual behavior, he was here. Her lips tingled with remembrance of the kisses they had shared.

"Huntingdon," she forced herself to say, "what in heaven's name are you doing, following me in here? If anyone were to come upon us, it would be the scandal of the decade."

"I needed to speak with you in private, to apologize for my unpardonable actions," he announced, dashing any futile hopes she had been harboring that he may have followed her so he could kiss her again.

"You kissed me," she said calmly, as if those kisses had not changed her world.

In truth, his refusal to speak honestly of what had transpired between them infuriated her. His *unpardonable actions* had been everything to her, drat his beautiful hide.

"It was a mistake, what happened," he said, talking far too loudly.

"Hush, or someone will hear you." If Helena snapped at him, it could not be helped. He had just called kissing her a mistake, as well. She longed to slap him. And then kiss him some more. "You truly must go, Huntingdon. This is quite unlike you."

"I have been able to think of nothing else but what happened." He reached for her, then frowned and withdrew his hand before making contact, almost as if his body had a will of its own which did not match his mind. "Thinking of how wrong and dishonorable it was of me to act as I did. I cannot forgive myself, even if Lady Beatrice has."

The mentioning of his betrothed had the effect of a bucket of ice being dumped into her soul. "Surely you are jesting, Lord Huntingdon."

"Jesting?" He blinked in owlish fashion. "Of course I would never jest about a matter of such great import. You must know I desire you…er, *your respect*. As an old chum of Shelbourne's, of course."

Her foolish heart thumped with greater abandon, clinging to his misstep.

What if it was not a misstep? What if Huntingdon does desire you?

He did not kiss like a man who did not desire her. If anything, his kisses had been proof of the opposite.

She searched his deep-blue gaze, trying to find the answers she sought and finding only more questions instead. "You have always had my respect. Until you began this nonsensical meddling in my affairs, that is. You cannot continue following me about. I have settled upon my course."

"Ruination," he muttered, disgust evident in his voice.

"It is that or commit myself to a miserable existence as Lord Hamish's bride," she countered.

Why, oh why, would none of the men in her life see reason? Why could none of them understand how little power and hope a woman truly held? She was at the mercy of her father and his ludicrous plan she marry a man of his choosing.

"Shall I speak to Northampton on your behalf?" he asked. "Or Shelbourne, perhaps?"

Frustration blossomed once more.

"And what shall you tell them, hmm?" she demanded. "The same thing you told Lady Beatrice?"

Hated name, leaving her lips. A name she wished she had

never heard. A woman she wished did not exist. But those wishes were futile. Every bit as futile, it would seem, as her attempts to create a scandal so she could have her freedom. She was so certain her father would not turn her away and cut off her pin money if scandal kept Lord Hamish from wanting to offer for her hand. And surely, *surely*, she could find a more suitable arrangement, given the time and opportunity thus far denied her.

"I did not tell Lady Beatrice about you, specifically." Huntingdon's voice sounded thick, his words lacking their usual crisp elocution.

Somehow, seeing him in a state of alarming imperfection made her want him more. Or mayhap it was the fact that her traitorous lips knew the way his felt molded to hers.

"*Quelle* relief," she said bitterly. "Please, Huntingdon. Just return to the gentlemen and your port and cigars. You have already done more than enough damage."

"She forgave me," he said, running a hand through his dark hair and leaving it rakishly ruffled.

Some hated part of her longed to reach out and smooth the wayward strands. But she would not—must not—touch him. "How lovely for you."

Helena could not bear another minute of discussing Lady Beatrice. She had endured more than enough, thank you. If Huntingdon was not going to leave the lady's withdrawing room, she would go.

Helena sidestepped him and moved to sweep past.

But his arm shot out, hooking her waist and hauling her to him.

The motion was so fast, so unexpected, so un-Huntingdon, that Helena lost her balance as she whirled to face him. Though the earl clutched at her waist, his inebriated state did nothing to help his ordinarily impeccable coordination. The two of them fell like a downed tree in the forest.

She landed atop him, the breath leaving her lungs in a whoosh.

At the last moment, she braced her hands on his chest to keep from knocking her head into his. It did nothing, however, to keep his head from striking the polished floor beneath them. He winced and let out a groan.

"Huntingdon, have you injured yourself?" she asked, struggling with the weight and layers of her evening finery to remove herself from him.

Deuce take fashion.

She was wearing flounced skirts and a full tournure, and she felt as dizzied as an upended chicken. But his grasp clamped on her waist, mooring her to him when she would have removed herself and scrambled to her feet.

"Hold still, Helena, will you?" he growled.

"You must let me go." She moved again, attempting to free herself from his hold.

Mayhap the fall had knocked him senseless and that was the reason he would not allow her to go. But this position was...far too intimate. Far too tempting. She wriggled with greater persistence.

"Stop. Moving."

He gritted the directive with such force, Helena stilled. "Are you hurt, Huntingdon? I do believe you may have hit your head."

"I am aching," he said, his voice wry. "Mayhap next time I should try to hit it with greater force. Amnesia would be a boon. I am convinced of it."

Helena struggled to make sense of his words. His gaze was hooded, the color of the sky just before the stars began to appear in the night. From this angle, his supple lips were a greater temptation. The slash of his jaw, covered with the shadow of dark whiskers since his morning shave, was a thing of beauty.

"Just how hard did you hit your head?" She frowned down at him, worried.

"Definitely not hard enough." His fingers bit into her waist through her corset. "Thank the Lord you are wearing your undergarments today. I suppose you were not planning an after-dinner ravishing in the lady's withdrawing room?"

Was that the true reason he had followed her here? To ward off further attempts at achieving her own ruin?

She frowned down at him. "I always wear my undergarments, my lord."

Being so forward was unlike him, even in his cups. Indeed, she did not think he had ever said anything so decidedly improper in her presence.

"Cease moving," he said on a groan, as if in desperate pain. "You were not wearing a corset that day."

She struggled to understand what he was speaking of. "Have you addled your wits?"

"That day in the carriage," he elaborated, "when I saved you from giving yourself to that worthless reprobate Forsyte. You were not wearing a corset when I touched you then. I could not help but to wonder…damn, damn, *damn*. This is all your fault."

"All my fault?" The outrageous man! He *must* have struck himself silly. "You are the one who arrived at dinner in his cups and then proceeded to drown himself in wine and follow me into the lady's withdrawing room. This is, indisputably, *your* fault, my lord."

But then, the rest of his words gradually permeated her mind. He had recognized she had not been wearing a corset on the day she had gone to meet Lord Algernon at his bachelor's residence. And he had been thinking about it, apparently. And he had kissed her, just yesterday.

And his gaze, at this moment, had slipped to her lips once more.

She licked them instinctively.

He groaned again, and beneath her, she detected an unmistakable ridge. A prominence she had read about in the books she had thieved from Shelbourne's collection. Her breath caught. She inhaled swiftly, and a rush of corresponding warmth slid through her, slow and molten. Could it be that he was not as unaffected by her as he pretended? That he did not, in fact, think of her as he would a sister?

Yes, said the wicked voice inside her. *Huntingdon desires you.*

"My weakness is your fault," he countered, his hands sliding up her spine, fingers sinking into the careful upsweep of her coiffure.

His fingertips skimming over her scalp elicited a frisson of pleasure. She never wanted him to stop touching her.

"How?" she asked, breathless. Need for him rose like a tide. "You are your own man. I have done nothing more than attempt to free myself of the unwanted betrothal my father is forcing upon me."

"Because you are so damned beautiful, and I should not want you, but I cannot help myself."

His guttural admission pierced her heart like an arrow. Warmth sluiced over her. She became more aware of her position atop him, his big body beneath her, the pulsing evidence of his desire pressed to her hip.

Helena stilled. So did the world, it seemed. "Huntingdon," she began, searching for the proper words.

What to say? What to ask him? Had she completely lost her senses? Could it be that this man desired her in the way she longed for him?

"Shut up," he said, and then he pulled her head down toward his.

Their lips met, fused, and she was lost.

* * *

Bloody, bloody hell.

He had done his damnedest to give the bottle a black eye today. Never had he ever acted with such recklessness, such disregard for himself, for his hosts, for those around him.

But as Helena's sweet mouth moved over his, kissing him back with every bit as much fervency, he could not muster the proper amount of regret. Indeed, not just the requisite sum of regret, but none.

Not a modicum of it.

All he could feel was relief. And desire. Fierce, overwhelming desire.

He cupped her head—even the shape of it was ideal, perfectly molded to his hands, and held her to him when she would have withdrawn. Because she wanted this every bit as much as he did. He could feel it in the eager response of her lips. He felt it in the bone-deep connection, the way their bodies melded together.

A realization hit him.

Struck him with the force of an unexpected blow.

He wanted her, as always. But he was not certain, now that he had tasted her lips and held her in his arms, that he could continue tamping down the need to have her. Resisting her, clinging to his honor and restraint, grew fainter, much like the stars of the night's sky as the sun rose on the dawn.

I am in my cups. This is wrong. Tomorrow, I will regret this.

And yet, he could not seem to stop. Even with the layers of their garments between them, there was an undeniable rightness to the way their bodies fit together. But he wanted to be atop her. It was a base urge, elemental. One he could not deny himself.

Later, he could blame his actions upon the blow to the

back of his head—still smarting—when they had fallen as one. Later, he could appease his sense of honor with the knowledge he would never pin Lady Helena Davenport to the floor of the lady's withdrawing room and have his way with her unless he had struck himself dumb.

But those insistences would be lies for the benefit of his conscience.

Because he was insensate to anything but his need for her, raw, uncompromising, all-consuming. He rolled them as one, without breaking their kiss. Slowly. Tenderly. Until she was the one on her back, and he was leveraging his body over hers, his tongue dipping between her lips to tangle with hers.

Lemon and bergamot filled his head.

And as before, he was on fire. Only this time, he was burning hotter than he could have imagined. Hotter than he ever had. Lady Helena Davenport would be the end of him. Half of him was certain he would not mind if she proved his demise, for he would die a happy man.

A wicked urge hit him, then. He wanted to know if she wore drawers. Gabe prayed she had not attended this evening's entertainment in the hopes of ruining herself yet again. His hand traveled of its own accord. He found his way beneath her voluminous skirts. His fingers connected with the soft, warm curve of her calf first. Covered in silken stockings. Lace-frilled drawers met his questing touch next.

His need for her was about to tear him apart. He would surrender every vestige of his pride, all his honor, to make her his. To take her here and now, although he knew quite well he could not. That he must stop.

And he would.

Soon.

But first, a small sampling of paradise. The paradise he had denied himself for far too long.

Ah, Lord. His palm slid over the delectable curve of her

hips. Perfection. Soft, lush womanly flesh. Her legs opened without any provocation, naturally, instinctively, welcoming him. And oh, how much he wanted to take everything she offered and more. How much he wanted to make her his.

Forever.

But that was not meant to be. And neither was this moment of desperate hunger between them. Their familial duties were calling them in twain directions. His inner confusion was more difficult to battle today, but tomorrow would be a new day.

For today…

He kissed her harder, almost with bruising force, his tongue sinking into her mouth as his fingers traversed the thin layer of fabric keeping the divine flesh of her inner thigh from him.

He groaned into her mouth. She hummed her pleasure. This was a mutual desire, consuming them both. He did not fool himself that it was one sided. Mayhap it was the recklessness of the moment, the excitement of their precarious assignation, the chance of being caught. Whatever the reason for her eager reaction to him, he thanked the heavens.

Some part of him balked at what he was about to do, but the rest of him took precedence. Helena filled his mind, his senses. She was all he could think about, all he could feel. To hell with honor. She was beneath him, kissing him back, making him wild. She was his, damn it.

Just as she should be.

No, that was wrong. She could not be his because he was promised to another. But as he struggled to recall Lady Beatrice and stop himself, he found he could not. He could blame it upon the whisky he had consumed after returning to his home. He could blame it upon Lady Beatrice's strange reaction at their meeting earlier today.

But the oddest realization of all was that he had no wish

to worry about a damned thing past this moment. For the second time in his life, he was going to do what he wanted and worry about the consequences later. He had Helena where he wanted her, where he had dreamed of her being, for far too long. He had been longing for her from the moment he had realized his friend's precocious younger sister had blossomed into an elegant, desirable woman.

He kissed the corners of her lips. And then he finally, at long last, skimmed his fingers over the slit in her drawers. Damp warmth seduced him. He was so close, desperately near, to touching her *there*. He could not stop himself. Another kiss, and his fingers were on her. Hot, wet, female flesh welcomed him.

Gabe swallowed her moan as he deepened the kiss.

He parted her, finding the bud of her sex. She was so slick, and she gasped, her hips jerking responsively. He knew this was wrong. Desperately wrong. But nothing had ever felt so right. He wanted to make her come undone. To feel her shudder helplessly as she surrendered to her release.

He wanted to be the man who made her spend.

He wanted to be the *only* man.

The realization hit him with the weight of a landslip.

He tore his mouth from hers and reared back, his breathing ragged, fingers still drenched in her beckoning dew. What was he doing? He could not be the only man. He had no right to touch her thus, to claim her for himself. She was not for him, and nor was he for her.

He was betrothed, for God's sake, and she nearly was as well.

He exhaled, forced himself to withdraw his hand from beneath her skirts. "Forgive me, Helena."

Another few minutes of mindless pleasure, and what would he have done? What was he capable of?

Once again, her lips were swollen from his kisses, her

emerald eyes dark with desire. Her breaths were every bit as ragged as his. She swallowed, and he followed the movement down the elegant, ivory column of her throat. His cock was stiffer than a ramrod in his trousers. He thought he would offer his soul to the devil for the chance to make her his.

"You seem to be making a habit of offering me apologies lately," she pointed out, a cutting edge in her contralto.

He was still atop her, he realized, a burst of shame blossoming in his chest. What a hypocrite he was. What an utter rogue. He had believed himself better than this. Had not imagined he would ever stoop so low.

"I will not take advantage of you again," he vowed stiffly, rolling to the side and standing before offering her his hand.

Which she promptly ignored, opting instead to leverage herself into a sitting position on her own, and then to rise to her feet. Her silken skirts were wrinkled from their tussle on the floor. His self-loathing was on the rise once more, rather in the fashion of the tides. Threatening to consume him.

She shook out her skirts. "I do not require your form of aid, Huntingdon. If you carry on in this fashion, you will be the one to ruin me. And what will your precious Lady Beatrice think of that?"

What indeed?

Up until their interview earlier that day, he would have sworn she would have been outraged. Now, he was no longer so sure. What he did know, however, was that his actions had been inexcusable. And wrong.

Before he could muster a response, Helena swept past him, leaving him alone in the lady's withdrawing room, wallowing in equal parts shame and lust. What the hell had he done?

More importantly, how was he going to make amends this time?

CHAPTER 7

There are those who would argue that women should be denied Parliamentary franchise because involving us in politics will prove damaging to our constitutions and characters. One cannot help but to wonder what people of such an opinion think of the characters and constitutions of men...
—*From* Lady's Suffrage Society Times

"You look utterly miserable, darling."

The words took Helena by surprise, and for a moment, she feared they had been directed at her. But much to her relief, Callie, Lady Sinclair, had issued her pronouncement to Lady Jo Decker instead.

The women were both newly married, and they were leading members of the Lady's Suffrage Society. She had become fast friends with them through their shared work, and Helena was keen to introduce Julianna to them now that she had returned to London. But first things first—they had gathered over tea.

And Helena was relieved for the much-needed distraction her friends brought her. Because those stolen moments in the lady's withdrawing room with Huntingdon had been...

Thrilling.

Wonderful.

Terrible.

Yes, all those words would be quite apt descriptors. Her unexpected kisses with him had left her once more in a hopeless state of inner turmoil. She wanted him, but he was betrothed to another. He seemed to want her, and yet he hated himself for doing so. Either way, she was not any closer to ridding herself of her impending marriage to Lord Hamish. As it was, she had all but fled the dinner at Lord and Lady Hartstock's, and she had not seen him since.

She forced herself to study Lady Jo now, who did seem rather Friday-faced for a new bride.

"You do look as if you just watched a carriage run over a puppy," Helena added.

Jo frowned at both Callie and Helena. *"Et tu, Brute?* The two of you are supposed to be my friends."

"It is because we are your friends that we are telling you that you look as if you are about to attend a funeral," Callie said.

"Or as if someone has just drowned your favorite kitten," Helena chimed in, fearing she looked little better herself.

Her future loomed before her, a forbidding pastoral of misery.

"What a grim lot you are," Jo grumbled. "Cease with your bleak similes, if you please."

"You ought to be on your honeymoon," Callie observed. "And yet, you are here in London. Is that the reason?"

"Of course that is not the reason," Jo said.

"Then what is the reason?" Callie frowned. "Is anyone else famished? I am going to ring for a tray of cakes and biscuits.

Is it wrong to suddenly be beset by the urge to eat quail eggs at this time of day? Do not answer that. Tell us what has you so distressed, dearest."

Callie was expecting her first child, though one could not tell to look at her. She was a petite, dark-haired beauty with a slender frame and an inimitable sense of fashion.

"I could eat quail eggs at any time of day," Helena offered as Callie went to the bell pull, not as much because it was true as because she had no wish for her friend to feel uncomfortable.

"I am in love with my husband," Jo blurted, surprising Helena, for Jo's marriage had been rushed and, as she claimed, not a love match. It had instead been another case of an overbearing lord browbeating a lady into doing her familial duty. If only someone would browbeat Helena into doing her familial duty with Huntingdon. She would more than happily accept.

But alas, that was not meant to be.

Unless...

No. Helena dared not contemplate such a manipulation.

Callie turned back to them all, looking pleased. "I knew you were in love with him!"

Helena blinked, thinking for a moment the words were meant for her again. They were not, however. She had been too preoccupied with the unsettling idea which had erupted in her mind, much like a volcano.

Dangerous and destructive.

She banished the thoughts, knowing them unworthy.

"How did you know?" Jo asked.

"You made it quite apparent the day I suggested Helena use Decker to cause a scandal," Callie said gently, returning to her seat. "That is wonderful, dearest! I know this marriage was a bit rushed, but I am relieved to hear the two of you are in love."

"Not the two of us," Jo said. "I fear I am alone in my feelings."

A hated state Helena knew all too well. Still, she had seen the manner in which Mr. Elijah Decker, the handsome businessman Jo had so recently wed, looked at his wife. If only Huntingdon would gaze at her with such longing in his eyes, rather than with disgust over his lack of gentlemanly decorum.

"But the way he looks at you," Helena argued, shaking herself from the unworthy thought, "I would be willing to wager you are wrong."

"I fear not." Jo sighed heavily. "He has never hinted at the slightest bit of feelings, and for a man of his reputation…"

That, too, sounded familiar. Huntingdon had never admitted to caring for her or for possessing any tender emotions toward her in the slightest. Of course he did not love her. Could not love her.

And yet, the idea was still there. The unwanted notion. Tempting. Taunting.

Did she dare? All this time, she had been attempting to ruin herself with other gentlemen, and the only one she had managed to behave scandalously with was the man she loved. And if she was faced with having no choice other than to marry Lord Hamish, could she truly be desperate enough to use Huntingdon's actions in the lady's withdrawing room against him?

She looked inside herself and the answer was undeniable: yes. She was.

They discussed Decker's past for a few minutes, and Helena was grateful for the diversion. Until the conversation turned back to her.

"Enough about me, if you please," Lady Jo said. "I am certain it shall all untangle itself as it ought. How is your campaign against the odious Lord Hamish going, my dear?"

Compromising herself to avoid marrying Lord Hamish had been an idea she and her friends had developed together. Heat crept over Helena's cheeks.

Here was her opportunity to consult her friends and see what opinions they held on the matter. "I do believe I may have convinced someone to aid me in my quest to be ruined."

"Tell us everything," Callie demanded.

A knock at the door heralded the arrival of a maid.

"After I arrange for my biscuits, cakes, and quail eggs, of course," she amended, grinning.

Helena waited for her friend to make her unusual request to the kitchens before explaining everything that had happened to her thus far, detailing Huntingdon's successful attempts to keep her from other gentlemen, up until the kiss they had shared.

"He seems dreadfully invested for a man who has recently celebrated his betrothal to another lady," Callie pointed out shrewdly.

The reminder of Lady Beatrice nettled.

"He does," she agreed miserably. "He had insisted he considered his actions a duty on account of his friendship with Shelbourne. And I believed him until..."

Lady Jo leaned forward in her chair. "Until? Do not leave us in suspense."

"Until he kissed me," she admitted, her cheeks going hotter as she made the revelation. Not because she was embarrassed, but because she could not help but to recall Huntingdon's kisses. "I had arranged to meet the Marquess of Dorset at the Duke and Duchess of Bainbridge's ball, and Huntingdon somehow discovered and met me in the library himself. I had arranged for Lady Clementine Hammond to walk in upon us and solidify my ruination. I scarcely had enough time to send Huntingdon out the door before Lady Clementine arrived."

"If she had caught you and Huntingdon in an embrace, all London would have known in the outside of ten minutes," Callie said.

"That is why I chose her." Helena smiled sadly. "Imagine her dismay when she walked in to find me alone, a volume of Lord Byron in hand."

"Everyone knows she thrives on scandal," Jo agreed. "I overheard her bragging about how many society marriages she is responsible for. Fifteen at last count. But let us return to the more salient information you have just provided. Huntingdon *kissed* you?"

"He did," she admitted, glancing down at her abandoned teacup as she struggled to decide how much she wished to reveal to her friends.

She trusted them implicitly, of course. But how could one properly say that a gentleman had pinned her to the floor of the lady's withdrawing room and slid his hand inside her drawers while ravishing her mouth with kisses?

"He has agreed to ruin you himself?" Callie guessed. "I confess, I am surprised. Huntingdon is such a cold man. Proper to a fault, as well."

Ah, there was the crux of the matter.

Huntingdon *was* proper. He cared a great deal about his reputation, his honor, and his familial duty. If she attempted to get him to ruin her, she would effectively set fire to everything he held dear. Including his betrothal to Lady Beatrice.

She could never do that. Could she?

She inhaled slowly. "He has not agreed to ruin me himself. I wish he had. Instead, he has apologized for his actions quite profusely. He told his betrothed about the kisses, though he did not reveal I was the one he kissed. He told me his actions were loathsome and unworthy. He insisted they would never be repeated. And yet they were."

Jo's dark eyebrows rose. "He has kissed you on two separate occasions, all while claiming he wants to protect your honor and keep you from causing a scandal? It sounds to me as if Lord Huntingdon protests too much."

Helena nodded, still at sixes and sevens over what had happened between them. "And that is why I am considering doing something drastic."

"How drastic?" Callie queried.

"I can refuse the match with Lord Hamish, but my father has vowed he will turn me out if I do not marry as it pleases him," she said slowly. "But causing a scandal and making certain Lord Hamish will no longer want to marry me has proven impossible to achieve thus far because of Huntingdon. There is only one option remaining. Huntingdon has already compromised me. If I go to my family with this information..."

She allowed her words to trail off. For the thought of what she must do was itself so daring, so damning, she was not prepared to give voice to it. Hungtingdon would be furious with her. So furious she was not certain if he would ever forgive her. Lady Beatrice would possibly end the engagement. But Helena herself would almost certainly be free.

"Your father may demand you marry Huntingdon instead," Jo pointed out. "Are you prepared for that?"

Hardly.

Yet Helena nodded as if she were. "If I am forced to marry anyone, I would choose him. For years, I have loved him from afar. He has no notion of my feelings for him, and nor does he return them. But I would happily marry him."

If only she could say the same of Huntingdon. He was attracted to her. He certainly felt the sort of base urges toward her she had read about in Shelbourne's naughty books. But lust and love were two different beasts entirely, and Helena did not fool herself that Huntingdon could ever love her. Especially if she revealed what had happened between them. It would be a betrayal of the first order.

Huntingdon prized loyalty, duty, honor. He wanted to marry a woman like Lady Beatrice, who would never dream of debasing herself to escape a marriage. A woman who was quiet and poised and ineffably lovely. One who had no doubt never rolled about on the lady's withdrawing room floor with him.

Yes, there was a definite possibility that in revealing everything to her family, she would suddenly have within her grasp everything she had ever wanted—her freedom and the man she loved. But in so doing, she would make him hate her forever.

"Lord Huntingdon is the man you choose above all others?" Callie asked.

Helena did not hesitate in her response. "Yes."

He would always be her choice. Even if she had never been his. Much to her shame.

"Then you know what you must do," Jo added.

"Follow your heart," Callie prompted.

Before she could say more, a knock at the door heralded the arrival of the biscuits, cakes, and quail eggs. Helena's heart was thumping as wildly as if she had just escaped a runaway carriage. But her answer and her course were clear and yet murky as mud.

She was going to save herself by ruining the Earl of Huntingdon.

* * *

Huntingdon was seated in his study, poring over correspondence from the steward of his Shropshire estate, when the door slammed open. All thoughts of falconry and repairs to the leaking western wing roof vanished as Shelbourne stormed across the Axminster. At his rear, Huntingdon's butler appeared quite out of sorts. But never mind. Shelbourne was a well-known visitor here.

Even as a sense of alarm swept over him, Huntingdon nodded to his servant, indicating he would not require anything else. He would speak to Lord Shelbourne alone.

"Sid," he greeted his old chum, rising in proper greeting. "I hardly expected you this morning."

"I dare say you did not," bit out his friend, an angry sneer curling his lip as he did not halt his stride. "Nor did you expect this."

Before he could react, Shelbourne's fist connected with his jaw with so much force, he bit his own tongue. Pain shot through him as the coppery tang of his own blood blossomed. *Bloody damned hell.*

Huntingdon rubbed his jaw, eying his friend warily. "What the devil are you about?"

But as he asked the question, suspicion rose. There was only one reason his oldest friend would rage into his study with the fury of an invading enemy army and plant him a facer. And that one reason was tall, blonde, and beautiful.

And perfidious, if what he suspected was true.

"Tell me it is all a vicious falsehood," Shelbourne spat, looking as if he were a heartbeat from hitting Huntingdon again. "Tell me you are not a villainous, spineless, maggot of a man! A man without any virtue or honor. A man without loyalty. One who would betray his friend's trust by abusing his innocent sister in cruelest fashion."

Helena.

She had told her brother.

He had spent every moment since his ignominious display in the lady's withdrawing room alternating between cursing himself and wishing he could be within that moment all over again. With Helena's supple curves beneath him. With her lips clinging hungrily to his. With her taste on his tongue and her scent filling his head. With desire coursing through his veins and the hot, sleek flesh of her cunny beneath his fingers.

He *was* a villainous, spineless maggot and every other aspersion Shelbourne would cast upon him. A vile, filthy man.

A disappointment to himself and everyone around him. For the first time, he was thankful Grandfather was no longer alive. At least he would not have to suffer the crushing blow of realizing Huntingdon was no more worthy of the title and the family name than his father before him had been.

Huntingdon had no choice but to admit his wrongdoing. To hope Shelbourne would forgive him for his trespasses.

He inclined his head. "I was trying to protect her."

"A damned excellent job you did," Shelbourne growled. "Was tossing up my sister's skirts truly essential to her *protection*, do you think, Huntingdon?"

Bloody hell. She truly *had* told him. Every sordid detail.

"My actions were inexcusable," he began, attempting to explain himself as shame burned through him. "However, in my defense, Lady Helena tripped and fell, which is how we ended up on the floor."

"On the floor? You dog!" Shelbourne took another swing at him, but this time, Huntingdon was prepared.

He dodged the blow. Apparently she had not given exacting detail. And now, he had just made the situation worse with his loose tongue. *Excellent.*

"It is not as bad as you suppose, Shelbourne. Allow me to explain," he said.

"You are supposed to be my *friend*, damn your hide," Shelbourne bit out, taking another swing. "The most honorable, decent man I know. I trusted you! I ought to beat you to a bloody pulp over this."

Huntingdon deflected his friend's fist. "I do not quarrel with your assessment of the situation. All I can say in my defense is that I recently came into the knowledge that Lady Helena was intending to ruin herself. The sole reason I was alone with her was because I was attempting to keep her from folly."

That was not entirely true, his conscience reminded him.

He had been alone with her on the last occasion because he had been inebriated and desperate. And he had kissed her because he had been unable to resist her.

"If that is true, you had an obligation to come to me with what you had learned," Shelbourne argued. "Not to follow her about and take liberties with her, damn you."

Shelbourne was not wrong in this. The devil of it was, Huntingdon had told himself the same thing. But he had followed Helena about like a dog in heat anyway. Because he wanted her. He had always wanted her. He had just never been able to have her.

You cannot have her now either, you conscienceless rogue. What of Lady Beatrice?

"It was my intention to seek you out." His excuse was thin. Pathetic, just as his resolve had been. "There was not the time, and in a delicate matter such as this, I was not certain of the best means of approaching you."

He was his father's son, was he not?

"And so you compromised her yourself instead?" Shelbourne's lip curled. "Just like your bastard of a sire before you."

Huntingdon inhaled swiftly. His fists tightened at his sides. The urge to hit back was strong, but he deserved his friend's wrath. He had earned every cutting word. Even if that last particular insult had the effect of a whip, lashing his miserable hide to bits.

"I am not like him," he denied hoarsely, Shelbourne's accusation bringing back a rush of bile.

Of old pain. Old shame. Of hatred and blame and loss and sadness. So much sadness. His chest tightened. His lungs burned. Not now. He could not have one of his fits here, in this moment, facing the man he considered a brother.

The friend he had betrayed in such villainous fashion.

There was a rushing in his ears, a dizziness seizing him. Suddenly, there was a fist connecting with his jaw. There was a blinding flash of pain.

And then, there was nothing.

CHAPTER 8

Fortunately, we have many allies in men who are not afraid of the prospect of women's suffrage. To that, we say a resounding hear, hear.

—*From* Lady's Suffrage Society Times

*H*elena cried out as she saw her brother's fist flying toward Huntingdon's jaw. The manner in which the earl had tensed, and the dazed expression on his countenance, had alerted her that Huntingdon was having one of his spells. Her warning had not pierced the fog surrounding his mind. Instead of feinting left or right or blocking her brother's blow, Huntingdon received the full brunt.

His head snapped back, and he crumpled to the floor. The sickening thud of Shelbourne's knuckles connecting would forever haunt her. This was her fault.

All of it.

Why had she not foreseen her brother's reaction? She had

intended to banish any chance of a betrothal with Lord Hamish. But she had never meant for Huntingdon to suffer violence.

"Shelbourne!" She raced forward, unthinkingly, breath hitching, intent upon reaching the earl. "What have you done?"

Her brother turned to her, his expression dazed, his knuckles bloodied. "What are you doing in here, damn you? I told you to wait in the carriage."

Yes, he had. But she had remained where she was for ten minutes before fear had constricted her heart. When she had gone to Shelbourne with her confession, she had never imagined his reaction would be so intense. Nor so violent. He had trembled with rage for the entirety of their carriage ride to Wickley House. She never should have allowed him to call upon Huntingdon alone.

She raced past her brother and fell to her knees at Huntingdon's side. He was already moaning and moving, regaining his senses, lashes fluttering. A dark, hideous bruise blossomed on his jaw. She gently caressed his hair, attempting to calm him.

"Huntingdon," she said. "I am so sorry."

"You owe this scoundrel no apologies," hissed Shelbourne, seizing her elbow in an attempt to force her to her feet once more. "Rise, damn you. Let him rot."

But she was not going anywhere. Her brother would have to drag her across the floor if he wished to put any distance between herself and the man she had unwittingly brought violence upon. She owed him that much, at least. What he had done had been wrong, but what she had done was worse.

She had never meant for Huntingdon to get hurt.

"I will do nothing of the sort," she denied, casting a glare in her brother's direction. "How dare you do him violence?"

"How dare *I*?" Shelbourne's indignant voice cracked

through the study. "How dare *he* do what he has done is more the question you ought to be asking, sister. He is lucky I did not demand satisfaction."

"Dueling has long been outlawed," she reminded him grimly. And thank heavens for that.

"Helena?" Huntingdon's confused croak had her turning all her attention back to him.

She brushed a fallen forelock of hair from his forehead. "Huntingdon? Are you in pain? Shall I ring for a physician to be sent? Pray forgive me. I never imagined he would attack you with such brutal ruthlessness."

Huntingdon's pupils were wide and dark in his brilliant, blue gaze. His lashes fluttered again, his brow furrowing. Why had she never noted before how lush his eyelashes were? She caressed his cheekbone next, marveling at the elegant architecture of this man, so beautiful and powerful at once. Masculine and yet almost pretty.

But then, he was suddenly alert. Swatting at her touch as if she were as tiresome as a fly buzzing about him. Sitting up. Rubbing his jaw. Glaring at her.

"What have you done?" he demanded, his voice sharp.

His anger was not a surprise. The abruptness of it, however, took her aback. In her haste to tend to him and her guilt over his injuries, she had almost forgotten Huntingdon would be irate with her for telling Shelbourne about their indiscretions.

Not that she had described what had occurred to her brother in vivid detail. No, indeed. She had ventured just enough for there to be no doubt. Just enough that she had hoped he would go to their father. Instead, he had flown into a rage and come here, barging into Huntingdon's study and thrashing him.

Had Huntingdon offered up a defense? Likely, he had not.

He would never raise a fist in such a conflict. That much, she knew.

"My lady," he bit out when she failed to answer him, taking her elbow in a punishing grip. "Have you nothing to say for yourself?"

"Unhand her," demanded Shelbourne. "You have no right to touch my sister. Not after what you have done, how deeply you have betrayed not only me but your own sense of honor. God rot you."

Huntingdon winced and released Helena at once.

But Helena was not moving from his side. Guilt and the undeniable magnetism she had always felt for the earl kept her from leaving. Still, she knew she needed to explain. Not that she could with her brother hovering over them like an irate gaoler.

"I am sorry, Huntingdon," she said softly. "I never intended for him to attack you. Seeing you hurt is the last thing I would ever wish."

"Then it would seem you made an err in judgment, my lady," he said cuttingly.

She deserved his scorn in part, she knew. For she had understood what going to her brother would mean, although she had not fully comprehended what it would entail. She had known Shelbourne's friendship with Huntingdon would be tested. But she was not alone in the kisses and embraces they had shared. He was every bit as complicit in what had occurred between them as she had been.

Rather, it was the betrayal of trust—far more than the actions—which set them apart. Trust was important for Huntingdon, and in going to her brother, she had proven to Huntingdon that he could not trust her.

"The err in judgment was yours." Shelbourne's angry accusation split the silence. "What were you thinking, compromising an innocent lady? Your friend's sister? *My* sister, damn you. You are all but wedded to another, and her betrothal is imminent."

Helena huffed out a sigh, turning her attention to her brother once more. He hovered over herself and Huntingdon like a grim, forbidding angel. "He knew I did not want to marry Lord Hamish, and he was trying to aid me."

"Aid you," her brother repeated, incredulous. "By ruining you himself?"

"Enough!" Huntingdon rose to his towering height once more. "Cease your arguments, if you please. My head is aching. What has happened is not in dispute. I have compromised Lady Helena. However, no one need know what has transpired beyond the three of us. Shelbourne, you now know that Lady Helena is on a mission to ruin herself, however she must. She does not want to marry Lord Hamish. My actions are inexcusable, but they hardly necessitate any more rash a response than those which have already been undertaken."

Helena rose to her feet belatedly, shaking out her skirts, as a chill swept over her. He was acknowledging his own wrongdoing but suggesting they keep it a secret—the three of them. And what a tidy secret it would be. His indiscretions with Helena would be forgotten. She would still be forced to marry the odious Lord Hamish.

Her heart thudded.

Huntingdon had left her with no choice.

She had not been certain she could dare, that she would willingly lie to her own brother. That she would cast Huntingdon's reputation and his honor to the ether. But his words had filled her with a desperation she could not shake. As before, during the tea she had taken with Lady Sinclair and Lady Jo, she knew she had to do what was best.

Follow her heart.

Save herself.

There was only one way. A hate, awful way. Her sole chance…

"I am with child," she blurted.

And then she instantly prayed the Lord would forgive her for issuing such a monstrous lie. And praying that Huntingdon could too, in time.

Huntingdon's stare swung to hers, accusing, irate. Glacial. "What the devil?" he asked.

"What the bloody hell?" Shelbourne demanded in unison.

Oh dear.

What the devil and what the bloody hell, indeed? In for a penny, in for a pound, however. If Huntingdon intended to carry on as if nothing had occurred between them beyond that which would could be expiated by fisticuffs to defend her honor, she would have to change courses.

"I need to marry," she fibbed, avoiding her brother and Huntingdon's probing gazes. "Lord Huntingdon is the father, so it is only right that it should be him."

She heard Huntingdon's swift inhalation. Felt her brother's wrath as if it were another creature loose in the chamber, prepared to attack. But she was desperate, and she was staying the course.

* * *

She was desperate.

Gabe rubbed his throbbing jaw, studying Lady Helena Davenport, who notably refused to meet his gaze, as comprehension hit him with the force of an anvil to the head. There was no other explanation. Her betrothal to Lord Hamish White was looming, and she had seized the reins he had so foolishly left in her hands.

Part of him could not blame her for what she was doing.

But the rest of him seethed.

They were both complicit in this tangled, unacceptable mess. But what she was doing was a different sort of betrayal entirely. She had just told an immense falsehood. If she were truly pregnant, there was no possibility he was the father.

There was the chance she had managed to ruin herself with another.

The thought made him cold.

His mind was still sluggish after Shelbourne had knocked him out. But it was damned difficult to wrap his thoughts around such treachery on her part. Helena was wild and unruly and reckless. She was bold and brash and outspoken. Everything he did not want in a countess. But he did not think her to be the sort of female who would lie with one man and then pin her bastard child upon another.

Not that such a supposition was a commendation.

But he did not have long to contemplate further, because Shelbourne launched himself at him once more, spurred by Helena's ludicrous confession. This time, Helena threw herself between them, acting like a shield.

Foolishly so.

Shelbourne nearly planted her a facer in his boundless rage.

"Stop this, Shelbourne!" she commanded her irate brother. "No more violence, if you please."

After she had already incited all this madness with her ill-planned attempt to force him into marriage, her protestation was rich.

"He needs to answer for his sins, curse him," spat Shelbourne.

Huntingdon wondered if their friendship could weather this betrayal. Whilst it was true that he had not gone as far as Helena claimed in compromising her, he was guilty of lusting after her. Of kissing and touching a woman he had no right to want. His own friend's innocent sister.

There was only one means of ameliorating this disastrous affair.

He settled his hands on Helena's waist and moved her to the side so he could face his outraged friend without her acting as a barrier between them. He was not a coward, damn it, and he would face Shelbourne on his own.

"What would you have me do?" he asked, already knowing the answer.

"You have to marry her," Shelbourne said. "It is the only way."

Yes, he had trapped himself quite neatly in a mess of his own lustful making. What he had not done, Helena had completed.

He did not flinch, and neither did his gaze waver. "I will marry her. However, I ask for some time. I will need to inform Lady Beatrice of the change in circumstance, and I will need to approach your father formally."

Shelbourne growled. "How could you have done this, damn you?"

He could deny he was the father of Helena's supposed child. But what good would the disavowal do him? It was plain from the virulence of his friend's reaction that Shelbourne would never believe him.

"There is no explanation," he said grimly, unable to keep the irony from his voice.

He cast a look in Helena's direction. Her lovely face was stricken, the full lower lip he had so enjoyed kissing caught between her teeth. She looked as if she were torn.

Guilty. That was how she looked.

"Shelbourne, let me speak with Huntingdon for a moment," she said then, shocking him with her bold request.

"Absolutely not," Shelbourne rejected flatly. "You cannot

believe I would allow you to remain in this vile seducer's company alone for another second."

She wanted to speak with him, did she? Gabe was tempted. He had quite a bit he wanted to say to the manipulative baggage. When he could swallow down his anger, that was.

Helena refused to meet his gaze. Her chin lifted in that defiant gesture he had come to know so well as she faced her brother. "Please, Shelbourne. A few minutes, no longer."

Shelbourne shook his head. "No."

But Helena persisted, wedging herself between Gabe and her brother once more. The sweet scent of her invaded his senses. His head felt as if it were suddenly too light for his body. His jaw ached. Thoughts remained slow. He must not, above all else, allow her to affect him as she had done in the past.

He had to keep his sangfroid firmly in place. Even if part of him wanted to throttle her and the other part wanted to kiss her.

"I need to speak with his lordship," Helena said softly, allowing a hint of tears to enter her voice.

If Huntingdon had been inclined, he would have offered her applause. She had the flair of a lifelong actress. He ground his jaw to keep from making a tart response and then winced as it made his headache more pronounced.

"I am hardly in a state to ravish her," he offered wryly.

Shelbourne snarled in the fashion of a rabid animal, which was apparently the sole response he was interested in giving.

"Shelbourne," Helena pressed, sniffling for good measure, Huntingdon supposed.

"Five minutes to plan your impending nuptials," Shelbourne relented bitterly. "And only because I hate it when you weep. I will be in the hall, counting the seconds. If you touch her, Huntingdon, I will thrash you to within a breath of your life."

He inclined his head in deference to his friend's threat. The moment Shelbourne had left the chamber, Helena whirled to face him. Her expression was still a study in misery.

"Explain yourself, madam," he demanded.

"Please do not be angry with me," she said, reaching for him.

He shrugged away from her touch—touching her was what had gotten him into this infernal mess in the first place. "Anger does not begin to describe what I feel at the moment, my lady."

"I had no choice. My father was preparing to announce my betrothal to Lord Hamish, and thus far, I have only had an opportunity to ruin myself with one man," she countered, dashing a tear from her cheek.

"Cease your theatrics," he ordered coldly. "Your brother is out of earshot and they are no longer necessary to facilitate his pity."

"Please, Huntingdon," she begged, those big, verdant orbs filling with unshed tears, as if on cue. "I did not know what else to do."

A growl emerged from him. "I can damn well assure you that telling your brother you carry my bastard was not the proper solution. Tell me, are you carrying a child? Because if you are, we both know it is not mine."

She blinked, wringing her hands in her distress.

More of an act?

He could not be sure.

Hell, he could not be sure of anything any longer. Except for that he never should have kissed her. Never should have followed her. Never should have given in to his lust. Never should have slid his hand beneath her skirts, found the slit in her drawers…

Damn her to perdition. She was like an infection in his blood.

"I am not with child," she admitted, *sotto voce*. "If you wish, I will admit the truth to Shelbourne. I feel dreadful for the way he attacked you."

Her claim of compassion did nothing to quell the fires of his ire. "I deserved the trouncing he gave me for touching you and kissing you. I will own my sins. But even if you did tell him the truth now, he would not believe you. No, indeed. The seed of our collective doom has been sown."

"I never intended—"

"You have what you wanted," he interrupted, driven by the need to lash out at her. "And now we must both pay the price."

The door to the study opened before either of them could speak. Shelbourne returned. "When will you be speaking to my father, Huntingdon?"

"With as much haste as possible," he decided.

But first, he needed to see Lady Beatrice and pray she would understand.

CHAPTER 9

It is just and reasonable for women to enjoy the same rights as men.
—*From* Lady's Suffrage Society Times

"I wish to God Lady Northampton had conceived a son instead of a disappointing, scandalous, amoral daughter. I have never been more ashamed of you than I am in this moment, facing you, knowing you have squandered all the careful plans I made to ensure your future contentedness."

Helena flinched at her father's rancor-laden pronouncement, issued with such vehemence that spittle flew from his mouth along with its utterance. She had long been aware she was a disappointment to her father. As a female, her worth to him had only been in the marriage he could arrange for her. A marriage with a man of his choosing. A man in his image. She would not have been content. She would have been wretched.

Ruining herself meant that she was no longer of any worth to him at all.

She had told herself she must prepare for his outrage, for his disgust. But his words still found their way into the small corner of her heart where hope he would change dwelled.

"I am sorry for my actions, my lord," she said solemnly.

Her apology was partially sincere and partially not. Her conscience still pricked her, hours later, over what she had done. Not because she regretted her father's reaction or the wrath she had incurred. But rather, because of what she had done to Huntingdon. He was a man who prized his reputation, and she had just dashed it to bits in the name of her own preservation.

What she had done was selfish and wrong.

"I do not believe you are sorry at all, you conniving jade!" her father shouted. "You have been cunning and wild. I ought to have taken harsher measures with you, as I wanted. But Lady Northampton advised against it, as did Shelbourne. Look at where all our good intentions have landed us. Smack in the midst of ruin!"

Where she had landed herself was where she wanted to be.

But she bowed her head and feigned humility and contrition just the same. "I hope that in time you might forgive me."

"You are deuced fortunate the man with whom you have sinned is the Earl of Huntingdon. Lord Hamish would not have you as his wife now, nor would I pass on soiled goods to him. If Huntingdon had not agreed to marry you in haste, you would not be beneath this roof, my lady." Father slammed his fist on his desk to punctuate his rage.

This time, she did not jump, for she was expecting it and more. She was almost inured to anger now. She had been facing hours of it. Huntingdon's words came back to haunt her then.

You have what you wanted. And now we must both pay the price.

His icy fury filled her with trepidation. She was in love with a man and she was marrying him. But none of it was happening in the way it ought to have done. And she had stolen from him his right to wed a bride of his choosing. She had escaped one miserable situation for another. At least she would not have to suffer Lord Hamish's supercilious soliloquies and ridiculously frustrating misconceptions of women at large.

Her victory seemed rather hollow from where she stood.

Escaping her marriage with him had been vindication. The aftereffects of her decisions, however, were decidedly not.

"Have you nothing to say for yourself, Lady Helena?" Father demanded, his voice hoarse from all his exclamatory outrage. "I had never thought you slow-witted, but now I cannot help but to wonder. Lord Hamish would have made you an excellent husband. You could not have done better. Instead, you have squandered your chances for an earl who hails from one of the most sordid, disreputable families in the kingdom. If not for the former Lord Huntingdon, this one would not even be worth a farthing."

Yes, she did have rather a lot to say for herself.

Suddenly, Helena found she could no longer hold her tongue. Mayhap it was the final verbal jabs he had offered. Perhaps it was the manner in which he had attacked Huntingdon himself.

Her chin went up. "I *do* have something to say, Father. Lord Hamish is a pompous, small-minded prig. The only reason you wanted me to marry him was to further your own political alliances. I begged you to keep from offering me to him as if I were a sacrificial lamb, and you refused to see reason. Therefore, I had no choice but to take matters and my own destiny into my hands."

"And naturally, Huntingdon, a man of tainted stock, would accept what you offered," her father sneered. "I cannot say I am surprised at his actions. His father was a rakehell and his mother bedded half of London."

"Huntingdon is a man of honor," she felt the need to defend him, for he was. He had kissed her on two separate occasions. And his hand had slipped beneath her skirts in the lady's withdrawing room. But his inner torment over his actions had proven he was not a conscienceless rogue.

"You are fortunate I have accepted his offer for your hand instead of sending you off," her father said then. "But fair warning, my lady. This marriage must happen with as much expeditiousness as possible. Else I will be forced to reconsider my leniency."

She took her father's warning to heart.

It meant she would have to wed Huntingdon with as much haste as she could manage. Supposing he was still willing to make her his wife after everything she had done, that was.

Huntingdon faced Lady Beatrice with the bitter weight of shame lodged in his gut. She had just inquired, in concerned tones, about the nature of the bruising on his face. And he had blurted the truth. The full, sordid truth. Or at least most of it.

His hopes for the same serene understanding she had exhibited when she had informed him she would support his taking of a mistress had fled. In its place was a stark, abject pain that ate away at his soul.

"You cannot marry me," she repeated.

How he loathed his lack of control. He had given in to his lust for Helena, and she had repaid him by betraying him and forcing him into an untenable farce of a marriage. Grandfather had wanted him to marry Lady Beatrice. Indeed, one of his final actions on his deathbed had been to secure Gabe's promise that he would take her as his countess.

And Gabe had agreed.

Now, he was being forced to break that promise. To take on a marriage that teetered on the brink of the same ruin his parents' union had faced.

"I cannot marry you," he agreed, choosing his words with painstaking care.

As they had on his previous visit, they were taking a turn about the gardens as her mother watched from the windows. For the last time. No such lenience would be allotted them from this moment forward. Indeed, he half-expected Lady Harthwaite to storm from the salon where she hovered, having seen the distress on her daughter's countenance.

A light mist began to fall, fitting for the moment.

For the task.

Lady Beatrice shook her head slowly. "I do not understand what has changed. I have already reassured you that I am more than willing to accommodate you, my lord, however I must. If I somehow failed to soothe your worries, I must apologize. How can I prove my devotion to you? You need only say the words, and it shall be done."

She was the most agreeable future wife in London. If he were honest, her willingness to send him off to a mistress and support his unfaithfulness in their union nettled. But that did nothing to ameliorate the sting of what he was about to do.

"I cannot marry you," he explained slowly, "because I must marry another. I have acted selfishly and disreputably, and I have...compromised a lady."

Oh, how he hated revealing the last—his utter moral failing. Though he had not done what Helena had suggested to her brother, he had done enough. He had trespassed. He had all but made love to her on the floor of the lady's withdrawing room. She may have been wrong to suggest he had taken her maidenhead and gotten her with child in the process, but he was little better, in the end, than she.

He had sacrificed his honor and his duty for the sake of his prick.

Just as his father had done before him. He could only hope the results would not prove as disastrous. He was prepared to do whatever he must to avoid such a ruinous end. He would have to control himself in Helena's presence, that much was undeniable.

Lady Beatrice's shock was evident on her lovely face. "This lady you have compromised. Is she the same one you spoke of before?"

He thought of Helena and her taunting scent and her divine mouth and her curves. Guilty heat flared over his cheekbones. "Yes."

Lady Beatrice's nostrils flared, absorbing the blow. "I foolishly supposed you were concerned about a mistress. It is common, and I expected no less. Who is she?"

For some reason, his first instinct was to protect Helena. To keep her identity a secret. But it occurred to him in short order that when he took her as his wife, the truth would be apparent.

"Lady Helena Davenport," he revealed.

Lady Beatrice's lips tightened, her shoulders squaring. "Ah. I suppose I ought not to be surprised."

Her reaction startled him. He had done his utmost to keep his desire for Helena at bay. Had he not?

"It was a mistake," he said. "And one I shall forever regret. But the damage has been done, I am afraid. I will be marrying her as quickly as possible."

Part of him balked at his explanation, at calling Helena a mistake. A regret. She had done him a great deal of damage with her reckless deceits. However, he could not, in truth, say he regretted kissing her. Touching her. Holding her. He merely regretted what had come after. Her betrayal. This godforsaken audience with Lady Beatrice. Going against his deathbed promise to Grandfather. The prospect of a marriage that would fare no better than his parents' ill-fated match.

"It is imperative that you marry her?" Lady Beatrice asked, with a note of hope. "I do not mind weathering scandal. As your countess, I will do everything in my power to stop tongues from wagging."

He could not reveal the sordid truth to her. So instead, he nodded. "It is imperative, I am afraid."

"But I thought she was all but betrothed to Lord Hamish White," she argued, her tone taking on an unnatural, shrill quality.

"She was," he agreed, his discomfort reaching new heights.

What was the accepted convention for speaking about one's future betrothed with one's recently jilted betrothed? He was sure there was none. This was no ordinary circumstance in which he found himself unceremoniously mired.

"She has broken her betrothal for you, then, just as she always wished," Lady Beatrice said bitterly. "I was warned. I saw for myself the way she looked at you, but I had believed you too honorable for her wiles."

The vitriol in her voice startled him, but he told himself it was to be expected. Even in a paragon such as Lady Beatrice. He could not deny that Helena possessed plenty of allure. However, Lady Beatrice's words gave him pause. He had never supposed Helena returned his attraction until he had kissed her. Had it been obvious then? Had he fallen into her trap?

Surely not. How could she have known Lord Algernon Forsyte would have been bragging about his impending conquest? Unless she was guilty of more damning manipulation and deceit than she had already proven.

He shook himself from the thoughts, from the suspicions. "I can assure you that what happened between Lady Helena and myself was not planned. Neither of us intended to do you harm. Indeed, hurting you is the last thing I would wish, my lady."

"And yet, you have," she pointed out. "You are standing before me, telling me you cannot marry me although you have already promised yourself to me. That you have compromised Lady Helena in such extreme you have no other option save marrying her. What am I to feel, my lord? I was settled upon you as my future husband, and you have reassured me of your own sentiments throughout the mourning period for your grandfather. I have been waiting for you."

She was right in her words, in her anger, in her outrage. All of it.

There was only one thing he could say, and it was not a defense, but the words and the regrets were all he possessed to give her. "I am so sorry, Lady Beatrice. I will not beg your forgiveness, for I am unworthy of it. My actions are unpardonable."

"Yes," she said coldly. "They are. If you will excuse me, my lord? I find myself unable to bear another moment of this conversation. Naturally, you will make the necessary explanations to my father and mother?"

"Of course." He bowed to her, hating the pain etched on her face.

She turned in a flounce of skirts and fled from the garden, hastening down the path they had so recently trod together.

CHAPTER 10

Why is it that a woman must pay taxes and yet she is denied the right to vote for members of Parliament? How odd that, after years of fighting for equal representation, we remain at an impasse. One must wonder at the reason why.
—From Lady's Suffrage Society Times

$\mathcal{H}$elena would have supposed that, following her fall from grace, her father would have watched over her with the keen precision of a general going to battle, ready to rout the enemy. However, she continued to enjoy the ordinary freedom of movement which had been hers prior to the announcement of her revelation. Perhaps it was because Father believed the worst of her and was persuaded she could not further compromise herself. Perhaps it was because he no longer cared for her reputation now that she would no longer be the sacrificial offering to Lord Hamish.

Whatever the reason, she was heartily glad for the opportunity it afforded her to watch and wait for Huntingdon to emerge from his interview with her father the following afternoon. She was hiding in the library, awaiting the earl's long-limbed strides, face pressed to the crack in the partially opened door.

Her back was beginning to ache from the awkwardness of her posture when, at long last, Huntingdon stalked into view. His expression was grim, the dark bruising mottling his jaw doing nothing to detract from his handsomeness. He looked more serious than she had ever seen him, and she was the source of his bleakness.

Her heart gave a pang.

She rushed from behind the door and seized his arm. "Huntingdon, wait," she pleaded in hushed tones, casting frantic glances about to make certain no one else was about.

The hall was blessedly empty. But that did not mean Shelbourne was not hiding in the wings, ready to storm out of the shadows with his fists swinging once more. Or, worse, Father coming to hail another barrage of insults upon her. She tugged the earl toward the open library door.

"I need to speak with you," she told Huntingdon.

"Helena," he gritted, balking at her attempts to get him to go where she wished him. "What the devil are you doing?"

Being foolish, it would seem. And reckless. But that was hardly a new state for her.

"Hush," she ordered. "This way, if you please. I must talk to you, and I fear this is the only chance I shall have."

"There is nothing to be said," he denied, remaining rooted to the carpets in the hall. "It has been a long day for me as I had to make innumerable sudden plans, and the last thing I wish to do is prolong it any further. I am taking my leave."

There was everything to say, as far as she was concerned. He was still angry with her, and she could not blame him. She had not expected him to forgive her with haste, of course. But she could not help but to feel that if she made another attempt at explaining herself to him now, when the wounds were freshest, that it would be better for the both of them.

"Please, Huntingdon," she said, pleading with him for the second time in as many days. "I cannot bear to leave things between us as they are now."

"Curse you, Helena, have you not already done enough damage?" he demanded, his voice curt. Angry.

His words stung, because he was right—she had caused a great deal of damage for the both of them. His blue eyes flashed with fire, and this time it was not the sort derived from passion, but rather from rage. But she would not retreat.

"A few moments of your time," she pressed. "No one will ever be the wiser. They think I am off in my chamber, napping and hiding from the shame of the last two days. No one is looking for me."

At least, not as far as she knew. Her mother had been horrified by the impending scandal. She had taken to her rooms with the megrims the day before, and had yet to emerge. Helena suspected her mother's absence had far more to do with her father's ever-growing cloud of rage than with Helena herself.

Huntingdon's jaw tightened, but he cast a look around and then relented. "A moment. No more. But cease touching me, if you please."

His directive hurt. She withdrew her hand just the same. What choice did she have? If she were in his position, she did not know how she would feel.

Helena ventured into the library once more, all too aware of Huntingdon's presence at her back. The man simply simmered, whether he was furious with her or not. He could be on the moon, and she would still long for him desperately.

All she could do was pray she had not ruined every chance of making a match between them succeed.

Supposing he had formally agreed to offer for her, that was.

She spun about to face him, taking a deep breath. "What have you decided?"

He scowled, keeping his distance. "That is what you wished to discuss? With your actions, you have already stolen the freedom of choice from me. Unless you have so soon forgotten the melee in which I found myself yesterday following your false revelations to your brother?"

"They were not all false," she defended.

"The worst of it was," he countered. "Tell me, was this your plan all along, to fool me into keeping you from courting scandal and then seduce me yourself?"

His accusation took her by surprise. "*You* kissed *me*, Huntingdon, not the other way around, and if you will recall, I was quite put out with you for interrupting my plans on every occasion."

He raised a dark brow, eying her impassively. "Or was your outrage yet another act? I confess, I cannot be sure, my lady. All I do know for certain is that I shall soon have a wife who is an excellent actress, instead of the bride of my choosing."

Relief washed over Helena, along with the accompanying guilt and twinge of jealousy at the reminder of Lady Beatrice. He had offered for Helena, then. There was that. He must have also ended his betrothal.

"My outrage was not an act," she said, collecting herself. "How can you think otherwise?"

"Your actions leave me with no choice but to question everything I know of you." His voice was bitter, his expression shuttered.

His revelation struck her with the force of a slap. "Can you not forgive me?"

He remained icy and aloof, a damning stranger who had once kissed her with a lover's unrestrained passion. "I cannot say, my lady. What I do know is that it will take time. You can hardly expect your lies to be forgotten after a mere night's sleep."

He was not wrong about that. Nor had she expected him to so easily move past her actions. But what she had been seeking now was a glimmer of hope that her sins would not forever haunt them. Would not forever taint their marriage.

"I understand it will take time," she said then. "All I can hope is that you will come to understand the reason for my actions."

"I can promise you nothing. Now, if you will excuse me, I must go."

When he turned to leave, she chased after him, heart tight in her chest. She caught his sleeve, intercepting him. "Huntingdon, do not go yet."

"Damn you, I told you not to touch me," he snarled, turning back toward her with so much festering anger, she faltered.

"Do you hate me that much?" she whispered, humiliated by the rush of tears in her eyes.

This was misery in its truest form. She finally had what she had always wanted almost within her grasp, but she had ruined it utterly. She had taken what should never have been hers. She saw it clearly now. Huntingdon would not forgive her for this breach. For forcing his hand. For making him betray his cursed sense of honor and duty.

"I do not hate you," he said coolly. "All I have ever felt for you, Helena, is pure, base lust. It aggrieves me mightily that I was drawn to a woman willing to go to the lengths you have stooped to."

She flinched. "If you think so little of me, why should you agree to marry me?"

"Because, *darling*, you have told your entire family you are carrying my child," he sneered. "Which you and I both know to be a spurious lie."

"I only told Shelbourne, and I recognized it for a mistake as soon as I uttered the words," she said truthfully. She still did not know where her lie had sprung from in that wild moment, save overwhelming desperation and fear her father would still somehow find a way to bind her to Lord Hamish. "I cannot convey how sorry I am for what I said and did."

"Apologies do not make a difference, Helena," he snapped. "Do you not see? This is not some sort of bloody game. I was engaged to another woman. She was planning her trousseau, and I had to go to her and cry off yesterday. My own inexcusable lack of honor was bad enough, but to allow her to think the worst of me, to hurt her when she has only ever been the soul of virtue, is akin to swallowing a live coal."

She reeled, for she had not once considered he may have been in love with Lady Beatrice, nor she with him. If he had been, he would not have kissed Helena, would he have? His impassioned response had her more uncertain of herself than ever. Suddenly, she needed to know.

"Do you love her?" she could not keep herself from asking.

"What I feel for her no longer signifies," he said. "Just as what I felt for you no longer does either."

Felt.

Past tense.

He turned to go once more.

* * *

Huntingdon had to escape from this bloody library. From her bloody presence.

Because although he despised himself and his weakness for her, and whilst he loathed her lies and machinations, he wanted her still. Damn him to his soul. And damn her, too.

"Huntingdon," she called after him in her throaty contralto that never failed to curl around him like smoke.

Cloying, he told himself. Irritating.

Seductive, whispered a voice within. *Delicious.*

And she would soon be *his*. Not that he could rejoice in that fact now, when he had spent every waking hour in the past two days attempting to right the wrongs they had committed together and against each other. Not that he could rejoice in it ever, he amended. Because Lady Helena Davenport was dangerous. He wanted her too much. Felt too strongly. There was every chance she would lead him to ruin.

He had to do everything in his power to keep that from happening.

"Huntingdon, please." The swishing of silk and her soft footfalls alerted him to her hurried pace in the moment before she threw herself between him and his only means of egress.

She was pale, and he could not help but to take note of the faintly purple half-moons shading the delicate flesh beneath her glorious emerald eyes. He had never known another female who called to him the way she did. Who made him both want her and despise her for that base need. Who undid him without lifting a dainty finger.

He had spent the last few years desiring her. Now that he would have her at last, he could not help but to feel guilt at his own sinful actions, which had led to his ability to make her his wife. If he had never touched her, never kissed her, he would have been able to look his friend in the eye and swear Helena was lying without a hint of compunction.

It would have been the truth.

But no. He had given in to his base desires.

"What do you want from me?" he ground out, feeling the beginning of a massive headache blossoming.

Ever since his friend had dealt him twin blows the day before, his head had been throbbing at irregular intervals. Being forced to deal with the ramifications of Helena's revelations had not helped the matter.

Her bright eyes widened. "I...oh, drat you. I do not know what I want, my lord. But what I do know is that I cannot bear for you to be so angry with me."

"Mayhap you should have considered that before telling Shelbourne I got you with child," he pointed out, unable to keep the acid from his voice.

He would own all his sins. But he would be damned if he would suffer the consequences for those which he did not commit. Shelbourne was his oldest friend. They had been through much together. Shelbourne had helped Huntingdon through some of his darkest days. Days he would not think about now, lest those memories bring him low once more. He could not afford to be weak in Helena's presence. Not now. Not again.

"You kissed me," she blurted, a becoming flush stealing over her cheeks.

He had, and he had done more. And he would do more again. *By God*, he would do everything. He would have her in his bed, at his mercy. The side he had always kept at bay rejoiced. But the rest of him banished all such notions. The rest of him clung to the tattered shreds of his honor, to the man his grandfather had been proud of, to the man he had tried so bloody hard to be.

"Kissing you is not the same as bedding you," he told her,

not giving a damn if he shocked her. "You cannot get a babe in your belly from a kiss. Did not your bawdy books teach you that, my dear?"

He was taunting her. Throwing down the gauntlet between them. He could not help himself, it seemed.

Up went her chin. "Of course I know the difference. I was merely reminding you that you are not as innocent in this tangled web of ours as you would like to pretend."

She dared to mock him.

The effect upon him was perverse. Unwanted. His cock swelled to stiff attention, pressed to the fall of his trousers. He had yet to indulge in the paradise he had been charged with enjoying. For a fleeting, mad moment, he thought of leading her to the far wall of the library, of pressing her to the bookcase, taking her lips, kissing her throat. Of raising her skirts to her waist and plunging into her willing heat.

Somehow, he knew she would be ready. He knew she would be slick. *Damnation*, he already knew the way she felt. He *dreamt* about it. Ever since he had touched her—and yes, even last night as he lay alone in bed, much to his shame, he had taken himself in hand to the memory of her silken flesh. Had thought about doing far more to her.

It was too much to bear.

Before he knew what he was about, he slid an arm around her waist, hauling her into him. He was awash with a complicated combination of yearning, desire, shame, and anger. Her breasts collided with his chest. Despite the impediment of her corset, her every curve seared him.

"You are a witch," he said, using his free hand to cup her jaw.

To tilt her head.

Her skin was soft and warm and smooth. Her scent enveloped him.

And he was once more baptized in a pool of flame.

His need for her was stronger than his next breath. The knowledge he was alone with her in the library, that at any moment her father or brother or an errant servant could cross the threshold and catch them alone together, was not enough to stop him. He was beyond control.

She had made him this way, brought him to this.

Sunk him, like a ship tossed upon the rocky shoals off the shore in the depths of the darkest night. In the midst of high winds, storm-ravaged seas. She was the siren, luring him to his painful, inevitable demise. He could not let her.

"We should not," she said, but her arms had encircled his neck. And her lashes had fluttered against her cheeks. Her head was tipped back, those lush lips his for the taking.

He had not come here for this, for her. But now that she was in his arms, not even his raging anger at her actions could keep him from seizing what he wanted: her lips.

Her.

"No, we should not," he agreed. "Indeed, we never should have, and that is why we currently find ourselves at this damnable impasse."

And yet…

His head dipped. Their mouths met. She tasted as sweet as ever. Her lips clung to his. He had known other kisses in his life, but none had held a candle to Helena's. Mayhap it was the time he had spent longing for her in secret. Mayhap it was the way her mouth moved against his. Mayhap it was merely the woman herself.

Whatever it was, indefinable as it was, she had it. This woman in his arms. This woman he would wed.

She had the power to bring him to his knees. To dismantle everything he had previously believed about himself. He hated the power she had over him. He hated it, and he longed for it. Whilst he resented what she had done, he could not deny the way he felt for her. Or the way she felt in his arms.

Too good.

Perfect, in fact.

He kissed her hard, with almost bruising force, wanting to punish her lips. To punish *her*. To please her, also. Her mouth opened, her tongue moving tentatively against his. A throaty sound of surrender tore from her throat. He wrapped his hand around the back of her neck, his fingers plunging into her silken hair. Need for her thundered through him. He caught her lower lip between his teeth and tugged.

Another mewl escaped her. He dragged his lips lower, down her throat, finding her pounding pulse, the evidence she was every bit as moved by their embrace as he was. All the doubts which had been eating away at him since his interview with Lady Beatrice gave way. There was nothing— no anger, no fear, no bitterness. There was nothing but desire.

"Helena," he whispered her name against her neck, then kissed a path to her ear, his lips grazing the shell.

"Huntingdon, please." She gasped when he bit her fleshy earlobe, then almost purred when he licked the hollow behind it.

She trembled in his arms, pressing herself nearer. His cockstand was hard and insistent in his trousers. Not even his self-loathing could abate the swift rush of lust coursing through him. He ought to be better than this, he knew. Lemon and bergamot twined around his senses like the cloying constriction of ivy vines. He was aflame.

The floor of the library creaked as they moved together, the frenzy of their embrace heightening. The sound was a reminder of the reality in which they found themselves. They were not alone. They were not wed.

Good God, they were all but making love in her father's library when they were already being rushed to the altar to avoid scandal. He was stupid. So bloody stupid. Powerless, at the mercy of his need. Like his father before him.

This would not do.

He had to put a halt to this madness before he took things between them any further. Before they wound up in a tangle on the floor. Before someone caught them. Before the web in which they had been ensnared grew more complicated.

Summoning all the control he possessed, Huntingdon ended the kiss. He tore his lips from hers and set her away from him. As before, her eyes were dazed, cheeks flushed, lips dark. He wanted to despise her for what she had done, for the lies she had told, and yet, he could not.

"We will be wed in one week's time," he told her, his voice ragged. "I think it is for the best if we refrain from seeing each other until that day. Prepare yourself as you must."

Confusion dawned on her expressive face. "But Huntingdon—"

"For once in your life, listen to me, Helena," he interrupted. "I am taking my leave now. I shall see you on our wedding day."

How strange the words felt.

Not as strange as they should.

Huntingdon bowed, and then he turned and stalked away from her. He was going to have to figure out how in the hell he could gird himself against his future wife.

CHAPTER 11

The House of Lords must be won if we are to have any hope of victory.
—*From* Lady's Suffrage Society Times

The last occasion upon which Helena had been at the Earl of Huntingdon's townhome, she had been a trespasser, stealing inside for fear of what her brother would do. This morning, she returned as its new mistress.

Impossible as it was to believe, she was the Countess of Huntingdon.

Her fingers were clasped tightly in her lap as the elegant barouche, which had carried them from the wedding breakfast, halted before the imposing edifice. Huntingdon had not spoken a word to her for the duration of the journey from her father's townhome.

Wickley House loomed, her future.

Or mayhap more appropriately, as Huntingdon had warned, her doom.

"We have arrived," he said grimly.

Unnecessarily as well. She could see quite plainly where they were. But Helena supposed three words were better than none.

She cleared her throat. "So I see, my lord."

His attention had been carefully diverted from her for the ride. But he looked at her for the first time since he had spoken his vows to her in the church, his baritone ringing low and clear and firm, despite the misgivings she knew must have been inwardly churning. His jaw was a rigid slash, covered in a dark shadow of whiskers to hide the bruising still evident. His blue eyes were cold.

"I will introduce you to the household and make certain you are otherwise situated before I take my leave in the morning." The tone of his voice was sharper than the blade of a knife. Cutting. Frigid, too.

She knew he blamed her for the situation in which they found themselves. He had been willing to accept the responsibility of his own actions, but he had not been able to accept her betrayal. Helena could hardly fault him for the latter. She had lied to her brother, all to obtain her own freedom.

But she was nevertheless startled he did not plan to spend time acquainting her with her new home and duties. "You will be taking your leave, my lord?"

"Yes." He raised an imperious brow, as if daring her to question him. "I will be journeying to Shropshire to attend to matters on my estate. I am taking a train out of Euston Square Station just after breakfast."

Shropshire? He was...*leaving* her? On the day after their wedding? No honeymoon, no time together to speak of? She understood his fury, but this must be a mistake. Perhaps she had misheard. Would he not wish to at least spend more than one evening together as husband and wife?

"But...we have only just married, Huntingdon. Surely your trip can wait," she ventured.

"It cannot," he clipped with finality.

He was punishing her, she realized. Escaping her. But she refused to allow him to flee her with such ease. If he left in the morning, she doubted whether their marriage could ever recover. She knew him well enough. He would go away, wallow in his shame and his self-loathing over his own lack of restraint. His wounds would fester instead of healing.

"Then I shall go with you," Helena decided.

"That will not be necessary, my dear," he said smoothly, flashing her an insincere smile.

"Of course it will." She smiled back at him with forced brightness. "You are my husband. I travel where you travel, as a matter of course."

"Helena." His sensual lips thinned to a forbidding line once more. "I do not want company. I wish to be alone."

She swallowed against a knot of emotion. This was to be expected, and she knew it. She had hurt him with her actions, wounded him by suggesting he had acted far more dishonorably than he had, that he had committed the ultimate sin against his friend's own sister. And she had done that which no other before her had managed to accomplish: she had pierced his armor of honor. She had brought him low.

Now, he wanted to make her pay.

"But I am your wife now, Huntingdon," she pointed out, trying to maintain her calm.

"Yes, you are, thanks to your scheming. I find I require time to adjust myself to the notion of being tied to you."

Her thoughts churned with misery and unwelcome realizations.

He did not want her as his wife.

He never had.

He did not love her.

And now, after what she had done, he never would.

She tried to tell herself it was just as well. That having him this way was better than not having him at all. But the protestation was a hollow one. Because it did not feel right. Because the Huntingdon seated in the barouche with her, the man who had stood with her at the altar and stiffly spoken his vows, was not the same man who had kissed her with such unexpected passion, even if he was now her husband.

In his place, remained the detached stranger who had been so forbidding and cruel in her father's library until he had given in and kissed her. He was a fortress, and she would have to determine the best way to breach his fortifications.

"How much time?" she asked.

"Do not ask more of me than I am willing to give, my lady," he warned. "You have already taken more than enough."

They descended from the barouche in a decided lack of fanfare. He offered her his arm with practiced gallantry, but his expression remained aloof. Helena felt as if a fog of gloom had enveloped her. Little wonder the skies opened and a drenching mist began to fall as they made their way up the walk. The gray misery reflected her mood. Mayhap her future as well.

"Huntingdon, you cannot be serious about leaving me in the morning," she tried again.

"I am as serious as you were about spreading your ruinous lie," he countered calmly. "You wanted me for a husband, and now you have me. Mayhap you shall find you would have been more content with a different choice. However, the dye has been cast, and here we are. Do smile for the staff, if you please."

Before she could formulate a response, the door swept open to reveal his butler and a gathering of servants assembled in the entry hall. So many sets of eyes were upon her. Some of them had seen her before, and in a rather ignominious circumstance. The whirlwind of the last week had not left her with enough time to prepare herself for the reality of her new role.

She endured the introductions in a state of semi-wakefulness, feeling as if she had just been dredged from a deep sleep. Although Helena had stood with Huntingdon in the church and exchanged vows before joining him at the wedding breakfast, nothing seemed more real than this—the affirmation that everything was about to change.

Just how much remained the question.

Because she had a husband who had no wish to be a husband.

Or, to be more specific, no wish to be *her* husband.

By the time the formalities were observed, her cheeks ached from the feigned smile she had kept upon her face. Huntingdon led her upstairs, away from the welcoming domestics. He remained silent and forbidding, stern and tall and strong. His presence seemed a rebuke.

She waited to speak until they were alone in the hall. "Will you not change your mind about leaving me in the morning? What will the servants think? Or my family, for that matter? The rest of London?"

Not that she cared what the rest of London thought. Or most of her family. She did care about Shelbourne. He was her brother. And she cared about her mother's opinion as well. Indeed, part of her had hoped that in her marriage, she would be able to enjoy a closer relationship with Mama, apart from Father's draconian marital plans for her, which had been hanging over them like a storm cloud for far too long.

Huntingdon's handsome mien still showed nary a hint of emotion. "Your family already thinks the worst of me, Lady

Huntingdon. The domestics may believe what they wish, and the rest of London can go to the devil for all I care."

Lady Huntingdon. The title was unfamiliar. Unexpected. It was her—the Helena she was now, not the Helena she had been. The ultimate symbol she was no longer living beneath her father's less-than-benevolent thumb.

But nothing her husband had said gave her pleasure or reassurance.

She supposed she deserved no less of a response. "And what of me? Do you not care what I think, what I want?" Something horrid occurred to her then. "Do you have a mistress awaiting you in Shropshire?"

He smiled, but the expression held neither warmth nor mirth. "It is rather too late to concern yourself over such a question, do you not think, my lady? We are already wed."

She raised a brow, refusing to bend from this new question which would not cease nettling her. "I do not think it too late for such a query. As your wife, I have a right to know."

The mere utterance of the phrase *your wife* was foreign and unfamiliar. Almost unbelievable. And yet, real. True. Her foolish heart rejoiced anyway, because it loved him still. No one could persuade that stubborn part of her he would not one day return the sentiment.

He studied her, his sky-blue eyes dark in the low light of the hall where they had paused for their impromptu discussion. "I have pressing matters awaiting me in Shropshire. That is all you need know, my lady. Now, would you care to see the countess's apartments?"

How dismissive he was. *Pressing matters* indeed.

She swallowed down a rush of resentment at his iciness. "Of course, Lord Huntingdon. Proceed as you wish."

"Excellent." He stalked down the hall abruptly, taking her by surprise as he hauled her along with him.

They crossed the threshold of the countess's apartments just as Helena's slipper caught in her flounced hems. One moment, she was struggling to keep up with her new husband as he all but dragged her into the chamber, and the next, she was pitching forward.

Huntingdon was there to catch her before she fell. He pulled her into his arms, against his chest. Her hands settled upon the fine fabric of his coat. His familiar scent washed over her, along with a startling rush of longing.

She clutched his coat. "Forgive me for my lack of grace."

His lips thinned. "Intentional?"

He thought she had thrown herself into his arms?

Helena frowned. "Hardly, my—"

His mouth swooped down on hers in the next breath, stealing her words.

* * *

Dear God, her lips.

Gabe had missed them beneath his.

The feeling of them, soft and supple and warm, obliterated all his good intentions. There was a fever in his blood, setting fire to every warning he had painstakingly issued to himself for the last bloody week.

Although he had told himself he must go into this marriage keeping his distance from her, that he must do everything in his power not to succumb to his fervent needs, he could not stop himself from kissing her. Kissing her in a way he had not permitted at the church, following their exchange of vows.

As if she were finally his.

Because she was.

But that did not make this right. Nor did it ameliorate what she had done. He could not trust her and he knew it. He ought to stop. And he would.

But first…

First, his tongue dipped between the seam of her lips to taste her. He told himself she was a liar. That the goddess in his arms was the same conniving woman who had told his oldest friend—now likely his former friend, judging from Shelbourne's coldness at the wedding—that he had gotten her with child. That she had forced him to betray his grandfather's wishes and his own sense of duty and honor.

Yet, her arms twined around his neck. Her breasts were two ripe temptations pressed to his chest. She smelled as delicious as ever, and she kissed with the wild abandon he longed for. And he could not keep himself from kissing her harder, from owning that mouth, from crushing her nearer, taking everything she so sweetly offered.

Even if it was a lie.

Yes, his darling liar was an elixir he could not seem to get his fill of. He could not shake from his mind an image of her in the church, standing before him in a slat of sunlight, her gown as golden as her hair. She had been the most glorious sight he had ever beheld. For a moment, he had forgotten he had not wanted her as his bride, forgotten the means by which she had landed at the altar with him. For a heartbeat, he had simply been in awe of her beauty.

That same, foolish response reawakened in him now as he plundered her mouth. The urge to punish her was there, almost as strong as the urge to take her. He nipped her lower lip with his teeth harder than he ought to have done. Her surprised whimper into his kiss told him so.

Gabe's mind swirled with what seemed a thousand questions. What must the servants think, their master's abrupt defection from one bride to the next, disappearing immediately into the bedchamber with his new Lady Huntingdon? Was the door still open? Could anyone see or hear what they were about? *By God*, did he care?

Then, the most salient question of all.

Why could he not cease kissing her?

Just one taste of her, and all his determination was dashed, his resistance obliterated. He was made of sterner stuff than this.

He tore his mouth from hers at last. She was so lovely, he ached just looking at her. Why should perfidy be so beautiful? He reminded himself he must cling to his anger, his distrust. Lust was a deceptive bedfellow.

"Here are the countess's apartments," he said through a throat thick with need. "I will leave you to get settled."

That was when he should have gone, and yet he lingered. She appeared dazed, the fringes of her lashes fluttering over her vibrant eyes for a beat too long. In her wedding gown, she still dripped with golden, ethereal perfection. The rise of her bosom was a tantalizing promise only partially hidden by the blonde lace lining her décolletage.

His cockstand—already rigid after those kisses—grew harder. He did not think he had ever wanted a woman more. *Damn her.*

"No," she said then, her husky contralto doing things to his senses no mere voice should be capable of implementing.

"No, Lady Huntingdon?" he repeated, hating the title on his tongue, how right it felt.

Mine, said the reckless part of him he had never quite been able to stifle from the moment he had so stupidly touched her.

Stubble it, warned his common sense.

"No," she repeated, then paused, seeming to think better of her words. "That is, please do not go, my lord. I am not ready to be alone just yet, and I wish to have a frank conversation with you about your plans to leave for Shropshire."

Not this again. She could argue with him all she liked, but the maddening female was not accompanying him on his journey. A month or two of rustication in the countryside—hours of travel between them—was what he required to rein in his wild impulses and get his imprudence under control.

He sighed. "There is no conversation to be had, my lady. I am leaving in the morning, and that is that."

"If you insist on leaving, I will follow you," she countered, defiant to the last.

Her stubborn little chin rose, making him want to kiss her again.

Stupid cockstand.

Mayhap he should leave tonight. Or spend the evening at a hotel. Far, far away from this maddening creature he had wed.

"You will do nothing of the sort," he told her. "I do not give you permission to trail along wherever I go, and since I am leaving *because* of you, it stands to reason that London is where you shall stay."

"You cannot keep me from following you."

The daring wench.

"Of course I can keep you from following me," he countered. "Why not remain and enjoy the misbegotten fruits of your treachery?"

"Because I am your wife."

He pinched the bridge of his nose. "I hardly need reminding of that fact, my dear."

The color fled her cheeks, and he knew a moment of regret over the sharpness of his words. "Will you never forgive me?"

"We have been married for—" he fished out his pocket

watch and consulted the timepiece—"less than five hours, madam."

Her lush lips compressed to a firm line as she absorbed his words. For a moment, he thought he had won the argument and that he might reasonably extricate himself from this damned chamber before he did something more foolish than kissing her.

"Would you have treated Lady Beatrice so coldly?" she demanded next, shattering the delusion.

Her words sank their barbs into his heart, not just the reminder of his former betrothed, but the realization that he had not once thought of Lady Beatrice all day. His every thought had been of Helena. She consumed him.

This dratted obsession had to stop. She had betrayed him, manipulated him. Why could he not stop wanting her, in spite of what she had done?

Bitterness rushed through him. "I suppose we shall never know how I would have treated Lady Beatrice if she were my wife, shall we? You made certain of that, Lady Huntingdon."

"Cease doing that, if you please."

Her request had him grinding his teeth. "Cease doing what, forcing you to acknowledge the repercussions of your deceit?"

"Stop acting as if I am the only one at fault between us." Her emerald eyes were flashing with fire now. "I may have embellished upon the extent of my ruination, but you and I both know what happened in the lady's withdrawing room."

Shame mingled with the maelstrom of other emotions warring within him. She was not wrong about that. He had lost control. He had touched her intimately that day.

And he wanted to again now.

No. He had promised himself he would not consummate their marriage today.

He frowned at her. "That regretful interlude was dishonorable of me, and I gladly admit to my sins. However, I remain unconvinced you did not orchestrate your entire plan just to catch me in your web."

Like a beautiful, cunning spider.

The color returned to her cheeks at last. "I never wanted you to take Lord Algernon's place. Nor did I invite you to follow me about London, ruining all my opportunities to create a scandal. You took it upon yourself, my lord."

"So you say," he allowed coolly. "But you have already proven yourself capable of duplicity. Why should I believe a word uttered from your lips?"

They stared at each other, having reached yet another impasse.

"Oh, do forgive me, Lord and Lady Huntingdon," said an unfamiliar voice then. "I did not mean to interrupt your tour. I thought to see some of her ladyship's belongings settled."

He turned to find a female servant hovering uncertainly on the threshold of the chamber. Here was the invitation to escape he required. He had to remove himself from his wife's presence before he did something desperately ill-advised.

Like kiss her again.

Or, worse, make love to her.

"We have just finished our tour," he said to the servant before bowing to Helena. "If you will excuse me, Lady Huntingdon, I will take my leave and allow you to settle in. I will see you at dinner."

With that, he beat a hasty retreat from the countess he could not stop wanting.

The countess he should have never had.

He needed time, distance, and a plan.

CHAPTER 12

*I have yet to hear an excellent, or rational, argument opposing
women's suffrage. To those who suggest most women do not want
the same rights accorded their male counterparts, I say show me
their numbers. Men are, by nature, no more capable of making
sound decisions than women are. Indeed, on many occasions, they
have proven themselves far less capable...*
—From Lady's Suffrage Society Times

*H*untingdon was not coming to dinner.

Helena had always possessed a hopeful
nature. Or mayhap she had merely clung to her naiveté with
a little more tenacity than she should have done. Whatever
the case, during the course of the afternoon, she had allowed
herself to be distracted by the unpacking of her garments
and assorted *bric-à-brac* which had been sent over to begin
her new life. She had told herself she would see her husband
again over their evening meal as he had promised when he

had fled from her chamber as if Cerberus were nipping at his heels.

When she had received his note one hour to dinner advising her that a matter was delaying his return, she had maintained her composure. In her first official act as Lady Huntingdon, she had requested Monsieur Mallette defer dinner for half an hour.

In her second official act as Lady Huntingdon, she had asked Monsieur to postpone dinner an additional half hour.

In her third official act as the Countess of Huntingdon, she had requested dinner be served at ten o'clock in the evening.

And now, she sat alone, trying not to cry into her *gelée à la Belgrave*.

Huntingdon's chef was as excellent as she had expected. His dining room was decorated tastefully in subdued damask. The table was polished to a shine. The servants presiding over the lonesome affair were above reproach. If any of them pitied their new mistress for taking dinner alone on the day of her wedding, their countenances masked all such emotion. She could not find fault with a single detail. The silver epergne held nary a hint of tarnish.

Everything was perfect.

Except for the empty chair mocking her. The chair where her husband ought to be.

He had neglected to send a second note after the first. She could read his silence in several ways. None of them were promising.

Her dessert was sweet on her tongue. Realization, however, was bitter.

"I do believe I have had enough of dinner," she announced to the footman nearest her. "Please give my compliments to Monsieur Mallette."

The chef had outdone himself. Her inability to consume

more than a few bites here and there was not in any way reflective of his culinary prowess. But rather, her lack of appetite.

The only sensation gnawing away at her insides was apprehension, not hunger.

Withdrawing from the dining room, she kept herself from making a discreet inquiry into whether or not his lordship had returned or if he had sent further word. Instead, she made her way to the library which she had only briefly had occasion to explore during her several attempts at delaying dinner.

She sighed as she made her way toward the beckoning wall of books. Perhaps some reading to distract her...

A strange sound cut through the stillness of the chamber.

A sound that was low and growling and emanating from the chaise longue at the opposite end of the room. That was when she noted the unmistakable sight of large, stockinged feet and long limbs emerging from the scrolled back of the furniture piece.

Someone was sleeping in the library.

The sound had been snoring.

Helena moved toward the trespasser. Surely it was not her errant husband who was the source. Surely he had not eschewed dinner with her to fall asleep in the library. But before she rounded the chaise longue to find Huntingdon sprawled on the green velvet cushions, her instinct told her it was him.

And when she saw his handsome face relaxed in slumber, his sensual lips parted as he emitted another light snore, something inside her—the hope, the foolishness, whatever it was—broke. She had spent all evening wondering where he was, awaiting him, eating dinner without him, and here he was.

Asleep like a babe in the library.

She drew nearer to him, and the scent of spirits was redolent. As was tobacco smoke.

Strike that. Make that asleep like a *drunken* babe in the library.

That was when she took note of the almost empty decanter on the floor at his side. Helena's irritation and disappointment turned to ire. The urge to brain him with the nearest available object rose within her. But doing him violence would solve none of their problems.

She bent down and nudged his shoulder in an attempt at waking him.

The man was harder than a boulder. Truly, was every part of him hewn from granite?

"Huntingdon," she said, giving him another nudge.

He snored louder and shifted on his back, his eyes never opening. "Mmm, bubbies."

Had she misheard?

"My lord," she tried again, harnessing some of her irritation to give his shoulder a shake.

He groaned again. "Sweet, lovely bubbies. Let me touch them."

Dear heavens, she had not misheard. Not only was her husband soused and asleep on the library chaise longue, but he was talking in his slumber. In quite inappropriate fashion. About bubbies.

Whose bubbies was he speaking of? And just whose bubbies did he want to touch?

They had better be mine, said a wicked voice within her.

But never mind that voice, and never mind the nonsense Huntingdon was spewing in his sleep. Because none of that was her most pressing concern at the moment. No, indeed. Her most pressing concern was that he had abandoned her on their wedding night. He had left her to dine alone in favor of drinking himself to oblivion.

She knew he was angry with her for forcing their marriage, and Helena understood his anger, appreciated it even if some of it seemed rather hypocritical in nature. She had been willing to allow him to cling to his resentment, to work on his ability to forgive her. But what he had done this evening was to humiliate her, before all his servants.

She could practically hear the belowstairs whispers now. *Lord Huntingdon got drunk in the library on his wedding night instead of joining her ladyship for dinner.*

Mustering all her outrage, she shook him more forcefully. "Wake up, Huntingdon!"

Her voice carried, echoing from the high ceiling of the room.

He gave a violent start, his eyes opening to reveal a bloodshot sky-blue gaze and big, dark pupils. The confusion on his handsome face would have been charming in any other circumstance.

"Helena?" He blinked.

"Indeed," she said drily, standing to her full height once more.

His gaze traveled over her, lingering on the fullness of her bosom. Her evening gown had been chosen with care. Red silk trimmed with lace and beads, the pointed bodice showing off her waist to perfection. One of her best gowns, a dress that never failed to make her feel lovely. Chosen with him in mind. Suddenly, she wished to tear it away and thrust it into the nearest fire.

She would have done, had not it been the midst of summer, no fire in the grate.

"What are you doing in my bedroom?" he asked thickly.

The clod.

"We are in the library, my lord," she informed him. "I found you here following the dinner you neglected to join me for."

"Dinner?" More owlish blinks. "Not hungry."

"I dare say not." She wondered if he had eaten anything since the wedding breakfast that morning, and then she told herself she should not care. "Only thirsty for whisky?"

His brow furrowed. "Gin first, whisky second. There may have been a splash or two of Moselle somewhere along the way. And champagne, too. Celebrating my nupshells, don't y'know."

His *nupshells* indeed.

Helena entertained a brief fantasy involving overturning the remnants of the decanter on his handsome head.

"You have a strange way of celebrating, your nuptials, my lord," she observed coolly. "Where were you this evening?"

"Egggshellent question," he said affably. "Excellent queshtion. Er, question."

The fantasy returned.

"You do not know where you were this evening?" she demanded. "The matter that required your attention, which initially caused your delay, must have been of great import."

"Hmmm." He scowled. "You make my head ache, woman. Amongst other things."

As he spoke, he ran his hand casually over the fall of his trousers. To her shock, Helena could see, quite plainly, the outlined evidence of his words. Surely that was not...

Yes, it most definitely was.

"Lord Huntingdon," she chastised, as the undeniable glow of desire began burning within her.

There was something wrong with her, surely, to be seduced by the sight of a drunken husband who had avoided her all evening after announcing he was abandoning her in the morning and taking a train bound for Shropshire.

She loved said drunken husband.

That was what ailed her, she thought miserably.

Fortunately, Huntingdon appeared to collect himself

enough to realize the inappropriate manner in which he was palming his anatomy. He moved his hand on a gusty sigh. "Forgive me, hellion."

"Helena," she corrected grimly.

"I haven't forgotten your name." He closed an eye. "Hellion's what your name ought to've been. Damnation, there's still two of you."

Oh dear. Once, Shelbourne had drunk too much champagne and vomited in their mother's prized orangery orchids.

She frowned down at him some more. "Are you going to be ill, my lord? Shall I ring for a chamber pot? Your valet, perhaps?"

His other eye fluttered closed. "Let me sleep, will you? I was having the most glorious dream."

And she knew what his dream had involved. She swatted his shoulder, perhaps a bit harder than necessary.

His eyes shot open as he made a grunt of pain. "What the devil are you doing, hellion? That hurt."

"Helena," she gritted. "And I am keeping you awake so I can get you to your chamber. If you sleep on the chaise longue, you will have an aching neck and back."

Once more, she was not sure she ought to care. A back and neck that pained him were well deserved at this point. Particularly if the breasts he had been dreaming of had belonged to Lady Beatrice instead of her.

"I am comfortably perfect here," he announced. "Off with you, hellion."

She gritted her teeth. "I do believe you meant to say you are *perfectly comfortable*, my lord. However, I am certain you will change your mind in the morning. Believe me, when you wake in the comfort of your own bed rather than cramped upon this small piece of library furniture, you will be more than thankful."

"This library furniture piece of small feels bloody lovely." His eyes closed.

Was boxing his ears out of the question?

"Up with you, my lord," she ordered in her sternest voice.

"Mmm," he answered, and promptly began to snore.

She sighed and tapped his shoulder. "Huntingdon."

No response.

"My lord."

Another snore.

She decided upon a different tactic and moved to his stockinged feet. Careful to use only her fingernails, she trailed her fingers up the soles, tickling him.

He kicked and jolted awake once more, looking like a surly bear. "What the devil?"

"It is time to go upstairs." She moved back to the other end of the chaise longue and offered him her hands. "Come along, my lord."

It was rather the same fashion in which she might have spoken to a recalcitrant child. But it seemed suiting in the moment. The dangerously seductive husband of earlier, the one who had kissed her breathless and then stalked off to get himself thoroughly inebriated, was nowhere to be found. Drat him if there wasn't something ridiculously charming about him, even when he was thoroughly in his cups.

Even when he was planning on leaving her in the morning.

She still had not determined what she could do about that. She had been hoping to use dinner as a means of offering persuasion in her favor. It would have been an excellent opportunity to attempt to explain to him. Or to at least convince him to allow her to accompany him on his trip to the country. Instead, she had been left all but weeping into her soup course.

"Playing the part of wife quite well, hellion," he said then, grinning drunkenly at her. "What else do you have for me, concern from aside?"

Once more, he was speaking nonsensically. But she knew what he meant. Her cheeks went hot at the frank innuendo in his gaze. She was not about to attempt to encourage him to consummate their marriage while he was so thoroughly sotted, however.

"Come with me and you shall see," she said, wiggling her fingers expectantly.

At long last he accepted her offer, taking her hands in his. The shock of awareness when her bare skin met his was, as ever, electric. It seemed he could drink all the spirits in London, and she was still aflame for him. As helpless to resist this man as she had ever been.

She pulled, steeling herself against the unwanted longing unfurling within her. Attempting to help Huntingdon to his feet was akin to pulling a piano uphill. He was making no effort to aid her. And his grin was wider than before.

"Help me, drat you," she snapped, giving him another tug, using all her weight to haul him to his feet.

This time, he did as she asked, helping her to pull his reluctant body from the chaise longue. The haste with which he complied took her by surprise, and she stumbled backward, Huntingdon crashing into her. His hands settled on her waist, and his head dipped to her throat, his mouth finding her bare flesh.

"Mmm," said her husband.

She knew the feeling. But this was neither the moment nor the place for lovemaking. She jerked away from him as if he had scalded her.

"None of that, my lord. We must get you upstairs."

"Upshtairs," he agreed, giving her a drunken leer. "Er, upstairs. Will you help me to disrobe like a good wife?"

How convenient for him that he only wished to consider

her his wife in more than name when he was soused.

"You have a valet for that honor, my lord," she said crisply, taking his arm as he swayed.

As if she would not enjoy aiding him in the removal of his garments. As if she would not wholeheartedly delight in seeing what that sturdy male chest looked like, divested of his clothing. Or that pronounced rigidity outlined by the fall of his trousers…

No, Helena. You must not think of that.

"But what if I want *you*, hellion?" He stumbled into her, bringing with him his scent, which overpowered the faint tobacco smoke and spirits, and his infernal heat.

What indeed? her lonely heart whispered.

Before her head chimed in.

Not with the hellion nonsense again.

She wished she could say that she was entirely unaffected by his proximity. That his tap-hackled state had drained the river of longing flooding through her. But her body was intensely aware of his, and her heart still loved him desperately. Neither his avoidance and suspicion of her, nor his inebriation and plans to leave her on the morrow, affected the way he made her feel.

Her heart was pounding just from his nearness. She clung to her anger and her resolve as she swept him toward the door.

"You cannot have me this evening," she informed him. "Not after spending our wedding night fleeing from dinner and drinking yourself to perdition before falling asleep in the library. To say nothing of the manner in which you are planning on abandoning me in the morning."

"Didn't intend to imbibero—to over-imbribe—er, over-*imbibe*," he said pleasantly, sliding an arm around her waist as if it were where it belonged.

The most foolish part of her loved the possession in that

touch.

Possession he would both regret and abandon tomorrow when he woke, she had no doubt.

"But nevertheless, you did." Her voice was impressively firm and solemn as she steered him over the threshold and into the hall.

The staircase was next.

A footman hovered in the shadows, but Helena did not care for the intervention of servants who were unknown to her. She was certain Huntingdon did not make a habit of appearing drunk before his domestics, and though she wanted to believe his staff impeccable and incapable of wagging their tongues, she nevertheless found herself protective of him.

Undeservedly so, at the moment.

But he was a good man, the Earl of Huntingdon. An honorable man. At least, he had been until he had begun kissing her senseless all over London. A campaign which she could not truly offer complaint about. His kisses were wondrous.

She dismissed the footman with a nod of her head, signifying that she would not require assistance. The footman bowed and made haste in leaving Helena and Huntingdon alone.

Her husband nuzzled her neck as they made their way up the first step.

A frisson skated down her spine.

"Mmm," he murmured against her neck. "You smell so bloody good. Is it witchcraft? Shorcery? That is to say, sorcery?"

Another two steps and Huntingdon's hand crept up from her waist, sliding to cup her breast. She nearly toppled backward at the jolt that ran through her at the touch. Her corset and all her layers of silk and linen kept his hand from what she wanted most, his long, elegant fingers curling over her bare skin.

What would it be like for him to touch her there, in the absence of barriers, in the privacy of her chamber or his? No watching eyes hovering in the wings, no staircase to fall down and break her foolish neck? Grimly, she reminded herself that with the manner in which their union had begun, she would likely never know.

"It is hardly sorcery, Huntingdon." Up several more steps they traveled. "It is my perfume."

"It makes me wild."

His confession, in perfect, crisp English with nary the hint of an inebriated slur, was uttered into her neck. The fingers on her breast moved higher. Until his hand connected with her bare flesh.

Was it possible to be seduced on the stairs?

Helena wondered if any of her friends who so recently wed—the Countess of Sinclair or Lady Jo Decker—ever had found themselves at their husband's handsome mercies on such an unfortunate architectural feature.

Guard your heart, Helena. He did not want to marry you. He does not trust you. He will never love you. He does not know what he is saying.

Likely, in the morning, he would not remember a word he had spoken or a single shuffled step up the staircase beside her. He would simply rise, see his packed valises loaded into a carriage, and make his forbidding way to Euston Square Station and from there, Shropshire. Far away from her.

Where he could forget all about the unwanted burden of the bride he had never intended to take. If he had married Lady Beatrice, would he have drowned himself in all manner of spirits before coming home to snore in the library? Helena thought not.

The reminder of her husband's former betrothed—the paragon—was just the impetus she needed to guide Huntingdon up another flight of stairs until they reached the floor where the lord and lady's apartments dwelled.

Down the hall they went, Huntingdon becoming more of a dead weight with each step. He was leaning on her, kissing her throat. Nibbling her ear. Sucking on her flesh, then scoring her with his teeth. Whispering sweet, sinful words to her. Some which made sense. Others which did not.

By the time they reached his chamber, Helena was breathless from a combination of exertion and Huntingdon himself. *Drat him, drat him, drat him.*

She managed to close the door at their backs. The warm glow of the lamps bathed his apartments, illuminating the strange new territory. For a moment, the realization hit her. She had never been in a man's private room, aside from Lord Algernon Forsyte, and then he had not been present. Only Huntingdon had.

But that had been different. She had been a bundle of anxiety, needles, and pins. Nervous about what she had been about to do. And then, it had all been for naught. The sole man in attendance had been Huntingdon himself.

Being in his chamber now was different. Far more intimate. Because he was her husband, and he was at her side, still kissing her throat. Dear sweet Lord and all the angels above, was that his *tongue*?

Yes, yes it was. And it was marvelous, curse him.

"You taste better than the finest dessert." He kissed her ear again. "Everywhere."

Everywhere?

She thought of the moment he had slid his knowing fingers inside the slit of her drawers. When he had touched her in the lady's withdrawing room. *There.*

"I tasted my fingers that night," he said, seeming to read her thoughts.

Helena's cheeks were ablaze. "My lord, you must not speak such improper thoughts."

He licked the sensitive hollow behind her ear, nibbled at a particularly responsive cord on her neck. "Do you know what is improper, hellion? *Truly* improper? Every last *fucking* thing I want to do to you."

His sensual growl curled deep inside her, reaching a place she had not previously realized existed. And she knew his vulgarity and coarseness should have repulsed her. At least, that was what she had been taught. But when had she ever liked doing what she was supposed to do? When had she followed rules or cared for propriety?

She forced herself to tamp down the longing rising within her. To tamp it so far down. To ignore it. At least for tonight. At least until she knew where she stood in this new marriage of hers. With the man currently wreaking such havoc upon her senses and her ability to resist him.

"You need to go to bed, my lord," she told him.

"Yes," he agreed, swaying into her once more. "That is preshishly what I need. Ahem. Precisely. What. I. Need. You. But not you. No, indeed. I do not need you. I cannot trust you, hellion. You lied to me and forced me into this godfor-shaken...godforsaken union."

She had forced him, yes. And it was for the best that he had seized that moment to recall it, for the both of them. Because he was desperately drunk. And she was just... desperately, pathetically in love.

She disengaged herself from him, knowing that no good could come of this evening. Not when he resented her and was so thoroughly inebriated. Not when he intended to leave her so soon. Not after everything that had come to pass between them.

He swayed, then sank into a wingback chair with a lusty sigh.

Even his sigh affected her.

Helena debated ringing for his valet. This was decidedly not the manner in which she had imagined she would spend her wedding night, and she knew next to nothing about properly preparing a gentleman for bed. But then...how difficult could it be?

"Hellion." Her husband's eyes fluttered closed. "I cannot stop seeing those perfect, pink lipsh...lips. Do you know how many times I have imagined them wrapped around my cock?"

Oh dear.

He was speaking inappropriately once more.

It seemed that whilst sober Huntingdon was a rather staid affair, intoxicated Huntingdon was a wanton rakehell who uttered all manner of wickedness with nary a hint of a flush. Helena wished she could find his decidedly inappropriate speech detestable. Instead, all it did was fuel her hunger, her ardor.

Images settled into her own mind, mingled with the images already present after having read those bawdy books she had filched from Shelbourne. Images of her lips on her husband's magnificent manhood. What would he look like, freed from the fall of his trousers? What would he feel like, taste like? Her mind whirled with everything she should not wonder.

He looked raffishly handsome in repose, his long legs spread wide as he sprawled in the chair. Difficult—nay, almost impossible—to believe this man was her husband now. But not hers yet. Not truly. Mayhap not ever. As irritated as she wanted to be with him, she could not deny the sudden rush of tenderness that swept over her as she began to undress him.

First, his coat, which he aided her by shrugging out of. Then, his waistcoat. She found the buttons of his shirt, plucking the line from their moorings. As she worked, she bit her lip, trying to keep unwanted feelings from overwhelming her. Her fingertips grazed his heated bare skin, and she was suddenly flushed all over from the mere touch.

No matter how much she wanted to remain impervious to him, she could not.

She became aware of his regard, scorching her, searing her from the outside in.

She paused in the act of unbuttoning his shirt. "I ought to call for your valet."

"Not yet."

His denial gave her pause. "My lord, I know nothing about helping a gentleman disrobe."

"I want you," he argued stubbornly.

Of course, he was not saying the words in the sense she wished to hear them. But just the same, they filled her heart with stupid, incipient warmth.

"I shall do my best," she relented, continuing her task. "But you must help me."

Together, they managed to divest him of most of his attire, right down to his smalls. Helena could not escape the observation that every part of her husband was handsome. Even his feet.

She led him to his bed, and he fell into it like a downed tree.

"Mmm, hellion," he muttered. "Don't go."

As she tucked the counterpane around him, he began to snore. Helena studied his profile, noting the dark prickle of whiskers shading his strong jaw, the slope of his nose, his well-defined lips. Those dark lashes that were too long for a man, his rakishly ruffled hair.

And slowly, inspiration struck. Along with it came a plan.

CHAPTER 13

There is nothing more infuriating than someone who refuses to accept reason.
—*From* Lady's Suffrage Society Times

Gabe woke to a throbbing head, a roiling stomach, blinding white light, and the voice of an angel.

Strike that. The voice did not belong to an angel at all, but rather to the gorgeous bane of his existence.

Helena.

"Thank you, Bennet. Would you be kind enough to see a tray brought up for his lordship?" she was asking his valet.

He had no idea why she would be arranging anything on his behalf with his own manservant. Where was he? What time was it? And why did he feel as if an omnibus had run over his entire body, from head to foot?

Most importantly of all, why was he not on a train bound for Shropshire?

Bloody hell, his travel plans.

Remembrance washed over him. The wedding. Helena was his wife now. The breakfast. That interminable barouche ride to Wickley House. His flight to his club. Drowning himself in Moselle and champagne and everything else. Had he dreamt that she had helped him to bed the night before?

He had not consummated their union, had he?

He sat up and instantly regretted the haste of his movements. His stomach lurched, and he feared he was going to cast up his accounts. Helena swept toward him across the Axminster of his chamber, a gleaming ray of sunlight catching in her golden tresses. A goddess at any hour, curse her.

The window dressing had been pulled aside to invite the unusual brightness of the day. Even his soul cringed at the offending light.

He pinched the bridge of his nose. "What time is it?" he asked, taking note that she looked far too beautiful for her own good this morning.

Or mayhap for his own good. He had to continue his campaign of resistance, damn it. Supposing he had not already dismantled it the night before, that was. The sight of her in an afternoon gown of light-green silk that served to heighten the vibrancy of her emerald eyes did not help the matter. Her lush curves were on glorious display, and although he still felt as if he had been dragged through the streets beneath an unforgiving pair of hooves, an answering spark of awareness lit within him.

"It is half past one in the afternoon," she informed him blithely.

Impossible.

He must have misheard.

He frowned, but the movement of his forehead inspired a fresh spate of pounding in his skull until he softened his expression. "I beg your pardon?"

"Half past one." She reached his bed and settled her rump upon it, arranging her tournure so it fanned out behind her in an elegant wave of silk. "How are you feeling? You look rather green."

Fitting that he should match her dress and her eyes.

And she had repeated the same time. His train had already left the station by now. But he was not on it. Instead, he had been slumbering away in his bed. Which begged the question...

"Bennet knew what time I wished to wake this morning in preparation for our journey to the station." He narrowed his eyes at her, but this, too, created more physical agony. At this point, the roots of his hair hurt. "Why did he not wake me? Why did he not pack my trunks and satchels in preparation for leaving?"

Helena reached out then, her cool fingers kissing his feverish brow. "I told him to let you sleep. You were resting so peacefully."

She had told Bennet to refrain from waking him for his journey? And his valet had listened to her?

"Damnation, Helena. I have missed my train!" He winced after issuing the exclamation, for it was louder than he had intended and set off a salvo of pain in his head.

"You were in no condition for travel this morning." She stroked his sweat-damp hair back from his forehead in a tender motion.

Her wry observation was not wrong, he had no doubt. For he was still not in any condition for travel. However, that was beside the point.

He gritted his teeth. "Stop petting me as if I am a lost mongrel you are attempting to comfort. You went against my plans, curse you."

Her lips pursed, and she withdrew her touch, settling her hands in her lap instead. "I was acting in your best interest, my lord, as is my place as your wife. Someone had to do so. Mr. Bennet was going to wake you at dawn. The hour was unconscionably early."

"The hour was early so that I would not miss my bloody train," he growled, doing his utmost not to mourn the loss of her caresses. "Which I have now done, thanks to your interference."

It was not the first time the vexing minx before him had interfered in his life, causing a diversion from his predetermined path. He had a distinct feeling it would not be the last.

"Actually, if you will but think upon it, I do believe you missed your train because of your own foolish actions yesterday," his wife dared to correct him.

Her tone was gentle, the sort she might employ upon a child.

Her scent chose that moment to curl around him.

Why did she have to smell so damned good? Why did she have to be so beautiful? So tempting? Why had he poured all that damned Moselle down his throat? Had there been gin as well? He rather thought there had, more fool he.

"On the contrary, my lady," he countered tightly. "I missed my train because you instructed my valet not to wake me as previously planned. You gainsaid me. Just as I did not marry my betrothed because you informed your brother that I had gotten you with child. Will your manipulation know no end?"

He was being a churl, and he knew it. But the bile was rising in his throat, his head was aching, his mouth felt as if it had been stuffed with a sour pair of stockings, and his plan to escape the wife he could not keep himself from wanting had been dashed. He was not in an excellent mood.

"You missed your train because you spent the evening drowning yourself in spirits instead of joining me for dinner. I delayed it for hours, waiting for you until I finally gave in, only to find you in the library, snoring and soused on a chaise longue." Her eyes had darkened, the swirls of stormy gray hidden within their vibrant depths coming to life. Twin spots of color stained her cheeks. "And after your poor treatment of me on our wedding day, I still helped you up the stairs and into bed. You are welcome, my lord."

Her tone was biting.

When she phrased it thus, he was being a cad. But she had forgotten an important part of their unfortunate circumstances.

"I left you yesterday because I could not reconcile myself to the fact that I was tricked into a marriage with you," he countered, snarling.

She flinched, her expressive face showing just how deeply his awful words had cut her. And although it had been his intention, his own cruelty gave him no pleasure.

A subtle rapping at the door interrupted the tenseness of the moment.

Helena rose from his bed. "Enter," she called.

Bennet had arrived with a tray in tow. Huntingdon had not had cause to over-imbibe so egregiously since the days of his youth; he was not a man given to excess. However, on the rare occasions when he had, Bennet had always proven a boon. Nothing like a bath and a shave, along with some restoring tonic, to have a man feeling human again.

Helena glanced in his direction, her expression unreadable. "I will leave you in Bennet's capable hands, my lord. You can find me later in the library, should it please you."

It did not please him to find her anywhere. Not the library, not in his life. Most especially not in his chamber.

Actually, that was a dreadful lie. He wanted her *everywhere*. However, there was lust and there was common sense, and he knew which one he ought to heed most.

He watched her sweep from the chamber. If only he knew which one he *would* heed.

* * *

She ought to have poured the rest of the whisky on Huntingdon's head last night when she had the chance. Indeed, she ought to have left him to rot on the chaise longue so he could awake with a stiff back and neck.

Helena stalked the length of the library once more, a practice which had done little to distract her or lessen the sting of her fury as she awaited her husband's presence. If he deigned to join her, that was.

Should he appear, she would be sorely tempted not to toss a book at him.

Although her plan had worked and he had not abandoned her in favor of Shropshire just yet, he had been not only rude when he had risen this afternoon and realized she had thwarted him. Indeed, he had been cutting and cruel.

Part of her could not blame him. She had no doubt he had felt perfectly dreadful after the spirits he had consumed. However, any sympathy she would have felt in that direction waned the moment she recalled he had been drinking himself to oblivion on their wedding day.

To avoid her.

His words from earlier returned, bitter and needling. *I left you yesterday because I could not reconcile myself to the fact that I was tricked into a marriage with you.* But that was not entirely fair, was it? She had hardly tricked him. She had merely gone to her brother with the truth—a truth which she had admittedly stretched in a moment of panic.

"You will wear the carpets threadbare if you continue

pacing like that, and then I shall have to buy new Axminster in addition to another set of train tickets."

The grim baritone had her spinning about to face the subject of her ire.

"My lord." She dipped into a perfunctory curtsy, noting that he was unfairly debonair after an evening of carousing.

He had bathed and Bennet had shaved him. The bruising on his jaw from Shelbourne's punches was fading. His bright-blue eyes settled upon hers, and that same old spark lit her from within.

"My lady." He bowed, effortlessly elegant.

"You still intend to go to Shropshire?" she blurted.

"My intentions have never altered." He prowled nearer, stopping too far away to touch. "I was merely once more the victim of a hellion."

"A victim of us both, I would argue," Helena countered. "Although you do enjoy painting yourself as an innocent, I am not the only one of us at fault. If you had never kissed me or touched me, and if you had never disappeared last night to drown yourself in drink, you would not currently find yourself where you are."

He stroked his jaw, his stare burning into hers. "Because I am a fool."

"Is it so foolish to kiss your wife?" she dared to ask him.

"It is when she is as trustworthy as an asp, and need I remind you that you were not yet my wife then?"

His quick reply stung.

She bit the inside of her lip. "You need not be so cruel. What is your pressing concern in Shropshire?"

His countenance remained cool. Aloof. "It is far from you."

"You are not the only one capable of taking a train," she pointed out.

"Do you intend to follow me there, Helena, knowing I have no desire for your presence?"

His question should not hurt. Nor should his anger come as a surprise. Their impasse was nothing new, though the day was. Her husband, momentarily diverted from his intended escape, was every bit as unavailable to her as ever.

She decided a change of subject was in order. "When are you going to show me the rest of the house, Huntingdon? Yesterday's tour was regrettably brief."

While she refrained from reminding him of the heated kisses they had shared in her apartments, the sudden clenching of his jaw told her he was remembering. *Good.* Let him pretend he felt nothing for her but disdain all he wished; she knew what it felt like to be held in his arms.

"I suppose we may as well go now, since I will be leaving for Shropshire as soon as I am able. Bennet is seeing to new tickets."

"You need not sound so grudging about it, my lord," she told him. "I am your wife now, and this is my home, when in London."

His nostrils flared, the only sign her words had affected him. "Come, then, if you must."

She settled her hand on his arm. "Hating me will not make our marriage any less a reality, Huntingdon."

"As I said, I do not hate you, my dear." His response was smooth as he led her from the library with long-limbed strides. "I trust you are already familiar with the library?"

He spoke nonchalantly, as if they discussed something of no greater import than the clouds in the sky rather than his enmity for her.

"Not as familiar as you are," she returned sweetly, unable to resist the verbal jab.

If he wanted for them to be at odds, she could play this game every bit as well as he could. Indeed, she would have to, for what other choice did she have? She needed to harden her heart.

"Do not all husbands spend their wedding night on the library chaise longue?" he asked, leading her up the staircase they had traversed together the night before.

"I regret to inform you that is not my understanding of the manner in which a husband ought to proceed with the night of his marriage," she said, cursing herself for her breathlessness.

She could only hope he would ascribe it to their ascent of the stairs. This afternoon, it was much easier to travel at his side since he was not leaning on her so heavily. She had to admit, she rather missed his face buried in her neck.

Bad Helena. Do not lower your guard yet. He may be your husband, but he still intends to desert you forthwith.

The thoughts crowded her mind, the worries, the doubts, the fears. Unpleasant and unkind. All the feelings she had been able to thrust aside yesterday in the madness of their wedding day buffeted her now, like the winds of a storm.

He never wanted to marry you.

He may be in love with Lady Beatrice.

Tender emotions for his former betrothed, coupled with Helena's actions, could certainly be responsible for his coldness.

"And how do you have any understanding of what should have transpired, hmm, hellion?" he asked as they reached the next floor.

She opened her mouth to answer him, but he was quicker than she.

"Never mind," he growled. "I should not have asked. I am certain Lady Northampton would have informed you. If you have been indulging in the middling literary talents of Shelbourne's bawdy books once more, I do not wish to know."

"How do you know they are middling?" she asked flippantly, wondering if it was possible that a paragon such as the Earl of Huntingdon could have flipped through the same pages.

He most certainly kisses like he has, trilled a wicked voice she promptly expelled from her mind.

That voice could not be trusted, and it most certainly had no place in her cautious dealings with her new husband today. He was not being terribly hateful at the moment, and nor was he inebriated. But that hardly meant she could fall back into his arms. Her battered heart could not endure much more rejection.

"All lewd treatises are." He guided her into a long, large room that overlooked the street. "If their authors possessed an inkling of talent or creativity, they would not write such twaddle. Behold, the crimson drawing room."

"One wonders why it is so named," she commented, taking in the scarlet damask walls, covered with familial portraits, and the matching settees and chairs. "And truly, Huntingdon, has it never occurred to you that what you deem twaddle, others enjoy reading?"

"Who could?" A suspicious tinge of color appeared on his sharp cheekbones.

"*I* could," she ventured, suspecting she was not the sole person in the crimson drawing room who had relished every wicked word and scenario upon the page. "And I dare say you could as well if you would only cease being such a prig."

"You go too far, madam."

She slanted an unrepentant glance in his direction. "I could go further, I think. And so could you. Indeed, you have. Need I remind you?"

His color deepened, and he looked away from her, working his jaw. "I would prefer to forget my folly."

She was not certain if he was referring to the occasions

upon which he had kissed her, the books he may have chanced to read, or their wedding. Mayhap all three.

Helena decided not to ask. She turned her attention instead to the chamber, releasing his arm to take a turn about. The fireplace was fashioned of black marble, the mantel lined with the requisite clock. A massive gilt chandelier hung from the decorated plasterwork of the ceiling. A polished grand piano crafted of rosewood occupied one wall.

"Do you play?" she asked him.

"I am afraid not," he clipped, sounding so stiff. So aloof.

Beneath the carpets covering the floor, slashes of gleaming, intricate parquet peeked. Although the sun shone in the well-dressed window, the damask wall coverings did not appear to be faded, and neither did the floors.

Helena turned back to find him standing in the middle of the drawing room, looking distinctly uncomfortable and so alone. "Did your mother decorate this room?"

He inclined his head. "She did. As the new mistress of Wickley House, you may change it as you see fit, just as the countess's apartments."

He was acknowledging she was his wife at last? Giving her leave to make changes, even?

She studied Huntingdon, sensing his discomfort. He was a man who kept to himself. It occurred to her that she knew shockingly little about his family, aside from what she had gleaned over the years and whatever bits and pieces Shelbourne had offered.

"You were not close to your mother, were you?" she pressed, though she was aware she likely ought not push him too far.

Entrapping him in marriage and making him miss his train were sins enough, were they not? Now, she had forced him to conduct a tour. The least she could do was have mercy upon him and—

No, what was she thinking? This was also the man who had all but tumbled her on the lady's withdrawing room floor and then blamed her for telling her brother about what had happened. The man who had spent last evening lolling about in the library, cup-shot and dreaming about bubbies. She still did not know whose.

If he had been thinking of Lady Beatrice, she would never recover.

"She lived her life in the manner that pleased her," he said, his voice taking on a deeper chill. "She did not care for her husband or her children."

At the mention of children, Helena thought back to that moment in the gardens when Huntingdon had frozen after she had so carelessly mentioned his having a sister. Her gaze settled upon a portrait hung on the wall opposite the piano. A young, lovely brunette in a beautiful court gown stared back at her. The resemblance to her husband was undeniable.

Helena found herself drawn toward it, moving before she realized what she was about. "Is this Lady Lisbeth?" she asked softly, though in truth she did not need to ask.

"Yes." One word, succinct. The tone cold and forbidding, suggesting she was not welcome to probe.

And yet, she could not help herself. The more Huntingdon wanted to hide himself away from her, the more Helena wanted to unveil everything there was to know about him.

"She was quite lovely, my lord. I am sure you must miss her dreadfully." There had been some rumor surrounding her prior to her death, Helena knew. But Lady Lisbeth had been older than Huntingdon, and both she and her scandal had been long gone by the time Helena had made her presentation at court.

Since Huntingdon was Shelbourne's old school friend,

she had always known he had lost a sister. Had known, too, the devastation that surrounded her death. Shelbourne had instructed her never to mention it in Huntingdon's presence. And yet she dared to now. Not so that she might hurt her husband, but so that she might, at long last, learn something about him.

Find a glimpse of the man hiding beneath the impenetrable façade.

She glanced back at him to find the color had leached from his countenance. He was pale and gray, stony-faced. A stranger who refused to confide in her.

"She was," he agreed. "And I do. However, missing her will not alter the facts surrounding her death. Shall we move on to the emerald drawing room?"

His abrupt change of subject told her everything she needed to know. Everything, that was, except for his own emotions.

Would he ever lower his walls enough for her to see the real him?

Helena stifled a resigned sigh. She had asked for a tour, and it seemed he was intent upon the delivery of her request. "Yes, my lord. Lead the way."

CHAPTER 14

Make no mistake. We find ourselves at an important crossroads in our cause.
—From Lady's Suffrage Society Times

By the time he was back in the familiar comfort of his chamber that evening, Gabe knew he was in trouble. Clad in his dressing gown, he paced the length of the room, glass of claret in hand. He had learned his lesson the night before, and he had no intention of imbibing more than necessary to ease the edge of fraught tension within him.

He was coiled as tightly as a watch spring, and there was only one reason for his restlessness, the simmering tautness he could never seem to fully escape. Helena. His hellion. His *wife*.

He had remained in the presence of his new countess for the entirety of the day, largely against his will. However, each time he had attempted to extricate himself from her company, she had asked to see something else. The stables, the terrace, the guest chambers, the portrait gallery, the night nursery, the day nursery, and on and on, until he had squired her to the service closet and the linen rooms. Finally, at her behest, he had taken her to the larder, the kitchens, and the scullery.

He would not have been surprised had Helena requested to be taken to the roof. Or to the carriage house or the bloody coachman's living room. However, she had somehow restrained herself.

On a heavy sigh, Gabe drained the rest of his claret. He should have requested Bennet draw him a bath after the day he had endured. Mayhap a soak in the warm water would have soothed him. Or at least offered sufficient distraction.

Because he was acutely aware of the fact that only a dressing room and a door separated him from her. That was all. And he was itching to remove the barrier. To end the distance. To take what was his.

But no, he could not.

He had told himself he would not consummate their marriage until some time had lapsed. There was always the possibility for an annulment. If he bedded her as he longed, he would not be able to procure one. He had to cling to that grim realization. To remind himself of it with almost every breath.

Need for her battled with reason. Each step he took was a taunt.

Take her.

Do not dare.

Take her.

You must not.

Damnation. He paced the length of his chamber thrice more. But his body had a mind of its own. One moment, he was in the haven of his chamber where she dared not intrude, and the next, he was in the dressing room, hovering at the door to her apartments. Would it be open for him? What was she doing now? The light beneath her door suggested she was not asleep.

Turn around, you fool.

Go to sleep.

He knocked.

Softly at first, and then with greater insistence. He knew he should simply return to where he belonged, that there could be no temptation in separation and solitude. Bennet had procured new train tickets to Shropshire for tomorrow morning. One more night to resist her. That was all.

The chamber door opened.

It was as if an invisible fist slammed into his gut.

He forgot to breathe.

Helena's golden curls were unbound, trailing over her shoulders and down her back. She wore a cream nightdress that clung to her curves with sinful adoration. The garment itself was modest, with long sleeves that covered her arms and lace trim kissing her wrists. A small, wispy affair covered her breasts, held in place by a pink ribbon. He had never wanted to undo a knot more. Her nipples poked through the fabric, tempting him. Tormenting him.

She was, without a doubt, the most beautiful woman he had ever beheld.

"Is something amiss?" she asked, a confused frown creasing the pale smoothness of her forehead.

Yes, everything was amiss. The roaring in his head could not be drowned out. Nor could the fire in his blood be cooled.

"Helena," he said her name, hoarsely. It was all he could manage.

Her nose wrinkled. "Are you soused again?"

He deserved that query. And he wished he could blame the unwanted feelings roiling through him upon wine. But they had nothing to do with claret and everything to do with *her*.

Gabe swallowed. "I am not."

"Was there something you wished to ask me, then?" Her gaze searched his, so green and vibrant, like the promise of first grass in spring. "You have been behaving oddly all day. I know you are vexed with me for the circumstances of our marriage and for telling Bennet to allow you to sleep this morning so you missed your train to Shropshire. But I cannot bear much more of your—"

"Nor can I," he bit out, interrupting her swift rush of words.

He had a suspicion he knew what she was going to say, and he had no wish to hear it. He had been cool and aloof, bogged down by the weight of guilt and need and reckless want.

"Then what have you come to say this evening, my lord?" she pressed, her countenance solemn. "You have not come here to consummate our marriage."

He ought to agree with her. Ought to say something, anything worthwhile.

Instead, he reached out and caught one of the ends of the maddening pink satin ribbon and tugged. The bow fell apart, and the twain ends of the lacy scraps covering her breasts went slack. He hooked his finger in the left half, moving it to the side first. Then the right. He did not think he imagined that he could see the tantalizing hint of her pink nipples through the almost sheer fabric beneath.

Suddenly, the demure covering made sense.

"Huntingdon?" her voice was husky now.

The swells of her breast held him in rapt fascination. He ran the backs of his fingers over her nipple. The soft brush of cotton and the tight bud sent a new rush of lust slamming into him.

Curse her.

Curse this ceaseless want rotting his brain, infecting his mind like an ague.

"Say something," she murmured, a silken plea.

Instead of obliging, he caught her nipple between his thumb and forefinger, rolling it gently. The caress was simple. There was yet a respectable distance between them. No reason for the pounding of his heart. No reason for the prickles of awareness down his spine. He had only two fingers on her body, separated by a thin barrier of cloth, and he had never been hungrier for a woman in his life.

She had seduced him without moving.

Without trying.

"What shall I say?" he asked with more gruffness than he had intended as he tugged at her nipple, torturing them both.

He felt her stare, hot and hard upon him, searching, seeking. He forced his gaze from her breasts and fell into brilliant, sparkling emerald.

"Why are you touching me this way, if you do not want me?"

Because he *did* want her, damn her hide. Wanting her had never been the problem. Having her was.

"Do you want me, Helena?" he dared to ask, although he knew he should not.

Her lips parted, her gaze dipping to his mouth. "I have always wanted you."

The wickedest part of him rejoiced. Ration and reason ceased to exist. She was his wife.

His.

"Good," he said.

Then he crossed the threshold, venturing into her territory, the knowledge he would regret what he was about to do no match for the need thundering through him.

He took her in his arms, and he settled his mouth on hers.

* * *

His lips were firm and insistent, hot and wonderful. Helena fell into the kiss, winding her arms around Huntingdon's neck. It seemed surreal, the man who had been so cool all day long, burning against her. If this was a dream, she never wanted to wake.

Her fingers found their way into the silky softness of his hair. Every part of her was keenly aware of him. His mouth on hers, his teeth tugging at her lower lip, his hard chest crushing into her breasts, the thick ridge of his manhood prodding her belly. He filled her senses. Even his scent, musky, familiar, intoxicating, twined around her. His taste was sweet and smooth with a hint of claret.

She kissed him back with all the fiery, pent-up need within her. Kissed him with the anger and the passion, with the longing and the love. And as she clung to him and he fed on her mouth as if he were starved for the taste of her, she made herself a vow.

Tonight, she would not let him escape.

He would not run from her.

Would not put an abrupt halt to the desire catching flame between them.

No, indeed. Tonight, he was going to make love to her. They would lie together as husband and wife, and if he still decided to leave her in the morning...well, that was a worry for the light of the dawn sun. There was no room for fear or common sense in this moment. There was only space enough for the two of them.

Fortunately, Huntingdon did not seem any more inclined to put an end to this madness than she was. He guided them, backing her in the direction of the bed she had spent the last night in alone, wishing he had been there with her. His hands were on her waist, firm and possessive. His kisses never wavered.

This meeting of mouths was different than all the exchanges which had preceded it. This time, there was an undeniable carnal intent, heightened by their dishabille and the lateness of the hour and the fact that they were alone in her chamber, nothing and no one to stop them. He sucked on her lips, ravishing her with his mouth.

She could not quell the moan that rose from deep within. Every part of her was ablaze. Her breasts felt heavy and full, the place between her thighs throbbing and slick. She wanted him to touch her there as he had before.

As if he had heard her thoughts, Huntingdon broke the drugging kiss, lifting his head to gaze down at her. "Off."

She blinked at him, trying to understand his one-word command. "Pardon?"

It amazed her that she was capable of speech. Of coherent thought.

He tugged at her night rail, his eyes searing her. There was a new light within the blue depths, a hunger she had never seen. She shivered beneath the force of that stark desire. Not because she feared it, but because she wanted it to consume her.

She released him with great reluctance and obliged, taking the soft cotton in her hands and pulling it over her head in one swift motion. Cool night air bathed her skin. She was naked, from head to toe, nothing to hide her from him.

Though a wave of shyness hit, she refused to give in as Huntingdon's gaze traveled over her. This was her husband, the man she loved. The man she had loved from a long-ago moment when he had visited their country house as Shelbourne's school chum. He was hers to keep now, but he was also hers to lose.

And lose him she must not.

Therefore, she dared.

Calling upon some of what she had read in Shelbourne's pilfered books, she reached for her husband's dressing robe. If she was nude, it was only fair that he must be as well. The tantalizing swath of his muscled chest, finely stippled with dark hair, was not enough. Her fingers found the belt, undid the knot. Beneath it, he was naked.

"Helena," he protested, his hand catching hers to stay her progress.

But she was having none of it.

"Let me, my lord," she said, part demand, part plea.

She wanted so badly to touch him, the need an ache in her fingertips. Helena pushed the robe from his shoulders, gliding her hands along his firm, warm flesh as she did so. The garment fell to the floor. She continued her exploration. He was so male. So beautiful, all angles and cords and sinews. His hardness different from her softness, the blunt, angular lines of him nothing at all like her curves.

He stood still under her ministrations, allowing her to touch him as she liked.

Helena grew bolder. She pressed a kiss to his chest, directly above his wildly beating heart. Her hands drifted lower, seeking the part of him she had not dared to directly behold. She glanced over his firm, thick hardness.

On a growl, he caught her wrists. "Damn you, hellion, not yet."

There it was again, the reminder of the night before. She wondered just how much he remembered. But in the next instant, his hands were on her, his arms around her. She was suddenly floating above the floor as he carried her the rest of the way to her bed before laying her gently upon it.

He joined her, his body settling between her legs, his hands coasting over her skin and sending sparks shooting through her like stars. "You are every bit as ravishing as I imagined."

His low words dashed away any lingering timidity. He had imagined her without clothing before? She would have demanded to know when and how often, but his head dipped, and those sinful lips of his latched on her nipple. An exquisite rush of sensation sent her reeling as he sucked.

Her back arched from the bed, her hands settling on his shoulders. She had read about such matters, but reading them and experiencing them herself, Huntingdon's mouth hot and wet upon her...there was no comparison. Nothing could have prepared her for the sleek suction.

Nor the next sensation he unleashed when those long, elegant fingers of his slipped between her already parted thighs and he teased her pearl with slow, tantalizing circles. Her hips bucked, seeking more. And he gave her more, releasing her nipple to flick his tongue over the distended bud while he rubbed her sensitive flesh harder below.

"Oh," was all she could manage to say when he moved to her other breast, torturing that nipple as surely as he had the first.

A sea of pleasure was running through her.

Delicious, overwhelming pleasure.

And she wanted to drown in it.

"So wet," he murmured against the curve of her breast, his voice dark with seduction and a note of approval. "Will you welcome me, Helena?"

Did he need to ask?

Could not the man see she was out of her mind for him, that she had been all along?

She was about to tell him so when his fingers left her pearl and traveled down her seam, finding her core. He slicked her moisture as he went, painting her with her own dew. How strange and feverish she felt, almost overwhelmed by need, wanting him there. Inside her. Any part of him, all of him.

"Helena," he said again, his gaze finding and holding hers through the low light of the lone gas lamp she had kept lit. "I must be mad to be here with you, to be touching you like this. I promised myself I would not."

As he uttered those unwanted words, he slid a finger inside her sheath. Just a shallow thrust. She inhaled at the sudden invasion. He moved slowly, rubbing her, allowing her body to stretch and relax around him. Readying her, it seemed, and with each knowing caress heightening her desperation to a raw crescendo.

"You..." she began to speak, but words fled her once more when he sucked her nipple again, then used his thumb to pleasure her nub while he moved in and out of her passage.

"I?" He prompted wickedly, lashing her with his tongue.

Think, Helena. What were you about to say?

She struggled to form thoughts, but making sense of anything with the weight of his body atop hers and his mouth and fingers working magic was an impossible feat. In and out, shallow dips, his thumb swirling.

"Yes," she managed, finding the word at last. The only word that mattered, aside from mayhap three others.

But she would save them for another day. For now, they remained her secret, locked deep within the hidden depths of her heart.

"Yes," he echoed, and then his fingers were gone.

Her throbbing core cried out at the loss. She had been so close to release, and now she was left aching and writhing beneath him. She pumped her hips upward, desperate to find him, to make contact.

He kissed a path down her belly. "Patience," he whispered as he went. "Have patience, hellion."

For some reason, the sobriquet, which she had supposed he used as an insult the night before, sent a strange frisson of something else through her now. Warmth. Longing. Love.

Different love, stronger than before. This connection between them—the physical bond—moved her in a new way. Deepened her emotions. Strengthened everything.

"Huntingdon, please." She was restless beneath his traveling lips. Wanting more.

He kissed all the way to her center. When his tongue flicked over her pearl, she jolted. His touch there had been incredible. His mouth was incendiary. It was shocking and wicked. She had read about this as well, but words could not begin to describe the delicious sensations coursing through her.

He drew on her there, just as he had done with her breasts. Then he feathered fast, decadent strokes over her, alternating between sucking, licking, and nipping. His hands moved as he pleasured her, caressing her hips.

Her fingers fisted in the bedclothes as he feasted upon her. She could not keep a low moan from rumbling free. His dark head between her thighs was at once startling and beautiful. His groan of desire vibrated her already pulsing pearl, sending a ripple of decadent desire through her everywhere.

She was helpless, pinned to the bed by need. His hands coaxed her thighs wider still, opening her to him. His tongue traced back down to her entrance, thrusting there in the same manner his fingers had worked her. She writhed, moaning, trying to get him deeper.

And then, his fingers were back upon her pearl, teasing her, taking her to the edge.

"Spend for me," he urged her. "I want your cream on my tongue."

The vulgar words should have shocked her, but she liked them. There was something so wicked about hearing them, so unexpected, emerging from Huntingdon himself. They made her wilder.

So, too, did his mouth. His tongue moved faster, his fingers swirling over her with increased insistence. And she was soaked, the sound of her wetness echoing in the chamber with erotic abandon. But the sounds mingled with her responses only seemed to increase his ardor. He buried his face deeper between her legs, his fingers biting into her hips.

It was all so good. Too good. And she was close. Too close… No, she was already there.

The frenzied rush of her release caught her by surprise. One moment, she was near, the sensitive place between her legs throbbing and pulsing. The next, she felt as if she had come apart. Her eyes slid closed, bursts of light dancing on her eyelids. Something inside her contracted, then pulsed. Wave after wave of bliss crashed over her.

A whimpered moan escaped her lips as she gasped to catch her breath. Her heart pounded as fast as the hooves of a spooked horse galloping into the distance. She was nothing more than splintered shards. And although she had touched herself in the dark sanctity of her own chamber on many nights, nothing had ever compared to this complete owning of her most intimate self.

Nothing wrought by her own fingers had ever brought such soul-gripping pleasure. Her eyes fluttered open to find his gaze on her. For a moment, she feared this was all he would allow, that he would flee back to his chamber as if this wicked interlude had never been.

But first, Huntingdon pressed a kiss to her sensitized flesh, and then he moved. Up her body, his mouth warm and wet upon her bare skin. Her hip bone, the curve of her belly, the hollow of her waist. Higher. Each breast. Her nipples. He sucked one again as his fingers found the secret places where she burned for him most.

She clutched at his shoulders, body bowing from the bed. Wanting more. Wanting him. Wanting *everything*.

And he was right there, settling over her, his powerful body once more a delicious weight. He kissed a path over her collarbone. Dragged his mouth up her throat. She trembled with the violence of her own need for him, not at all abated in spite of the pleasure he had already bestowed upon her.

"Huntingdon, please," she said. "I need you."

Inside me.

The last words were too bold, even for her. They hung in the air, though, unspoken yet somehow still there, vibrating with potency.

He kissed her ear. "If I consummate this marriage, we can never undo what has been done."

Had he intended to undo it? Her mind whirled, the spell of desire disrupted. There were no causes for divorce, so that meant he had contemplated an annulment. Perhaps that was the true reason behind his sudden trip to Shropshire.

Hurt lanced her heart. She could not help it. Helena wished he had not said anything at all. She ought to push him away, to stop this madness. Should she truly surrender her body and heart to a man who had been secretly contemplating abandoning her?

"Helena?" He lifted his head until his face hovered over hers.

She wished she could look away, but he stole all her attention as ever. There had never been anyone but him. He was the only one she longed for. The only man who had ever made her feel those queer little sparks fluttering through her, the tightening in her belly, the breathlessness and heart-fluttering moments when their eyes connected. And when he touched her, *good Lord...*

But still, she had her pride.

She cupped his face, the prickle of his whiskers, reemerging after his morning shave, stinging her palms in a delicious rasp. "Do you mean to annul our marriage?"

She had to know.

She did not want to know.

His eyes did not flit from hers. "I had considered the possibility."

No subterfuge from him, then. She could respect his honesty, if not his intentions.

They were almost as close as man and woman could be, their naked bodies pressed together, and yet, he still held a part of himself from her. She did not know if he would ever relent enough to allow her into his heart. To welcome her there. When she had spent the last few weeks plotting to rid herself of Lord Hamish, somehow, she had been desperate to do everything in her power to keep from marrying a man she could never love.

In her haste, she had never stopped to think about what it would be like to marry a man who could never love *her*.

"And now?" she asked him, needing to hear his answer, no matter the damage it would do her.

"I want you," he said, the raw confession sounding as if it had been torn from him. He moved, and for the first time, she knew the sensation of his rigid manhood rubbing over her, the tip of him brushing over her pearl until she quaked with a renewed sense of urgency. "Do you not feel how much?"

She did feel. And it was marvelous. Helena jerked against him, undulating her hips so that his length rubbed up and down her needy flesh. But still, he had not answered her question. She would not lie with him if he was uncertain about what he wanted, the lust inspiring him notwithstanding.

She understood well enough the way it was between a man and a woman. A man could want a woman without loving her, and the same was true for a woman. The problem was, in this instance, the woman was desperately in love with the man, and her heart could not bear to be split in two.

She was still holding his face in her hands. Her thumbs investigated the sharp delineations of his cheekbones as she studied his face. "That is not an answer, my lord. Do you wish to remain married to me, or would you rather be free? I cannot bear the thought of you spending the rest of our lives resenting me. If you shall hate me forever, then I set you free before we go too far."

"We have already gone too far," he told her, turning his head to drop a kiss upon first her left palm, then her right.

Still, this was not the answer she sought.

"I have to be inside you. It is a need which supplants all else. Therefore, I surrender. You have won." He lowered his head and sealed his lips to hers.

Helena did not want his surrender. Nor did she want to win. She wanted his love. But if there remained the chance she might ensnare that, surely she owed it to herself to try...

He licked along the seam of her lips. She opened to him. Their tongues tangled, and the musk of her sex invaded her mouth along with him. Her hands traveled from his face to his silken hair, then to his back. The muscles of his shoulders flexed beneath her questing touch, and she could not help but to marvel at the strength and softness of him. Smooth, warm skin encompassing rippling muscle and sinew.

It seemed at odds, much like the man himself.

One moment, he consumed her with the ardor of a lover, and the next, he viewed her with the cold reckoning of a scorned suitor. How could a man so hot also be so cold?

Any misgivings fell away beneath the power of his kisses. As he kissed her, he rubbed his shaft over her pearl again and again. She shuddered and quaked beneath him as a small tremor of renewed release passed through her. But it was not enough. Nothing was. Nothing ever had been.

Helena had been waiting her entire life for this claiming. For this man. For this night. She clung to him, kissing him back with all the frantic ardor clamoring through her. There would be no annulment. After this night, they would be bound to each other forever.

It was what she wanted. She would fret over the rest later. Not now. For now, all she wanted was this. Him.

He bit her lower lip, a low sound of need emerging from his throat. "Ready for me, hellion?"

"Always," she whispered, half promise, half plea.

He aligned himself with her, and then he was inside her. The tip of him at first. Slow and shallow. She inhaled swiftly, shocked at the size of him, so different from his fingers and tongue. So much more, in every way.

"More?" he asked against her lips.

"More," she agreed.

He moved again. Deeper. A small thrust. She burned. But still, she did not feel any pain. Only a slight discomfort at the newness of it all.

"More," she said again, moving her hips beneath him in an attempt to seat him fully.

But he was stronger than she was and, in this instance at least, possessed of greater control. He kissed her furiously, his tongue lashing at hers. Then he caught her leg and hooked it over his hip, bringing their bodies flush. He sank inside her a bit deeper. His encroachment was painstakingly slow. Helena was desperate for him. Her entire body clambered for more. Instantly.

She could not wait.

Growing impatient, she planted her right foot on the mattress and pushed herself upward. Huntingdon had not anticipated her sudden movement. The action lodged him farther inside her.

He grunted, then shifted, thrusting deeper still, and groaned. "Helena, I am trying my damnedest not to cause you pain."

She did not think pain possible. Discomfort mingled with ridiculous, all-consuming bliss. The feeling of him within her was wondrous and strange and good. So very, very good. But not good enough. Because beneath it all, she could not shake the sensation that he was withholding from her, that there was more to be had, more to be felt. She was not fashioned of porcelain, and she would not break. No, indeed. She was Helena Davenport, and she had been made for this man.

He only had to realize it.

"Just bed me, Huntingdon," she gritted. "Waiting is more torture than anything you can possibly do."

As she said the words, she bucked her hips again. The friction of him inside her sent a current straight through her. Rapturous agony. That was how she could best describe it.

"Damn you, Helena," he growled, and then he plunged inside her.

All the way. Deep. She knew it because of the sharp sting followed by the undeniable rightness. Pain mingled with pleasure, the two entwining into a heady, odd mix.

He felt so good inside her. Filling her. He reached a place she had not realized existed. Sparks skittered. She held him to her tightly when he would have withdrawn, the leg hooked around his waist keeping him lodged within her.

"Make me yours," she commanded against his lips.

On a growl, he began to move again. His hips withdrew, then slid inside her once more. Between their bodies, his knowing fingers played a steady rhythm on her pearl. All the while, he kissed her. Lips and tongue and teeth. In and out. The pain receded and all that remained was the pleasure.

And it blossomed and grew. Another tremor of ecstasy quaked through her. She tightened on him, kissing him hard as she reached her pinnacle. He groaned into her mouth, his body stiffening over hers, and then he was plunging deep, and a spurt of warmth filled her.

Huntingdon broke the kiss, his face dipping to her neck, his breathing ragged and hot. Helena clutched him to her, heart pounding, love and awe warring within her for supremacy, along with the remnants of pleasure.

Their marriage had been consummated.

He was hers now.

Finally.

CHAPTER 15

Those who feel women should be denied the Parliamentary franchise because of their intellectual inferiority should, perhaps, have their own mental acuity examined instead.
—From Lady's Suffrage Society Times

*H*e woke to his wife, naked and glorious, sleeping peacefully beside him. Even in her slumber, she encroached upon him, her slim ankle crossed over his calf, tendrils of golden hair on his pillow, her fingers grazing his shoulder. It was, he thought, rather symbolic of their marriage.

A marriage which he had made permanent and inextricable last night.

Excellent restraint, Gabe. Two days into your marriage, and you have already bedded her.

He winced at the realization. It was his fault, everything that had happened over the last few weeks. From the moment he had touched her for the first time, he had been lost. There had never been any hope of this conflagration between them ending in anything other than the rumpled bed upon which they now lay.

Still, as he watched her, slumber softening her lovely countenance, a riotous blonde curl on her cheek, the resentment and shame that had been his almost-constant companion was supplanted by a rush of tenderness instead. He longed to tamp it down, that unwanted emotion. But it had taken hold, like a weed in a garden.

Making love to her had been a mistake.

He never should have done it. He could not wait to do it again.

His morning cockstand twitched at the thought of plunging into her tight, wet heat. Of waking her with kisses and then rolling her to her back...

No.

That would not do him a whit of good. For one, she may still be sore after their lovemaking the night before. For another, it would only further enslave him to her. He could not afford to allow his desire for Helena to cloud his mind. Time and distance, a polite marriage of mutual respect —*Shropshire*—remained what he needed.

Consummating their marriage did not have to change anything, including his plans. Taking care to keep from waking her, Gabe disengaged from her body and left the bed. His discarded dressing robe was easily found in the early morning shadows, abandoned where he had left it in a heap upon the Axminster. He stuffed his arms into the robe and fastened it, trying to banish the steam from his head, the poison from his blood.

The rustling of bedclothes and her sleepy sigh reached him as he lingered, breathing in the new scent of the countess's apartments. Bergamot and citrus and something that was purely Helena. Looking back to the bed he had left her in was a mistake. The pale curve of her rump was on display, and one of her full breasts had slipped free of the bedclothes, a pink, pouting nipple taunting him.

My God, how the hell am I going to leave her?

He was not going to.

Realization hit him right in his thudding heart.

He could not leave for Shropshire now. Anything he needed to discuss with his steward there could be conducted from afar. Traveling there had been naught but an excuse, an easy means of escape. After what had passed between himself and Helena last night, he knew he needed to resurrect his walls and sense of duty.

Because his duty was to her as well. When he had married her, she had become his family. She was his countess, for better or worse. Right or wrong, they were forever bound, and he was determined not to make the same mistakes as his parents.

Grimly, Huntingdon crossed the chamber, returning to his own. If he lingered here any longer, the urge to slip back into her bed would be unavoidable. And he could not succumb to his lust again so soon.

No matter how desperately he longed to.

Time and distance could be affected in different ways.

Helena awoke to light streaming through the cracks in the window dressing. She stretched her arms over her head and yawned as wakefulness gradually descended. Her body was sore in strange places, every part of her deliciously aware of her nakedness beneath the bedclothes.

Remembrance hit her.

Huntingdon had made love to her last night.

She sat up in bed, holding the sheets over her bosom, and searched the chamber for any sign of him. There was none.

Of course there was not.

Had she expected any less? *Silly Helena.* What had she thought, that he would spend the night in her bed and proclaim his undying devotion to her by morning light? The chances were greater that he was already bound for the train station, determined to depart for Shropshire and leave her alone in London.

Grimly, she rose from the bed and found a *robe de chambre* her lady's maid had laid out for her the previous evening. She secured each button in its moorings before taking in her appearance in the large, gilt-framed looking glass occupying one of the walls of her chamber.

The woman staring back at her was almost a stranger. Her blonde tresses were wild and mussed with the evidence of what she had done the evening before with Huntingdon. She attempted to smooth the strands down and gather her courage. The mantel clock told her the hour was yet early. Early enough, she hoped, to catch her husband before he attempted to flee her once more.

But a subsequent trip to his chamber—polite knocking which had reduced to rudely poking her head into the room only to find it empty—proved unsuccessful. She rang for her lady's maid and made haste with her toilette for the morning. On account of her pride, she held her tongue and refrained from asking whether or not Lord Huntingdon had departed for his journey. Helena was sure she already knew the answer.

He had wedded her, bedded her, and left her. The intensity of their lovemaking rendered the resultant retreat all the more insulting.

So it was that when she made her way to the dining room

to break her fast and discovered her husband seated at the head of the table, she drew up short. Shock flitted through her. He was handsome as ever this morning, dressed to perfection, his dark hair neatly brushed, his jaw freshly shaven.

He stood at her entrance and bowed. "Lady Huntingdon."

He was here. Not on his way to Shropshire, but with *The Times* ironed and spread before him as if this were just another ordinary day. As if he had no plans of leaving her. Was it too much to hope he did not?

Belatedly, she dipped in a curtsy, swallowing her shock. "My lord."

He nodded to the footman dancing attendance, and the young man quit the room, leaving them alone. Helena's face went hot as a new awareness of her husband hit her. They had been as intimate as a man and woman could be last night. By morning light, it was almost impossible to believe but for the memory of his touch and lips and tongue.

And him inside her.

At the last thought, her knees nearly turned to water.

"You are off to Shropshire this morning?" She forced herself to ask the question with as much studied nonchalance as she could manage. Quite as if she could not be bothered with his response, she congratulated herself. He could hardly know her hopes hinged upon his answer.

"There has been a change of plans," he responded with equal smoothness.

A change of plans.

Her puerile heart rejoiced.

She made her way to the sideboard where a dazzling array of breakfast foods had been laid out in generous display. "Oh?"

"Indeed. I will not be traveling to Shropshire today."

His deep baritone warned her, just before his presence at

her side made her body shimmer, that he had come nearer. She told herself she would not look. That she would calmly fill her plate. But when she picked up the china, long elegant fingers were there to pluck it from her grasp.

Startled, she turned to him, finding his bright-blue gaze studying her intently. "My lord?"

"Allow me to assist you," he said, rather than responding to her query.

"I can gather my breakfast on my own," she countered, girding her heart against this mysterious new Huntingdon before her.

He did not seem nearly as cold, nor as aloof. And yet, he still held himself apart from her. All had not been forgiven, although he had altered his travel plans.

"Nonsense," he clipped. "Only tell me what you wish, and it will be my pleasure to get it for you."

The word *pleasure* uttered in his silken baritone turned her insides to blancmange.

She swallowed against a rising tide of longing. This would not do. She still had no notion of where she stood with him. "Eggs, if you please. Strawberries and pineapple as well. And a rasher of bacon."

He carried her plate to the chair nearest his and laid it upon the table linens with care, then held out her chair. Helena sat, acutely aware of his presence at her back. But while the wickedest part of her yearned for him to lean closer and attempt to steal a kiss, she told herself she was relieved when he returned to his chair and resumed his consumption of both his own repast and the newspaper.

Breakfast continued in silence, interrupted only by the clinking of the cutlery on the fine porcelain and the periodic turning of *The Times* pages.

Helena's irritation mounted with each passing moment. They had consummated their marriage last night. She had fallen asleep with him by her side. And now, he played the gentleman, as though they were mere strangers meeting for the first time at a ball rather than husband and wife.

"When will you be traveling to Shropshire, if not today?" she asked at last, unable to bear another minute of silence.

"I have yet to decide," he told her calmly, lifting his gaze to hers.

She pursed her lips. "When will you decide, my lord?"

She did not think she misunderstood that they were speaking of far more than his trip to Shropshire.

He quirked a brow, a slight smile curving his lips. "Are you in a hurry to be rid of me, madam?"

It was not fair that he was so beautiful, and it was also not fair that he seemed no more inclined to forgive her this morning than he had the day before.

At least he is not on a train bound for Shropshire, whispered her heart.

And that was something, she supposed.

"Of course I am not in a hurry to be rid of you, Huntingdon," she said calmly. "You are my husband. I should like you to stay."

Because I am in love with you, you dolt.

Naturally, she kept that bit to herself.

His gaze searched hers, probing. "How are you feeling this morning, Helena?"

She knew what he was asking—how did she feel now that they had made love? A flush crept over her cheeks once more as she remembered those blistering moments of passion.

"Quite well, thank you."

She resumed eating her breakfast.

After an indeterminate span of time, he finished reading his newspaper and took his leave. Helena watched him go, knowing the chasm between them had not truly been breached. Of course it had not. What had she expected? One night of desire to change everything?

He still resented her for forcing him into marriage.

And she still loved him as desperately as ever.

* * *

Making love to his wife the night before had given Gabe clarity on two facts: he needed to attempt to make amends with his friend Shelbourne, and bedding her had not quelled his desire for her but rather increased it. He was not certain what to do with the latter, dangerous realization, but he damn well did know what to do with the first.

And that was why he found himself meeting with Shelbourne on neutral territory, their club, the Black Souls. A private room had been arranged, along with a lovely Sauternes courtesy of the club owner, Mr. Elijah Decker, himself a newly married man. Decker's wife, Lady Josephine, was a member of the Lady's Suffrage Society and friend of Helena. As such, Huntingdon expected Decker took pity on him.

"How is my sister?" Shelbourne asked coolly.

Gabe took note his friend did not refer to Helena by her new title. "Lady Huntingdon is well, thank you."

"No honeymoon?" Shelbourne prodded, raising a dark brow.

He drummed his fingers on the polished table. "No fisticuffs today?"

His friend's eyes narrowed. "You are the one who invited me here to speak. You are also the one who ruined my innocent sister and necessitated a rushed, forced marriage. Am I expected to be entertained by such a quip?"

He was not wrong.

And although Gabe had not lowered himself to the depths which Shelbourne believed he had sunk by getting a child on Helena, he had gone far enough. He had kissed her, been alone with her, *touched* her.

He took a long, slow sip of his wine, trying to gather himself, before returning his glass to the table. "That is the reason I wished to speak with you today."

"To invite me to plant you another facer?"

Huntingdon frowned. "To explain myself. To apologize. To make amends."

But his old friend's stare was flat, his countenance lined with stark disapproval and anger. "You cannot do so, Huntingdon. That horse is out of the pasture, jumped the fence. All you can do is promise to be a good husband to Hellie."

At the sobriquet Shelbourne used for Helena, Gabe knew another sharp spear of guilt. His friend and Helena had been close once. Shelbourne had doted upon her, and that knowledge had long been a part of what had forced him to think of her as nothing more than his friend's sister. A lady he must never want. A lady he could never have.

A lady who was now his.

Irrefutably.

Irrevocably.

He tried to find his place in the conversation. "I am doing my best to be a good husband to her."

His words were accompanied by the swift sting of shame. Was that true, however? He had been polite at breakfast. He had canceled his trip to Shropshire for the moment. But was that truly the sum of being a good husband? He thought not.

"If you hurt her, I will kill you, Huntingdon," said his friend as blithely as if they discussed the quality of the wine in their glasses.

The finest, as it happened. Elijah Decker would serve

nothing less than the best. But its excellence was lost upon him now. The stuff may as well have been fashioned of sawdust for all he tasted it.

Gabe inclined his head toward his friend in understanding. "I have no intentions of hurting her, Shelbourne. As my countess, she will want for nothing."

"As your countess." Shelbourne shook his head. "I can scarcely believe it. You have always been the most honorable man I know, above reproach. You were promised to another, and yet…of all the women in London, Huntingdon, my own sister. It is unforgivable."

Yes, it was. He could not deny the veracity of his friend's words. That knowledge, deep-seated, had been one of the reasons Gabe had avoided Helena for so long. He had long been intrigued by his friend's bold, beautiful sister. The more time he had spent in her presence, the more enraptured he had become. Chance encounters in the countryside where the strict London edicts were not nearly as enforceable, entirely inappropriate. Entirely wonderful.

Until Grandfather had reminded him of the wrongness of his feelings. Until Grandfather had expressed a desire to see Lady Beatrice as the next Countess of Huntingdon. His grandfather had been quick to remind Gabe of the ills that had befallen his parents, and, as a result of their selfishness, Lisbeth as well. The warning had been enough. He had not been willing to travel that same, unwise path.

"I cannot explain it myself," he said thickly. "I wish to God I had possessed more restraint."

Shelbourne took a sip of his own wine, then replaced his glass on the table, sighing heavily. "I wish I could say I was surprised. But in truth, I think a part of me has always known."

Gabe frowned. "Known?"

What the devil was his friend speaking of? It had only

been recently that he had acted upon his lustful urges. He had gone years without touching Helena, without once kissing her or being alone with her. By his own device, they had never danced.

"She was always besotted with you," Shelbourne said. "From the moment she first saw you, everything was *Huntingdon*. You were all she could think of. When you became betrothed to Lady Beatrice, I had hoped it would end. But what happened between the two of you proves it did not."

Helena had been besotted with him?

Helena?

Besotted.

With him?

Everything within him cried out with a resounding *no*.

"You are certain of this?" he managed, studying his friend's countenance.

Shelbourne's smile was grim. "Utterly. I never supposed you would return her feelings."

"Feelings?" Huntingdon repeated, more confused than ever.

"She fancies herself desperately in love with you," Shelbourne told him. "Surely she must have told you."

He did not miss the excoriating tone his friend used. But for the moment, all his thoughts hovered upon was one fact. One notion. Helena in love with him. It could not be. Surely Shelbourne was mistaken.

Unless…

"She told you she was in love with me?" he pressed, certain he had found his answer.

She had been desperate to avoid marriage to Lord Hamish White. Knowing Helena as he did, she would have told her brother anything that would aid her chances of avoiding the union.

"Long ago," Shelbourne said. "She was but a girl of sixteen

then. I expected the years to change her mind. Clearly, they did not have an improving effect upon her."

A girl of sixteen.

He remembered her then. That last visit to her family's country holding before she had been presented at court. He had spent much of his time shooting grouse and riding horses. But there had been a few, stolen moments when he had enjoyed the pleasure of Helena's company. Even then, she had been a beauty. Young, but sweet and vivacious, with a marked intelligence. He had been drawn to her, but she had yet to have her comeout. And afterward, Lisbeth had died.

Everything had changed.

Now?

Huntingdon reached for his Sauternes, swallowing down the rest of his glass in one vicious gulp. Helena had never suggested tender feelings for him. He had been convinced she had gone to Shelbourne to save herself because she considered him the lesser of all evils presented her. Their kisses had been mutual and heated, and he certainly hoped he was a better husbandly prospect than Lord Hamish White, whose outmoded views were more suited to the last century than to this one.

"Clearly, the years have not aided her, if that is truly the way she feels," he rasped.

His mind and his heart were a tumult of emotion.

Confusion. Longing. *Desire.*

Tenderness, too. In spite of himself.

He was a tangled web. And mayhap she was as well.

"You are not worthy of her love," Shelbourne said coolly. "At last we have reached a topic upon which we can agree."

"Indeed," Huntingdon agreed.

But his friend's words had already sunk into him, planting themselves deep, like a seed which would inevitably catch root. Except he did not wish for them to catch root.

Nor did he want a wife who loved him, *damn it*. Love had no place in a marriage that would survive.

"Huntingdon?"

He glanced up from the sight of his fingers idly tapping upon the table to find his friend watching him with a curious, searching stare.

"What is it, Shelbourne? You have already dropped the equivalent of a mountain on my head." The last was grumbled. But heartfelt, nonetheless.

"You truly had no notion? She did not tell you?"

No, his wife most certainly had not shared her love for him—or rather, her supposed love for him—with him. But discussing his marriage with his closest friend, when his wife was said friend's sister, was deuced uncomfortable.

So Huntingdon feigned a smile. "Of course she did."

Shelbourne, no fool, had already scented blood, however. He grinned. "She did not. I can read your face, old chum. You are an abysmal prevaricator, as ever."

What the devil was he to do?

"She did not," he acknowledged.

"Nor is she with child," Shelbourne guessed next, taking Huntingdon by surprise.

He said nothing, for acknowledging his friend's supposition would only suggest Helena had lied. Which she had, but...Huntingdon found himself hopelessly conflicted.

Instead, he brought his Sauternes to his lips, only to realize, quite belatedly, that he had already drained his glass dry.

"She was desperate to escape the match with Lord Hamish," Shelbourne added, lifting the bottle of wine and gamely replenishing the stores in Huntingdon's goblet. "I was furious with you when she suggested she was carrying your babe, but I also know her far better than anyone else, I think. As I know you better than anyone else, Huntingdon. It took me some time to calm myself and realize you are not the sort of man who would get a bastard on his friend's sister."

Curse it, he hoped he was not. But he could not be sure. There had been moments, when alone with Helena, that he had most assuredly lost all semblance of control. And now, his sense of honor demanded that he not reveal his wife's deceptions.

He met his friend's gaze. "None of that matters now. All that does matter is that Helena is my countess, and you are like a brother to me. I do not want our friendship to end. You have my solemn vow that I will do everything in my power to be a good husband to Helena."

"That is all a man can ask for," Shelbourne said.

He meant those words. He meant that vow.

"Friends?" he prompted.

"Friends." Shelbourne raised a brow. "You still do not deserve her. And I still do not forgive you for cavorting with her all over London while you were betrothed to Lady Beatrice."

Huntingdon's face flamed. "I was not cavorting."

His friend held up a staying hand. "I have no wish to hear the details. But know this, Huntingdon. If you hurt her, you will be answering to my fists once more."

Fair enough.

Huntingdon drank the rest of his Sauternes.

CHAPTER 16

If we wish to truly help anyone else, we must get the vote.
—From Lady's Suffrage Society Times

"How is it, life as a married woman?" Julianna asked Helena over afternoon tea in the blue salon.

Up until this particular query, Helena had been certain her first attempt at playing hostess had gone swimmingly. She had extended the invitation to her friend following breakfast and Huntingdon's departure. He had indicated she should not expect him until dinner, and since it was the wrong day of the week for her Lady's Suffrage Society meeting, she had decided to fill the void of her empty day by catching up with her dear old friend once more.

Helena pondered her response to Julianna's question.

Confusing.

Wonderful and terrible.

"It is hardly any different than my life as an unwed lady," she fibbed.

Julianna issued an indelicate snort. "Liar."

Honesty—raw, unapologetic honesty—was one of her friend's most notable traits. Not always a boon.

Helena winced. "My response depends upon the hour of the day. There. Are you happier now?"

"If you are being honest with me, yes, I am happy. And if Huntingdon makes you happy, then I am as pleased as can be. However, I must admit that I cannot fathom the notion of being tied to a man forever." Julianna settled her teacup into its saucer.

"With the right man, it is not so terrible a fate," Helena countered softly.

For she had to admit, whilst she had considered marriage to Lord Hamish an impossible encroachment upon her liberty, she did not regard her union with Huntingdon in the same fashion.

"The right man," Julianna repeated, a tinge of bitterness edging her tone. "That seems an impossibility. Similar to saying delicious aspic. Or delightful kippers. Or a lovely hailstorm."

"What happened while you were abroad to so harden your heart?" Helena asked her friend. "You wrote to me of nothing but delightful social gatherings and a whirlwind of entertainment."

"It was delightful," Julianna agreed. "Until it was not. But nothing happened to harden my heart, I can assure you. It was already harder than a rock before I ever left London."

There it was, the opportunity she had been meaning to seize.

Helena took a small sip of her tea, studying her friend. "And why did you leave London, my dear? I do not think you ever said."

In truth, she *knew* Julianna had never explained her sudden defection. She had simply been gone, in the midst of the Season, packed away on a steamer for New York City. Although her mother, an American by birth, had been living a separate life from her father for years in her home country, Julianna had never shown the slightest inclination toward venturing across the Atlantic.

Juliana avoided her gaze, fidgeting with her skirts. "There was no special reason. Need there have been one? I missed my mother."

"You had not seen her in some years, and the two of you could never abide each other's company."

Her friend's lips pinched. "You know the proverb. Absence sweeteneth the heart."

"Hmm." Helena sensed a deeper story there, something her friend did not wish to divulge. "If you shall not reveal the reason you left, mayhap you will explain your return."

"Are you not glad to see me?" Julianna teased.

But there was a tenseness in her friend's countenance that could not be ignored nor so easily dismissed.

"Of course I am," she said. "You know, I quite feared you would marry some dashing American and never return."

"Marriage." Julianna shuddered. "*Never.*" Then she paused, appearing to think better of her dramatic reaction. "Oh, forgive me, dearest. Pray do not take insult to my dislike of the institution. I am sure it shall suit you and Huntingdon well, but I have only to look at my mother and father for all the reasons why I have no wish to ever take a husband."

The Marquess and Marchioness of Leighton's union had been marked by bitter contention. The scandal was old, yet well-known. Lord Leighton had publicly accused Lady Leighton of bedding the architect tasked with refurbishing one of their country homes—an American, like the marchioness—and nearly sued for a divorce. The matter had ended quietly, with Julianna's mother returning to New York City and her father remaining in London. They had lived separate lives ever since.

"I understand your reticence," she told Julianna. "Indeed, I share it. However, faced with the untenable fate of marrying Lord Hamish White or binding myself instead to Huntingdon, I chose the latter."

"I would say the lesser of two evils, were not Huntingdon so handsome." Julianna frowned. "The earl was always such a proper fellow, bound by duty. Does he kiss well, Hellie? Please tell me he does. I cannot bear the thought of my dearest friend tied to a stiff-backed earl who cannot properly woo a lady."

Hellie.

It was not the first time her friend had used the sobriquet for her. But for some reason, the use of it stood out rather pointedly to her now. Only two people had ever referred to her thus. Shelbourne and Julianna.

Still, she had her friend's impertinent question to answer. Her face heated as she thought of all the delicious kisses her husband had visited upon her. And not just upon her mouth.

"He is hardly stiff-backed." Actually, he was, rather. But not always.

"You have not answered my question."

She frowned. "He possesses excellent talent."

Julianna laughed. "How prim you sound, and so delightfully English."

"And you sound almost American," she countered, having noted the same thing on their previous meeting.

How odd it was that they had been separated for years, for long enough that Julianna's properly aristocratic accents had been worn down, much like the pebbles in a stream.

"Never say it." Julianna laughed. "Poor Father would be

horrified were he to know anyone can detect a hint of the Yankee in my speech. He does hate Mama so."

The reminder of the enmity between Julianna's parents filled Helena's heart with sadness. Sadness because she feared much the same end for herself and Huntingdon if they did not sort out their differences.

But Lord and Lady Leighton had been married for five-and-twenty years. Helena and Huntingdon had only been wed for three days. Surely there was hope for her? At least hope she could earn back her husband's trust, if not his love.

"I dare say my parents are hardly shining examples of the state of matrimony either," she acknowledged grimly, trying to stave off the forbidding portent. "However, I do have hope that Huntingdon and I will find some semblance of happiness in our marriage. I do not expect him to love me, of course."

Julianna grew serious. "He ought to love you, Hellie. No one is more worthy of love than you. If he breaks your heart, I shall blacken his eye."

"Thank you." Helena raised a brow. "I think. However, Shelbourne has already blackened his jaw, and Huntingdon has only just recovered from his injuries. Leave me some time to work my magic upon my husband before you beat him, please."

"Shelbourne?" Her friend's expression shifted. "How is your brother these days?"

"He is Shelbourne." Helena's nose wrinkled. "He was not pleased with the haste or the necessity of my marriage to Huntingdon, particularly as they are friends."

Or rather, they had been friends. She could only hope they would one day find themselves capable of moving on from the rift she had created.

"I love you, dearest, I do, but Shelbourne has always been

an unfeeling prig." Julianna sniffed. "It sounds as if nothing has changed."

Her brother was not unfeeling. Not entirely. He was simply too much in Father's mold, which meant he held duty and honor of the highest import. But he did have a tendency to be a prude. Helena had to agree with that. Which was why it was so surprising he possessed a secret cache of bawdy books.

"He is not as awful as one might suppose," she defended lightly.

Julianna's laugh was bitter. "That is not a recommendation."

"Was I meant to recommend him?" Her brow furrowed. There was something distinctly odd about both her brother's reaction to her prior mentioning of Julianna and her friend's current reaction. "I did not suppose your paths had much crossed."

"We crossed swords, more like," Julianna grumbled. "But that is all in the past. It was a long time ago."

"You and Shelbourne?" Helena repeated, incredulous. Her mind whirled with the possibilities.

"Yes," her friend said, shifting in her chair as if she were suddenly uncomfortable. "Think nothing of it and do not, I pray, make mention of it to him."

Something was afoot, and Helena meant to uncover more. But she could plainly see Julianna had no wish to further discuss the subject.

She decided to pivot the conversation and return to the intriguing notion of her brother and Julianna another day.

"I would never dream of it," Helena reassured her friend. "Your every secret is safe with me, as you know. Let us speak of something else. Something of far greater interest than Shelbourne. There is a meeting of the Lady's Suffrage Society in two days' time, and I would dearly love for you to attend with me."

Julianna smiled. "The prospect of life in London has just become infinitely more attractive. Tell me all about it, if you please."

* * *

Gabe could not stop staring at Helena across the dinner table.

She was dressed in a fetching sapphire-blue gown that showed off her ample bosom to perfection—and distraction. Her hair was dressed in a softer style, a loose Grecian braid with wisps of blonde curls a halo about her oval face. She was ravishing. Stunning.

And she loved him.

Fuck.

"Is something amiss, Huntingdon?" she asked, eying him curiously.

Those emerald orbs bored into him, stoking the fires which had been simmering beneath his surface ever since he had left her bed that morning. And yes, the answer to her query was that something *was* amiss. He did not think it possible for him to suffer through another handful of courses without hauling her onto the polished mahogany, throwing up her skirts, and feasting upon her instead.

Curse her.

He cleared his throat. "Of course not. Why do you ask, my lady?"

"You are staring at me strangely." She settled her soup spoon in an elegant motion. "Have I inadvertently dripped some *potage à la prince* on my bodice?"

If she had, he would not be above licking it off. And then tugging down that indecent silken fabric and her corset with it, until her nipples popped free. She was so deliciously sensitive there…

But she had not dribbled soup. He was simply staring at her because his control had been dashed. Because Shelbourne's unwanted words were ringing in his head with the persistence of a bell. Because she was so deuced lovely, there was no other place he wished to look. Not even his own bowl, which sat before him, scarcely touched.

The only pangs of hunger affecting him in this moment could not be sated with food.

"You have not, of course," he told her. "I am merely attempting to accustom myself to the notion of sharing the dining table with my wife each evening."

He inwardly winced at his words.

She stiffened. "Is it because I am not the wife you intended to sit across this table from you?"

Lady Beatrice was ever a specter between them. One which grew increasingly dim to him with every passing hour.

"It is because having a wife is new to me," he countered.

As was having a wife who loved him. Because love had no place in a marriage.

But he must try to push that particular thought from his over-burdened mind. He still had no inkling of what to do with it. He had not been seeking a love match. He had been seeking a calm, rational union with a lady who would give him children and companionship, one who would never bring him scandal.

The perfect countess.

That was what he had been seeking.

What he would have had, if not for the siren seated opposite him. If not for his own helpless attraction to her, his stupid actions, his lack of restraint, her lie…

"I suppose I cannot find fault in that," his countess grudgingly offered now. "For having a husband is new to me as well. At the moment, he is not attempting to flee me in favor of Shropshire, and that is my small measure of success."

Gabe winced. "I was never trying to flee you. I was trying to put some time and distance between us, that we might find our places in this unexpected union of ours."

She pursed her lips. "That you might have our marriage annulled, you mean to say."

Damnation. She had not forgotten that.

"Helena," he began, attempting to explain himself as a tide of guilt threatened to drown him from within, "I never intended to annul our marriage."

At least, he did not think he had intended it, not truly. He had told himself it was an option because he had been so angry with her for lying to Shelbourne. And he was still angry with her for what she had done. For forcing him to break the promise he had made to Grandfather on his deathbed.

A man without honor is a man who has nothing.

One of Grandfather's favored adages returned to his mind, a mocking, silent reminder. For he had proven himself in painful dearth of it, both in his interactions with Helena and Lady Beatrice.

Helena cast a slicing look of disapproval in his direction now. "Do not lie to me to spare my feelings, Huntingdon. You have already confessed you considered it."

"Fair enough." He inclined his head. "I told you I considered the possibility. However, I decided against it. Either way, last night has decided the matter for the both of us."

Quite deliciously, too.

Before he could say more, the servants returned, robbing them of their privacy and their soup course both. The next course was laid before them. Partridge *rissoles* and fried parsley with a *macédoine* of assorted vegetables, swimming in a mushroom sauce. Ordinarily one of his favorites. But the rich scent wafting to him did not appeal at the moment.

All that did was the woman seated across from him.

He dismissed the servants against the instinct that warned him further intimacy with Helena could only lead to more mayhem and distraction. When they were once more alone, he could not wrest his gaze from her.

She sighed. "You are at it again, my lord."

Staring at her, she meant. Yes, he could not seem to help himself.

He took a sip of his wine, searching for a suitable response and finding none. He settled upon levity instead. "What am I at, Lady Huntingdon? The dinner table? Indeed, I am, as it is the ordinary place for the evening meal to be served."

Her lips pursed in a pout he could not help but long to kiss. "You know very well what I am saying. You are staring at me, as if I have dropped soup down my bodice, which I assure you I have not. Having experienced the sensation once before, I can promise, it is unmistakable."

He could not help but to laugh at the notion of her dripping soup down her bodice. "You are having me on."

"I am not," she countered. "It was guinea fowl soup, and it was quite dreadful. I had to spend the entirety of a dinner party with a hunk of celery firmly lodged within my corset. The more I wriggled in an effort to move it into a more comfortable position, the deeper it fell."

"Being a gentleman, I never considered the unfortunate prospect of such an occurrence." Gabe envisioned her squirming in her seat through a ten-course dinner. "Did not your fellow diners take note?"

He would have taken note, he thought. Never mind the lump of offending celery. He would not have been able to keep from being enthralled by the sight of her shimmying, those glorious pale mounds of her breasts swaying with her every movement.

"I do hope not, but my mother admonished me quite sternly for my fidgeting on the carriage ride home. I did not have the heart to reveal the cause of my agitation." Helena grinned, a pink tinge giving her cheeks some lovely color.

He was not entirely certain how they had so far diverged from the original path of their conversation to be discussing lost celery in bosoms, but he was grateful for the distraction. Helena's humility was refreshing. Lady Beatrice would have perished before she would have ever admitted such a faux pas.

"Are you certain a piece of celery is not now similarly lodged within your bosom, my dear?" he teased. "I would be more than happy to search for it in the name of your comfort."

Her color heightened, but there was a newfound warmth in her gaze that seeped into his heart and settled there to stay. "There was no celery in the soup course, Huntingdon."

"Do you think you might call me Gabe when we are alone?" he asked, shocking himself with the question as much as with the desire to hear her husky voice call him by his given name.

Last night, he had been inside her. He had consummated their union. And yet, this request of his somehow seemed more intimate, emerging from a deeper, more profound place. He ought to be alarmed.

"I would be pleased to call you Gabe if you wish." A shy smile curved her delectable lips. "Is that the reason why you have been staring at me so strangely ever since dinner began?"

Of course it was not. But somehow, broaching the topic of her feelings for him did not feel right in this moment.

"I was staring at you because you are beautiful tonight, Helena," he told her instead. Because this, too, was true. "And because it is difficult indeed to look anywhere else."

Her color deepened once more, but the smile she sent him, tentative and sweet, revealing the slight gap between her front teeth, hit him with the force of a fist. "Thank you, Gabe. That is the nicest compliment any gentleman has ever paid me."

"You are welcome," he said with matching politeness.

What an arse he was. Had he never told her she was lovely?

He would have to tell her more often.

Every day.

No. He was still angry with her for making him break all his vows to himself, his vows to Grandfather. Was he not?

That was the crux of it. Gabe was no longer sure. And the more time he spent in Helena's intoxicating presence, the more he wanted to cling to the future rather than the past.

CHAPTER 17

Change does not make us weak. Rather, it makes us stronger.
—*From* Lady's Suffrage Society Times

*H*elena settled into an overstuffed chair by the hearth in her chamber, book in hand, and told herself she must not be disappointed if Huntingdon did not come to her this evening. She would distract herself with literature. Books were lovely. Words were an excellent form of escape.

The book in her lap was one she had intended to begin reading some months ago, a memoir penned by an anonymous gentleman. All London was abuzz over it, and Helena herself had only managed to secure a third printing of it on account of the previous runs selling out within a day. Thankfully, her friend Lady Jo Decker's husband owned the publishing company, which had enabled Helena to finally get her own copy.

She had meant to begin reading it well before now. But

then, she had been distracted by her whirlwind marriage to Huntingdon—strike that, she corrected herself, *Gabe*. His invitation to refer to him by his Christian name at dinner had been unexpected, but appreciated nonetheless.

Still, she remained hopelessly confused with where she stood. Her husband had not wanted to marry her. He had preferred the paragon Lady Beatrice. He wanted Helena, and yet he seemed to loathe himself for the weakness.

She opened the book to its frontispiece, which bore an elaborate engraving of a handsome gentleman dancing with a lovely lady in a ballroom. The attention to detail was impressive, but her mind was still too occupied with thoughts of her husband.

Dinner had been surprisingly pleasant, peppered with moments of unexpected intimacy and shared laughter. Afterward, they had decamped to the blue salon, where they had shared some wine and chatted before her husband had announced he intended to retire. There had been a brief moment, when he had pressed a kiss to the top of her head before withdrawing, when she had sworn something more would happen.

And then, it had not.

Stinging disappointment had been her accompaniment for the rest of the evening thus far. Helena had finished her sherry alone, in the damning silence of the blue salon, surrounded by dismal pictures of bleak, dreary landscapes adorning its walls in overwhelming abundance. Truly, there were some aspects of Wickley House which needed the inviting touch of a woman. The blue salon was just such a place.

Helena sighed. She flipped to the first page of the book, trying to quell her irritation. She made her way to page three before she realized she had not absorbed a word she had read and turned back to the beginning of chapter one. How desperate she was, lingering in the glow of the gas lamps, her lady's maid already long since departed for the evening, herself clad in nothing more than a wispy night rail without benefit of a *robe de chambre*. Awaiting a husband who had no intention of visiting her.

A husband who resented her.

A husband who was impossible to read.

Much like this book.

On another sigh, Helena snapped the volume closed before settling it upon the table at her side. She rose to pace the Axminster, her bare feet sinking into the plush softness of the carpets. At least that was one part of the house she would not need to rectify—the Axminster was thick, plush, and new.

He was not going to come to her tonight.

Each minute that passed told her so.

How had she been foolish enough to believe they had somehow made progress? For every step forward, there were at least another three in retreat. Last night had been wonderful. Breakfast had been positively dreadful. Dinner had fared only marginally better. To say nothing of her foolish tale of dribbling soup down her dress.

"Celery," she grumbled beneath her breath as she made another turn of the chamber. "You utter fool."

What had she been thinking, to share such a humiliating story of gracelessness? She had not been thinking at all. Rather, she had been blurting.

"Celery is an erudite vegetable. I cannot fathom why you would be upbraiding it just now."

The low, amused baritone slipped over her like a silken caress.

Helena spun about to find the object of her tumultuous thoughts hovering on the threshold of their mutual territory. They shared a bathroom and dressing room, and the fact had not been lost upon her whenever she had spied his distinctly masculine accoutrements strewn about the spaces. To say nothing of his divine scent, which lingered like a particularly maddening taunt, long after he had inhabited a chamber.

"Huntingdon," she said, pressing a hand to her instantly fluttering heart. "I did not hear you."

"Gabe," he reminded gently, offering her a smile that hit her in the heart. "Am I welcome?"

Always and forever, my beautiful man.

"Of course," she said instead, giving him what she hoped was a practiced, serene smile.

Then she wondered at the protocol for such an event. Last night, she had been a tangled mess of nerves. She did not recall what she had done. Ought she to curtsy? In her night rail?

"I would hate to find myself at odds with you," he said lightly as he sauntered into her chamber after closing the door at his back. "Celery was doing quite poorly just now."

He was teasing her, and the slight lift in his sensual lips said so. Who was this version of the man she had married? She was not accustomed to lightness from him, nor levity.

Helena smiled back at him against a sudden onslaught of nervousness. "That is because celery found its way into my bosom, and I have never forgiven it since. Nor have I forgiven myself for sharing such a humiliating detail with my new husband—who already has considered annulling our marriage. After The Celery Incident, I can only imagine what he must think of me."

Gabe winced as he reached her, the distance between them scant. She tried not to notice he appeared to be clad in nothing more than a dressing gown once more. His bare calves and feet refused to be ignored. So, too, his broad shoulders. His robe this evening was of a dark, lush navy that complemented his eyes and rendered them more startlingly blue.

"He thinks you are an original," he told her. "Just as he always has. There will be no annulment, as I said at dinner. We have progressed beyond that option, and even had we not, I would not wish to pursue a dissolution."

Hardly words of undying love and devotion, but Helena would gladly take them. He thought her an original? Was that a good thing or a bad thing? *Hmm...*

"You are certain, my lord?" she asked, then recalled his request at dinner once more. "Gabe?"

"As sure as I can be of anything." He reached out, brushing a curl from her cheek and sending a rush of electric sparks skittering over her skin. "I spoke with your brother today."

The admission seemed torn from him, and it took Helena by surprise. The sparks should have faded, but they lingered. "Shelbourne? What did you speak about? I do not see any bruising, so I suppose he must have controlled himself."

She was still greatly displeased with her brother for attacking Huntingdon—*Gabe*. She felt largely responsible for the attack, and she wished she had possessed the foresight to realize Shelbourne would not react well to the news that his sister had been ruined by his best friend. She had known, all along, he would not be pleased. No man would. However, she had not anticipated such violent aggression on his part.

Her husband inclined his head, that brilliant gaze of his seeming to devour her. "We have reached an understanding, I believe."

"Good," Helena said on a rush of relief as molten heat pooled in her belly. "I could not bear the notion of the two of you being at odds, especially since I was the one at fault for suggesting I was carrying your child. I am not proud of myself for making that claim. Desperation is hardly an excuse."

"You were not entirely at fault," her husband corrected gently. "I compromised you, whilst I was betrothed to another. I hold myself accountable for everything that transpired. I hope we can begin anew tonight."

Tonight.

The heat burst into unadulterated flame.

She wanted to ask him if he could forgive her for what she had done, but the words would not leave her tongue. Instead, she searched his gaze, trying to find the answers she sought. His eyes were hooded now, obscured by the sweep of dark, too-long lashes.

"Gabe?" she asked hesitantly.

"Yes, Helena?" His fingers had lingered behind her ear, and now they skimmed lightly down her throat.

She summoned her daring. "Will you kiss me?"

* * *

Her skin was smooth and creamy. The sweet scent of citrus and bergamot teased his senses. And heaven help him, but that filmy night rail clinging to her curves was nearly transparent. The dusky circles of her nipples were on full display, the peaks stiff and wanton. Begging for him.

His fingertips traveled lightly over her in a slow caress, absorbing her heat, the frenzied beat of her heart. Her verdant eyes burned into his, so vibrant they took his breath. Her sweet, pink lips parted.

"Will you kiss me?"

The hesitant invitation had his cockstand rising to full attention beneath the cloaking drapery of his dressing gown.

He wanted to haul her into his arms. To give in to the frantic urges sweeping over him.

But this was only their second time making love. He did not wish to rush her. He intended to proceed slowly. To seduce her, to savor her.

He gently cupped her face and lowered his mouth to hers, giving Helena his answer. Kissing her was always a revelation. No matter how many times he felt her lips beneath his, each kiss felt new and more intoxicating than the last.

On a pleased-sounding sigh, she wrapped her arms around his neck, pressing herself against him. The voluptuous crush of her breasts sent an arrow of need straight through him. The tight buds of her nipples abraded his chest. He deepened the kiss, licking the seam of her lips until she opened, their tongues tangling.

She tasted of the sherry they had enjoyed in the blue salon following dinner and of something that was mysteriously, indefinably her. He allowed his hand to drift from her jaw, slowly coasting it over her breast and cupping her there. When he ran his thumb in circles over her hungry nipple, she arched into him and made a seductive sound low in her throat.

He was lost.

Desire overwhelmed him. His caress traveled lower, his fingers tightening on the soft fabric of her night rail to pull it slowly upward. All the while, he kissed her with the fevers raging within. He found the sleek curve of her hip, and he discovered she wore no drawers. Nipping her lip, he sought the heart of her, his fingers gliding over hot, slick feminine flesh.

She was drenched for him already, just from their kisses. From his fleeting touches. She was so responsive. He found her pearl and rubbed it in slow, teasing strokes until her hips undulated against his hand and she sucked on his tongue.

Her unabashed desire for him thrilled him more than he could have imagined. He tore his lips from hers and kissed a path down her throat, finding her collarbone, then settled his mouth over the hollow where her pulse pounded. All the while, he continued to tease them both, slicking her dew over her as she clutched him.

If he took her to the bed, their interlude would be over before it had begun, so desperate was he to be inside her. But Gabe was ever cognizant that she had been a virgin. He needed to be tender with her, to take her to the heights of exquisite pleasure. Their lovemaking could not be rushed.

He kissed behind her ear, nuzzling her throat, and an idea came to him. With great reluctance, he withdrew his fingers, allowing her night rail to fall back into place. He raised his head to drink in the sight of her, cheeks flushed, mouth swollen from his kisses, eyes glazed with desire. She had never been more beautiful.

He took her hand in his and tugged her toward the chairs settled by the hearth. "Come."

"What do you intend?" she asked, breathless, as she allowed him to pull her to the chair.

"Sit," he invited softly instead of explaining.

What he intended required no announcement or warning. He wanted to surprise her. Last night, he had enjoyed a taste of her, but tonight, he intended to savor.

"Gabe?" She frowned at him. "Do you wish to speak with me?"

The smile he sent her brimmed with sensual intent and he knew it by the way her color deepened. "Something like that, hellion. Sit, if you please."

This time, she obeyed.

He rather enjoyed watching his stubborn minx go soft for him, doing as he asked.

Gabe lowered himself to his knees, his entire body

acutely aware of every sensation. The Axminster beneath his bare calves was coarse yet plush. His cock was harder than granite, pulsing and aching to be inside her.

Not yet, damn it.

First, he wanted to make her spend. To worship her.

He settled his palms on her hips and realized he had a problem. "Scoot your bottom toward me, darling. Until you are seated on the edge of the cushion."

She placed her hands gently atop his. "Gabe…"

He loved the sound of her speaking his name. "Trust me. I want to bring you pleasure."

Hesitantly, she moved. He pulled her toward him, easing her movement, until she was positioned as he asked. "Lift your hem for me, Helena."

Her gaze never leaving his, she removed her hands and slowly bunched the material in both fists before hauling it up. The action must have taken her mere seconds, but as he watched, it seemed to go on for an eternity. Each part of her was painstakingly revealed. Slender ankles, shapely calves. Perfect knees. The pale, smooth tops of her thighs.

She pooled the fabric in her lap, keeping her legs closed. He began at her ankles, caressing her there, marveling at the delicate bones beneath his fingertips. Then gliding along her calves. Her flesh was warm and smooth and luscious. He found the insides of her knees and guided them apart.

He lowered his head to press a kiss, first to her right knee, and then her left. His fingers skimmed over her lush inner thighs, parting them more. She needed no further coaxing. She opened wider, and the scent of her desire mingled with citrus and bergamot to create the headiest blend he had ever known.

He caressed upward, lifting the hem of her night rail higher, until she was fully revealed to him. He took a moment to drink in the sight of her, pink and slick and welcoming, the prettiest, most decadent picture he had ever beheld.

And his.

All his.

He slid his hands beneath her bare rump, clasping handfuls of soft, womanly flesh that incited the fires within him to a crescendo, and dipped his head. His tongue flicked over the swollen nub of her clitoris first. The taste of her, as before, was sweet and musky and good. So good. His lips latched over her and he sucked.

She jerked against him, releasing a breathy moan that made his cock twitch. He licked lower, traveling down her slit until he found her channel. When he sank his tongue inside her, she cried out, bucking her hips and driving him deeper. Again and again, he licked into her. Wetness bathed his tongue. He lapped it up and then returned to her pearl, alternating between quick, fluttering movements and suction.

The raggedness of her breaths and the way she writhed against him told him she was already near to reaching her crisis. He nibbled lightly at her, then withdrew to blow a stream of warm air over her glistening flesh. For so many nights before they had wed, he had lain awake in his bed to thoughts of having her thus. Of touching her, kissing her, making her come on his tongue. Always, he had taken himself in hand, only to later wallow in shame for the desperation with which he lusted after his own friend's sister.

But now, it was no longer wrong. No longer forbidden. Because she was his wife.

"You are so beautiful," he told her, meaning those words. "I have never desired another the way I want you."

"Touch me, Gabe, please," she pleaded softly. "I ache for you."

And she would ache more before this night was through. But her impassioned pleas spurred him on. He buried his face between her curved thighs once more, gently nipping at her swollen bud, then suckling it and using his teeth to abrade it in slow, steady palpitations.

He knew the moment he found the most responsive part of her, for she stiffened, her body bowing into his, and came on a low, keening cry. He absorbed each spasm rippling through her with his tongue, savoring this moment, the silken warmth of her quim, the sheer decadence of her surrender.

When the last lashing of pleasure had seemed to ripple through her, he withdrew, kissing her inner thighs as he went. His cock had never been this rigid, his ballocks never drawn so tight with the need for release. Hastily, he flipped her gown back into place and then stood, offering her his hand.

He was almost beyond speech, past all capability of rational, coherent thought. If he was not inside her within the next few minutes, he swore he would explode. Wordlessly, he led her by their linked hands to the bed.

She tugged at the sash holding his dressing gown in place with her free hand. But her fingers fumbled on the knot. Her lovely face was a study in concentration.

"I can do it," he offered as she only seemed to tighten the sash rather than loosen it.

"I want to," she said softly, almost shyly. "Touching you pleases me."

He held himself still, heart pounding, as she used both hands to open the sash and then slide the dressing gown from his shoulders. The robe fell to the floor in a puddle around his feet. As they had the previous evening, Helena's hands roamed over him, leaving fire in their wake.

Her lashes fluttered low, shielding her gaze, as her hands

traveled with tentative lightness over his shoulders first. Then with growing boldness as she traced over his chest, down his abdomen. This time, when she neared his aching cock, he did not stay her. He wanted her hand wrapped around him more than he wanted his next breath.

She hesitated, one hand trailing around to his back while the other hovered, her fingertips kissing the skin just above his straining prick.

"Touch me wherever and however you like," he told her roughly, hoping she would be as daring as he wanted her to be.

She did not let him down.

Nothing, however, could have prepared him for the light grasp of her elegant fingers on his length. She brushed over him, stroking him, her thumb circling the tip where a bead of his mettle already leaked.

"I want to pleasure you as you did me," she said, shocking him.

Just the notion of her sealing her sweet lips around him, of being engulfed by the welcoming warmth of her mouth, was enough to make him almost lose control. He could not take much more.

A groan escaped.

She stilled, glancing up at him as she caught her lower lip in her teeth. "Does it not please you?"

"It pleases me," he growled. "It pleases me too much, and I mean to be inside you, hellion."

"What if I were to use my mouth on you?" she asked softly, giving him another stroke. "Or my tongue? Would it feel as wonderful?"

She nearly unmanned him.

Wonderful did not begin to describe the prospect. This woman was bound to be the death of him. But what a sweet death it would be. Still, he was not about to spend in his wife's hand on their second night of lovemaking.

He bit back another groan. "That shall have to be an investigation for another evening. Tonight, I want you naked and beneath me."

"But Gabe," she protested with a pout that made him want her that much more.

He silenced her with a lingering kiss. That turned into another, and then another. Until at last he tore his lips from hers.

"Now you," he told her, helping her to remove her night rail.

Together, they lifted the gossamer fabric over her head. And this time, it was his turn to trail his hands over every part of her he could touch. He cupped her breasts and dipped his head to take one of her nipples in his mouth.

"Gabe." His name was a soft, hungry sigh on her lips.

No more waiting. He had to have her. Now.

He kissed her again hungrily, and then he led her to the bed before joining her in it. Her arms opened, her legs parting to accommodate him. He could not help but to feel, as their bodies aligned, that he was coming home. That here with Helena, her as his countess, was what had always been fated.

Like it or not.

He covered her body in kisses first, finding every part of her skin where he could set his lips. Throat, shoulder. The curves of her breasts and belly. Her hard nipples, and when he lingered on them, playing his tongue over each stiff peak as he had before, she moaned, her body bowing from the mattress.

Making love to her was akin to playing an instrument. The sweet melodies he drew from her in response to each touch, lick, and suck, intensified his ardor. And he could not get enough. She trailed her fingertips over his back, sending heat shooting through him.

"Sweet Helena." He dragged his jaw over one milky swell, abrading her sensitive skin with his whiskers.

Her nails raked his flesh. Her lips pressed a kiss to the top of his head. Her fingers threaded through his hair, tugging.

"Kiss me again, Gabe," she urged. "Please."

There was no need to beg. His prick was rigid and throbbing against her sleek folds as he made his way back to her lips, sealing their mouths in a passionate union. Reaching between their bodies, he dragged his cock over her slit, coating himself in her cream. She was slicker than she had been the night before. Hot and welcoming.

As his tongue plunged into her mouth, he guided himself to her entrance. His control had been dashed as a ship upon rocky shores in the midst of a tempest. Licking her, bringing her to spend, her tentative touches, her unabashed embrace of her own sensuality, the sweet musk and perfume of her, the give of her curves beneath him... It all mingled together into one overwhelming sensation.

He scarcely dragged his lips from hers as the tip of him breached her.

"Ready for me, hellion?"

"Always," she whispered, and then his minx of a wife's wandering hands swept down his back to his buttocks.

Grasping him, she urged him forward.

And he obeyed. Or mayhap his body obeyed. He was mindless now. At her mercy. His hips thrust, and he was sheathed to the hilt. Her inner muscles drew him deep. The tight, wet grip of her almost made him spill. He could not remain still. There was a roaring in his ears. White-hot desire licked down his spine.

He pumped in and out, starting up a rhythm that only became more intoxicating when she joined him, thrust for thrust. So sinuously they moved together, one in body. Gabe's fingers glided over her pearl, exerting greater pressure when she moaned into his kiss and arched into him, driving him deeper still.

Their tongues tangled. She tightened on him, her channel constricting like a vise, and he lost himself as the ripples of her second release milked his cock, draining him dry. On a shuddering groan, he planted himself deep, filling her with his seed as he tore his mouth from hers and tipped back his head as blinding pleasure washed over him.

He stayed with her there, pinning her to the bed, and could not keep from falling forward once more for another kiss. Bracing himself on his forearms, he sealed their lips. She kissed him deeply, passionately, their ragged breaths blending.

It had been the most passionate encounter of his life.

Reluctantly, he withdrew from Helena and rolled to his back at her side, staring into the intricacies of the plaster-work in the ceiling as coherent thought returned. Having Helena as his wife was dangerous indeed.

CHAPTER 18

The strident voices of opposition so often ignore logic.
—*From* Lady's Suffrage Society Times

"*The utter darkness of woman suffrage,*" Lady Jo Decker announced to the informally gathered assemblage of the Lady's Suffrage Society. Bitterness and outrage laced her voice. "Can you believe it? He also called the politicians in favor *appalling in their gayheartedness.*"

"Who dared to write such nonsensical tripe?" Callie, Lady Sinclair, demanded. "And in *The Times*, no less!"

"Naturally, the coward remained anonymous," Lady Jo said, her lip curling. "His letter to the editor was signed with nothing more than an M."

"Of course he was a coward," Helena said, indignation rising like a tide within her until her hands trembled under the force of her reaction. "His opinion is not one which he ought to take pride in. Little wonder he hides behind an initial."

"There was also another letter supposedly from a woman who opposes universal suffrage," Lady Jo added. "She was horrified by the prospect of a woman who loses the 'weakness' of her sex. Can you fathom it? She claimed all the wrongs which have been done women have already been addressed and that allowing women to vote will do us more harm than benefit."

The Duchess of Longleigh spoke up then. "Shall I infer she, too, retained her anonymity as she attacked her own sex?"

"She signed her letter as *A Woman*," Lady Jo confirmed grimly.

"She should have signed it as *A Woman Who Has Abandoned Her Own*," Julianna added fervently.

"Indeed she should have," Lady Jo agreed.

"Although I dare say you are being kinder than *A Woman* deserves, Lady Julianna," Callie added. "In my opinion, something such as *A Woman with the Brain of a Trout*."

"Lady Sinclair, that would be an insult to all river-and-lake-dwelling fishes," Julianna countered, grinning.

Helena was once more gratified her friend had decided to join in the work of the Lady's Suffrage Society. Julianna complemented their fellow ladies as perfectly as sugar to tea, whether it was for a smaller circle meeting such as this evening's or a large gathering for all members. The ladies gathered laughed at her sally, seizing the moment of levity, before getting back to the serious nature of their meeting.

"These ridiculous letters have inspired me, however," Lady Jo continued when their laughter had faded. "In addition to the periodic publication of pamphlets explaining the necessity of universal suffrage, I propose we begin our own journal. Just think of it, a publication written by us, meant for other like-minded ladies. A means of apprising us of the latest news more regularly than the pamphlets are able to achieve. I have already spoken with my husband about the prospect, and he is keen for his publishing company to provide all the printing, just as he has been doing for our pamphlets."

A chorus of excited agreements bubbled up in Lady Sinclair's drawing room. The notion of a journal written and printed by the Lady's Suffrage Society appealed to Helena as well. It was an excellent idea, and a sure means of reaching more ladies than those who could attend their meetings, including working women.

"I wholeheartedly agree with your idea," Lady Sinclair said. "Jo, you are a marvel, truly. Have you suggested your idea to Lady Ravenscroft and the Duchess of Bainbridge?"

Those two ladies were the founding members of the Lady's Suffrage Society, though busy with recently born babes and not present for the afternoon's meeting.

"I have," Lady Jo confirmed. "They think it an excellent notion as well. My husband will print and distribute it free of cost as well, so that it cannot only be afforded by ladies of means. We want to reach every woman, not just those who can afford the penny to buy it."

"I would be more than happy to write for the journal," Julianna volunteered.

"As would I," Helena added, thinking it would give her some much-needed distraction from the state of her marriage.

And her inconvenient, hopeless, all-consuming love for her husband.

Which only seemed to increase with each passing day.

Who was she fooling? With each passing hour, minute, second, *breath*. Gabe filled her days and her nights, but a fortnight into their marriage, her husband still did not trust her. Helena could sense it. Worse, she knew that she alone—with her unnecessary, desperate lie—had caused his lack of confidence in her.

But she must not think of that now, those worries which had been weighing heavily upon her heart. Tonight, she was amongst friends. Their cause was good and right, and it deserved all her attention. Her whole heart.

"What do you suppose we shall call it?" the Duchess of Longleigh asked the room at large.

Petite, blonde, and beautiful yet soft-spoken, the duchess had the misfortune of being married to one of the coldest men in the Upper Ten Thousand. She was, as far as Helena had been able to discern, kindhearted and sweet. Entirely undeserving of the circumstances in which she found herself, tethered to a man she did not love. Though Helena had not often had occasion to speak with Her Grace, she knew from their few informal chats that the duchess was hopelessly ensnared in an unhappy marriage.

"*The Suffrage Journal*," suggested Lady Sinclair. "A serviceable, yet explanatory name."

"*The Journal of Equality*," offered Lady Jo.

"What do you think of the *Lady's Suffrage Society Times*?" Julianna asked the company. "That way, there is no mistaking the organization behind it."

"They all sound excellent," Helena said, keen to offer her opinion. "However, I do believe *Lady's Suffrage Society Times* would have my vote."

"I agree," Lady Sinclair said.

"Ever so much more cultured than *The Times*," Lady Jo agreed.

"*Lady's Suffrage Society Times* is the perfect name for it," the Duchess of Longleigh offered.

"Do we have a consensus, then?" asked Lady Sinclair, who had become a leader by default with the other members preoccupied by their growing families. "All in favor?"

"Aye," agreed a chorus of feminine voices.

The Countess of Sinclair grinned. "I cannot wait for *A Woman* and the mysterious *M.* to have a peek at the *Lady's Suffrage Society Times*. Undoubtedly, *A Woman* shall swoon with horror. *M.* will similarly shrivel up in disgust, I should imagine."

"Mayhap *M.* and *A Woman* ought to go boating together in the Serpentine," Helena suggested mildly.

"In a leaky boat," Julianna agreed.

"One outfitted with some fortuitous leaden weights," Lady Jo added.

"Do tell me where to stand," said the Duchess of Longleigh, "and I shall happily watch them sink. If only they would take His Grace along with them."

There was a moment of silence as all the women convened privately reckoned with the realization that the Duchess of Longleigh had just suggested she wished her husband would sink to the bottom of the Serpentine. It was one thing to imagine anonymous, invisible opponents slipping beneath the waters, but another indeed to think of a person they knew. No matter how dastardly he was.

"Forgive me," the duchess said. "I forget sometimes that I am the only one of us in an unhappy marriage. Do not allow my bitterness to ruin the excitement of the afternoon, I beg you. And if it pleases you, I would dearly love to write articles for the journal as well."

But *was* she the only one of them in an unhappy marriage?

Helena bit her lip as she contemplated that most unwanted thought. Lady Sinclair was hopelessly in love with her husband, and Lady Jo was every bit as smitten with Mr. Decker, and the husbands were equally besotted with their wives. That left only Julianna, who was not married, and Helena, who was.

She loved Gabe quite desperately.

But was she happy?

No, said a voice deep inside her heart.

Because loving someone without being loved in return was...*torture*. That was the word to describe this constant flux. Pure, utter, torture. From which there seemed to be no escape.

* * *

Torture.

That was the best means of describing each day in his new marriage.

Complete and utter. Delicious, awful, inescapable —*torture*.

He did not want to long for her as much as he did. Every day, he told himself he would keep his distance. And each night, he found himself going to her chamber just the same.

Until finally, Gabe vowed he would not do so tonight.

And that was why he was seated at his desk instead of on his way to his wife's bed. That was why his accompaniment was a glass of claret instead of Helena. He had told her he would not come to her this evening, that his attentions were required elsewhere.

He had taken note of the confusion in her vibrant eyes and the hurt in her clamped pink lips. But he had deemed some distance necessary. It was not Shropshire, but it was just enough to remind him that he must not allow himself to care for her too deeply.

On a heavy sigh, Gabe lifted the claret and took a generous sip. If there was anything he had learned from his parents' hellacious marriage, it was that even when a union began in love, it could quickly descend into destruction. Father and Mother had been a love match, once upon a time.

The heart was a fickle thing. Far too shallow.

He turned his attention to the reports from his steward in Shropshire. The repairs to the western wing roof were being undertaken. Unfortunately, the damage to the upper rooms was worse than what had originally been supposed, and some of the original eighteenth century plaster medallions and ceiling frescoes would require complete removal.

The estate in Shropshire had been a crowning jewel in the coronet of the Huntingdon earldom for centuries. Adringham Hall had been built upon the ruins of a former abbey. Grandfather had preferred it to the bustle of London, and Gabe had often sought his own solace there. His current presence in London had been down to Parliament being in session and his impending nuptials to Lady Beatrice.

The latter, of course, no longer being a reason for him to remain.

Damnation, he was accomplishing nothing save watching the hands on the ormolu mantel clock tick aggressively toward the midnight hour. Irritated with himself, with Helena, with the world and every bloody person within it, he finished his claret and rose. Turning down the lights gave him no pleasure. He made his way to his chamber, lost in his thoughts, no more settled than he had been before he had avoided his wife in favor of solace.

Solitude was not a cure for what ailed him.

As he mounted the steps and took himself upstairs, he came to the unwanted realization that there was no cure in existence. He was restless. Displeased. Randy as a sailor who had just arrived at port after a sojourn at sea. He was a man of too much contradiction and too little peace. He longed for Helena quite desperately, and yet he despised himself for that weakness, that yearning.

He had a wife he had never wanted or planned for, and yet desired more than he had ever thought possible. A wife who had, whether through her actions or his own, caused him to break his vow, his betrothal...

He reached his chamber, closing the door with more force than necessary at his back. The claret had done nothing to soothe the sting of the unrest rising within him. He stalked about his chamber, divesting himself of his attire. Bennet had seen to every preparation; the counterpane was turned down. The lights were low, a bowl and pitcher of water to splash upon his face awaiting him. More claret awaited him as well, further proof that the valet possessed an almost eerie ability to predict what Gabe wanted before he realized it himself.

Naked, he slid on a banyan and poured himself another measure of claret. His traitorous cock was rigid and insistent, making him eye the door connecting his chamber to the dressing area and bathroom he shared with Helena. Having to share the space was an inconvenience he had yet to accustom himself. Even so, the arrangement was not entirely unpleasant.

He had found he rather enjoyed the lingering scent of her garments and perfume in the dressing room. She had a tendency to leave her baubles everywhere, little traces of her he never failed to find and smile over before her lady's maid inevitably located them too and tidied them up. Just this morning, he had discovered a pair of emerald earbobs in the bathroom, suggesting she had removed them herself and then abandoned them wherever she had left them in the moment. Later, they were gone, whisked back to their proper place as if they had never been strewn about in distracted disarray.

Now that he was thinking of the bathroom, a nice, calming soak seemed just the thing. Taking his claret with him, Gabe padded to the adjoining door, pleasantly surprised to discover the bathroom engulfed in low light, warmth suffusing him from the waters of the drawn bath. The entire chamber smelled of the sweet perfume of citrus, an oil Bennet frequently used for his baths.

Bless the man. He had predicted Gabe's needs this evening far beyond expectation.

Gabe shrugged out of his banyan, allowing the cool silk to pool on the tiles at his feet. And then he stepped into the deep, ceramic bliss of the tub, sinking into the water up to his armpits on a well-pleased groan.

Hanging his arms over the edge of the tub, Gabe tipped his head back, allowing it to rest upon the lip. His eyelids shuttered. Hot water lapped at his skin, soothing him. Calming him.

Yes, drawing the bath had been an incredibly attentive action on Bennet's part. Gabe was going to give his valet a raise. He was, in every instance, a man who ventured beyond the call of duty to his master. He was a man who truly cared.

A man who—

"Gabe?"

The shocked echo of his wife's query had his eyes opening. There, on the threshold of the bathroom, stood Helena, clearly hesitating in her *robe de chambre*, cinched neatly at her waist. Her golden locks were unbound, cascading in a wild bevy of curls down her back and over her shoulders.

She looked, in a word, delectable.

He wanted to lick and kiss her from those burnished locks all the way to her toes. Her dressing gown left nothing to the imagination—and hell, he need not rely upon his mind but rather his memory anyway. Just last night, he had sucked the stiff peaks of those pink, pebbled nipples.

Belatedly, he realized he was staring. Devouring her with

his gaze as he longed to do with his lips. But, he cautioned himself, tonight he had decided to keep his distance.

Gabe sat up in the tub. "Have I disturbed you? Forgive me. I thought you long since gone to sleep."

Her gaze flitted over his shoulders and chest, warming every bit of skin above the surface of the water. And all the skin below it as well. *By God*, he was on fire, and it had nothing to do with the temperature of his bath and everything to do with the woman hovering on the threshold of the bathroom.

"I was not able to sleep," she said then, giving him a smile that was at once demure and seductive. "I read for a time, and then my lady's maid drew the bath for me. I see I tarried a bit too long and you discovered it before I could claim it."

Well, bloody hell. Bennet had not drawn the bath for him, nor entirely guessed at his needs before he knew them himself. The bath had been meant for Helena. And Gabe had greedily sunken himself into it.

A pang of conscience hit him. "Forgive me, my dear. I had no idea it had been drawn for you. I had supposed my valet had done it, guessing at what I would require after I retired. Would you...shall I remove myself?"

"Of course not." But instead of retreating to her own chamber where he most decidedly needed her to be, she moved deeper into the room. "You are already enjoying the waters, are you not? It seems a pity for me to require you to remove yourself on account of my whims. Selfish, even."

She was being most accommodating to a husband who had essentially informed her he wished to spend the evening without her company, albeit in more polite terms. He willed his aching cock to behave itself and wither. He had no wish for her to see the effect she had upon him. Or, worse, for him to lose control now that he had so deliberately set out to exercise it this evening.

"I can finish my bath in peace and then draw fresh water for you if you like," he offered. "I will not be but another few minutes, I promise, and there should be sufficient heated water to call for more."

"I would not dream of ejecting you from your bath prematurely," she countered as she reached the tub, bringing with her the seductive scent that was purely hers. And the decadently curved body that was also, purely, hers.

His fingers itched to seize her by the waist and haul her into the bath with him, dressing gown and all. It was only by the thinnest reminder of his intentions for the evening that he did not.

"You are hardly ejecting me," he forced out, gratified when he did not hear a hint of the turmoil secretly raging within him. "I am willingly abandoning the bath that was yours to begin with. It is hardly the selfless act of a martyr."

The selfless act of a martyr would be to remove himself from this chamber. This moment. Because he was finding it increasingly difficult to resist her. Or rather, to resist all the urges she brought to life within him. Wicked urges. Deep-seated urges. The same damned urges which had led to him compromising her and having to marry her.

He would never learn his lesson.

"Or," she said, trailing her fingertips over his forearm in a caress that made his cock stand at attention beneath the water, "you could remain in your bath, and I could aid you."

"Aid me," he repeated, then ground his molars as her touch skipped down to his wrist.

"Yes." Her pink tongue peeked out, moistening her lips. "I can wash you, if you like."

He had to stifle a groan at the thought of her passing a cloth over his body. Of her remaining near enough he could be tempted to haul her into the tub with him at any moment. His resolve was weakening fast.

"I am not certain that would be a wise idea," he said, irritated with himself for the hoarseness of his voice.

"If you would prefer solitude, I understand." Her hand settled atop his briefly before flitting away.

The notion of her going, now that she was here, filled him with a strange sense of loss. She had offered to assist him in his ablutions. He should agree with her that solitude was best.

She turned to go.

He hated himself for the hurt tone of her voice.

"Wait," he called out before he could think better of his decision. "Do not leave. Your company is welcome."

As is your touch, all over my body. Especially upon my cock.

Damnation, what was the matter with him?

Helena gave him a smile that lit him up from the inside. "I was hoping you might change your mind. I missed our usual tête-à-tête this evening."

So had he.

He cleared his throat to keep that maudlin sentiment from revealing itself. "I do believe Bennet keeps my soap and towels in the cabinet just over there, if you wish to have a look."

In his haste to slide into the soothing waters of the bath, he had neglected to take note that the soaps laid out were not his. If he had to spend the night smelling of Helena's soap, he would never get any bloody rest.

"Of course," she said, turning away to retrieve his soap and a cloth.

She was back in no time, proceeding to roll up her sleeves so she would not get them wet. The intimacy of the moment—the sweet domesticity of it—was not lost upon him.

He needed to distract himself. To keep his mind from wandering to unwanted places.

"How was your Lady's Suffrage Society meeting today?" he inquired.

There—an excellent subject for suitable distraction.

She dipped the cloth into the water and used it to wet the cake of soap. "It went well, and we are continuing to collect signatures for our petition for the second reading of the Franchise Bill. We are beginning a suffrage journal, written by us, to be distributed to like-minded ladies throughout London. Lady Jo's husband, Mr. Decker, has volunteered to distribute it for free. Lean forward, if you please, and I shall begin with your back."

Gabe obeyed her soft order. "That is remarkably generous of Mr. Decker." The extension of the Parliamentary franchise to women had been argued since 1867. It was a bitterly contested subject, and one which had been met with innumerable obstacles over the years, not the least of which was a Prime Minister who was not in favor. "I support the amendment to the Franchise Bill that would give women the right to vote, as you know. However, I greatly fear Gladstone will once more squelch it."

"I suspect you are right, much as it grieves me. Many liberal members have pledged they are in favor of women's suffrage. However, it is unlikely they will not bow under pressure. This all just makes the work of the Lady's Suffrage Society that much more important and imperative." The cloth passed over his shoulders in gentle, swooping strokes. "Do lean back now, if you please."

He did as she asked, and she began to spread the frothed cloth over his collarbone, affording him the opportunity to study her. "I admire you for your dedication to your cause, Helena."

She paused, her gaze flying to his. "Thank you, my lord."

Regardless of the muddle in which their marriage had begun, Helena was worthy of praise. She was intelligent, steadfast, and determined. Unfortunately, those traits had also led to her making some reckless decisions, which had in turn forced them to the situation in which they currently found themselves.

A situation which did not seem terribly unwanted at the moment, as situations went.

She passed the cloth over his chest.

He forced his mind to less-tempting matters. "Your work with the Lady's Suffrage Society is estimable. The cause is a worthy one, and I approve of your determination. Forgive me for not saying so before now. I am an abysmal husband, I fear."

She cast him a tentative smile. "You are not so abysmal. At least you did not abandon me whilst you ran away to Shropshire."

He grimaced at the reminder, though her voice held a light, teasing note. "That is not saying a great deal in my favor."

His former plan seemed as if it had been hatched a lifetime between then and now. So much had happened since. But with that thought came the steely reminder that he dared not allow himself to lower his guard with Helena. She had already crept past most of his defenses. The lesson of his parents' ill-fated match remained, however, a pointed rebuke.

But his wife chased any traces of rebukes and reminders from his mind when she leaned closer, so near an unbound curl fell into his bath. He plucked it up, holding the sodden hair as it dripped. A mistake, for it felt like warm spun silk, and he no more wanted to release it than he did to spend the night with only his hand for accompaniment.

This was getting increasingly more perilous, his obsession with Helena.

She stilled, those verdant orbs pinning him in their thrall once more. "Gabe?"

He swallowed down a knot of rising desire. "Yes, my dear?"

This he said as mildly as possible. As if he were discussing, say, a scuffed boot. Or mayhap the improvements to Adringham Hall. He impressed himself with his ability to sound so decidedly unruffled when inwardly, he was a conflagration. Every part of him wanted to kiss her. To pull her into the tub with him, have her ride him as water sloshed all over the tiles.

"I do not wish for you to think you are anything but an excellent husband to me." A sad smile flirted with her luscious lips. "I know our marriage was sudden, and that I am not the woman you originally chose as your countess. However, it is my hope that in time, we can find our way past these initial barriers."

She was not wrong in her words. Helena was a woman he was never meant to have wanted, let alone married. However, as he looked upon her now, he could not fathom any other woman being in this chamber with him.

There were so many things he could say. The words rushed to him, clamoring on his tongue.

"That is my hope as well," he told her thickly instead of revealing the full extent of his thoughts.

His response appeared to be enough, for she nodded and continued performing his ablutions for him. Slowly, tantalizingly.

Deliciously.

Her hand slid lower, the cloth traveling down his chest, across his belly. Anticipation rose, along with the almost feral urge to have her hands upon him. Until he forcefully reminded himself of the need to maintain his control.

"Helena," he growled in warning as the cloth moved to his thighs, in suspicious proximity to his erect prick.

He had to put an end to this before they both went too far. What was he thinking, to allow her to tend to him so intimately? To allow her to…

The cloth floated to the top of the water. He inhaled sharply as her knowing hand, already so adept at bringing him pleasure, grasped his cock. She stroked him from root to tip.

Yes, crooned the devil within as his ballocks drew taut with the need for release. A miracle, truly, for he had been making love to his wife every night since consummating their marriage. *Yes, yes, and more yes.*

Her thumb swirled over his cockhead. *All the yeses, in fact.*

He groaned, his hips jerking. Their prodigious amount of lovemaking only made him more randy.

"I love touching you," she murmured, her voice throaty. Laden with wicked invitation.

How was it that a woman so new to pleasure already could lay him low with more proficiency than a practiced courtesan?

"Helena, I meant to give you the evening to yourself," he gritted.

She stroked him again, her grasp tightening. "What if I do not want the evening to myself?"

Curse this beautiful, maddening woman he had wed who was all the things he should not want. Outspoken, rebellious, fiery, independent. Sensual. Because he was beginning to fear that she could prove to be everything he would ever want, now and forever.

"Devil take it, woman," he growled, standing abruptly, warm bath water traveling down his body in rivulets. "I have had quite enough of this bath for one night."

She rose to her full height, which was almost even with

his when they were both standing. He liked that about her—how tall she was, those long, luscious legs…

"I was not finished," she dared to protest.

"On the contrary." He grinned when he spied the exact moment her gaze settled upon his cockstand. "It would seem we are only just beginning."

CHAPTER 19

What we seek is not so different from that which man has sought.
Nor are we any less worthy of calling it ours.
—*From* Lady's Suffrage Society Times

*H*elena could not wrest her gaze from the sight of Gabe standing tall, proud, and nude in the bath. And erect. Her eyes dipped to the thick protrusion of his manhood, jutting upward, stiff and proud. That part of him, like the rest, was beautiful. She wanted to worship him there, to take him in her mouth.

In truth, she wanted to worship all of him, this man she loved. This man she had married. This man who looked at her as if she were the most glorious, seductive creature he had ever beheld.

The sudden surge of possession within her took Helena by surprise. He was hers. Even if he was difficult to understand. Even if he was a lover who scorched her with his passion by night and turned into a polite stranger by day.

The dichotomy was not lost upon her. But what she relished in this moment was that she had pushed the polite stranger he had been at breakfast and dinner, the man who had urged her to go to bed without him, over the edge.

There was no denying she had an effect upon him.

He wanted her.

Triumph soared, lifting her hopes along with it.

Her stare reluctantly returned to his, traveling up his well-muscled planes, lingering over all his sinew and maleness. Their stares met and held, his filled with so much heat, every part of her tingled in response.

"Shall I dry you off if you have finished your bath?" she asked him.

The decidedly naughty thought of licking the water from his skin occurred to her, but she kept it to herself. What would he think of such an improper suggestion? The lover who burned in her arms every night would be pleased. The cool stranger who spoke to her of the news over their morning breakfast would likely be scandalized.

Who was he? Which Gabe was he, deep within? Or was he a complex combination of the two men he presented to her?

"Damn you, woman, how do you make the most innocent of suggestions sound wicked?" he asked, stepping from the tub.

The towels which had been laid on the surrounding tile absorbed the water running from him. But Helena still could not help but to find the southward trajectory of those rivulets utterly fascinating.

Instead of answering him, she distracted herself by fetching a fresh towel and blotting off the moisture on his chest. The ends of his mahogany hair were damp and dark, clinging together and falling over his brow in a rakish manner that was utterly irresistible.

Tenderness and desire hit her simultaneously.

"Here now," he said gruffly, taking the towel from her. "You are not my manservant, and nor shall I expect you to tend to me as if you were."

He was attempting to resurrect the walls he had erected earlier at dinner. That much was plain to see. Helena, however, was in the mood for victory this evening. Neither defeat nor surrender were options, and they never had been.

She snatched the towel back. "I tend to you because I want to, Gabe. Because tending to you pleases me. You are my husband."

His jaw hardened, but he made no move to reclaim the towel. "You do not need to, Helena. I am not your duty."

"There it is again," she observed, drying off his well-delineated chest muscles. "Your favorite word, I dare say."

"Duty?"

"Yes." She dried his abdomen and then moved behind him, dabbing at the water running down his broad back with the towel next. "It seems to be a favored word in your lexicon."

His back was perfection. Strong and wide, tapering to his lean hips and his buttocks. Helena could not help but to admire him there as well as she dried his lower back.

"Duty is important," he said, his voice low. "It is the force that drives us through our every day, leading us on. And when we falter from it, duty brings us back to the course which we are destined to travel."

His response brought a twinge of sadness to life within Helena. She did her best to diminish it as she toweled off his rump.

"Did you falter from duty when you kissed me the first time?" she asked, for the question had been burning within her for some time now. She had come to believe she understood him, at least in a small sense.

"Of course I did. And from honor as well."

How stiffly he held himself now.

Duty was all-important to Gabe. It was why he had been betrothed to Lady Beatrice. Why he had fought his attraction to Helena so much. Why he fought it still. But there had to be other reasons, reasons which she had yet to unearth. Reasons aside from the lie she had told to force his hand. Reasons why he would make love to her so passionately and then withdraw by the light of the morning. She would simply continue digging until she discovered them all. Until she knew and understood everything there was about her husband.

On a wicked whim, she worked her way lower, drying off the firm backs of his thighs, the well-formed calves all the way to his ankles. Once there, she quietly knelt.

"Turn," she told him, summoning every bit of boldness she possessed.

He did as she asked, his blue eyes burning into hers. "Why are you on your knees?"

"It is most assuredly not because of duty." She tipped back her head, aware of every sense in a way she had not been before. The scent of him—citrus from the water, sandalwood from his soap—was heady on the air. Heat wafted from his bare skin. Steam rose from the bath, enveloping them both in a delicious mist. Even her own curls, trailing down her back until they tickled the soles of her bare feet peeping from beneath her bottom, were a cause of sensation.

"Helena." Though he said her name in a warning fashion, he stroked her cheek. "This was not my intention this evening."

Of course it had not been. His intention had been to send her away from him so he could continue clinging to the barriers he needed between them.

Pretending her only interest was in drying him, she

forced herself to apply the towel to his thighs. First the right, then the left. Then lower. Down the rigid slant of his shins. All the way to the tops of his feet.

Only then did she glance back up at him, marveling at his height and strength, the firm, decidedly masculine musculature and sinews of his body. She had seen her husband naked on numerous occasions, but most of those had been in low gaslight, with him poised above her. Here, now, she had the opportunity at long last to admire him as he deserved.

And more, she hoped.

Much, much more.

She wetted her lips as the warm, heady lure of desire unfurled within her. "There you are, my lord. All dried off from your bath."

He still cupped her cheek, the pad of his thumb rubbing her jawline in a slow, steady caress. "Thank you."

But he did not move.

And neither did she.

"Gabe?"

A muscle ticked in his jaw. "Helena?"

"I want to please you."

A handful of words. Not enough to explain everything she wanted. But enough, she hoped. There was something about the man she loved hovering over her, his expression inscrutable, his hand on her face, his body nude and ready for the taking, that had her at sixes and sevens.

"You do not know what you are saying," he argued. "This is not...we cannot...should not..."

Helena had endured enough of Gabe's denials. On the last of his attempts to enumerate the reasons why she ought not to give him pleasure this evening, she simply leaned forward and pressed a kiss to the tip of his cock.

"Damn," he swore.

It sounded like a good curse to Helena, the sort which he

permitted himself to utter in the throes of passion. Smiling, she extended her boldness by running her tongue along the length of him.

"Helena," he said on a groan. "This is...wrong. I cannot ask you to do this for me."

"You did not ask," she pointed out. "I want to do it."

Actually, she had simply begun doing what pleased her. And in this moment, what pleased her was touching and teasing him as he had done to her. He was so good at giving. Tonight, she wanted to return the favor. Whether or not the evening had begun with such an intention was irrelevant. They were here now. Together now.

Nothing had ever felt better or more right.

She did not await his response. Instead, she drew him into her mouth in the same way he had done to her pearl. Echoing his actions, she sucked.

His hips bucked, driving him to the back of her throat.

Helena gagged.

Her husband withdrew instantly. "Forgive me, my dear. That is not...I should have never allowed you to do that. The act is not for a wife, but rather for a mistress."

The word *mistress* made her cold. She stared up at him, the thought of him bedding another woman akin to a knife in her heart.

"Do you have a mistress?" she asked, not for the first time.

"Of course not, Helena." He frowned down at her, their disparate positions making it seem as if they were farther away from each other than they truthfully were. "Surely you know me better than to suppose I would have a mistress after marriage."

Thank. The. Lord. In. Heaven.

Helena exhaled slowly. "I do know you well, I think."

Just not well enough. She would like to know him better. To understand him.

Yes, that was what she wanted.

And to make him lose control.

His nostrils flared. "Do not remain on your knees, Helena. Rise, if you please."

His body, however, did not appear to share the demands offered by his lips.

And she was feeling decidedly stubborn. "I want to bring you pleasure. Cease being so stiff-backed and tell me what I should do."

Color tinged his high cheekbones. "I cannot control myself in your presence, as I have proven time and again. I dare not trust myself with you."

"Good." She wanted him to be mindless, and if he would not offer any assistance in the matter, she would merely follow her instincts instead. "I do not want you to control yourself. I want you to be as wild as you like."

Helena took the ruddy tip of him into her mouth, gratified by the hiss of his breath from above. She sucked, then tentatively swirled her tongue over him. Feeling brave, she took him deeper. Slowly, so slowly.

"Helena," he bit out. "Sweet God."

But instead of withdrawing or requesting she stand again, his fingers sifted through her unbound hair in a gentle, unexpected caress. It would seem his ability to withstand her seduction was diminishing more and more by the moment.

Excellent.

She'd had no plan when she had entered the bathroom and discovered him—quite propitiously—already enjoying the bath which had been meant for her. Already naked. However, Helena was no fool. When Fortune's fickle wheel gave her a good turn, she seized it. And so, any reason to remain in his presence had been excuse enough.

How she loved him. Loved the thickness of him in her mouth. Loved the way he smelled, tasted, felt beneath her questing hands as they skimmed his hips. Loved the low groans of reluctant approval torn from his proper lips. Loved the way he made love to her and brought her to passion's exquisite heights every night.

She was going to do the same for him now. Helena was determined. And she would keep the walls he sought to raise between them down. In the dining room and drawing room, they were the politest of society spouses. But at night, when they were alone, they were aflame. She wanted to keep him burning.

To make him forget all the reasons churning through his mind.

She worked her mouth up and down the length of him, paying close attention to the subtle cues his body and his responses gave her. Breathing through her nose, she took him deep once more, and his fingers tightened in her hair as he rolled his hips. The movement took him to the back of her throat once more. This time, she was prepared. She relaxed, held him there, and then withdrew.

He made another guttural moan. "Hellion. You will be the death of me."

Pleasure slid through her as she sucked and licked. Having this big, powerful man so completely at her mercy filled her with a swelling tide of desire. The more she tended to him, the more pronounced her own need became.

But just when she thought he was about to reach his pinnacle, he reached for her, drawing her to her feet. His gaze was dark and stormy as it clashed with hers.

"Gabe," she protested.

"Hush." In the next instant, his mouth was on hers, fierce and insistent.

The kiss was hard and claiming and deep, his tongue sweeping inside to tangle with hers. So drugging were his lips that she did not even notice he was removing her robe until the whisper of it slid down her arms. She shrugged out of it, allowing it to fall to the towel-lined floor as humid air greeted her bare skin.

He dragged his mouth down her throat, his hand on her waist, clutching her, it seemed, as if she were his anchor. "I need you."

His hoarse confession sent a frisson of desire through her. "Yes."

He spun her about, taking her hands in his and placing them on the lip of the high tub surround. "Now."

Helena shivered at the low tone of his voice, the sensual promise. He kissed the side of her throat, then her ear, pressing his body against hers. Helena arched her back. She wanted him inside her so much she ached.

* * *

Gabe wanted to be inside her so badly, he was going to make love to his wife standing up, in the bathroom. It was depraved, but so were half the things he wanted to do to and with her. Besides, after he had allowed her to suck his cock, any barriers he had been taught to believe existed for the prosperity of a marriage were effectively smashed to bits.

He was not certain if the failure was in Grandfather's teachings or in Gabe himself. Whatever the reason, he was beyond the point of being capable of fretting over right from wrong. All he wanted was Helena, as quickly and completely as he could have her.

He nibbled lightly on the creamy curve of her shoulder as he reached between them, parting lush folds from behind. She was deliciously wet, and the knowledge that taking him in her mouth had achieved her sodden state was enough to make his ballocks tighten.

He slid a finger into her heat, testing her readiness. Her inner muscles contracted, tightening on him in a welcoming grip he could not wait to feel upon his cock. A breathy moan escaped her. Gabe sank another finger inside her, massaging her in the place he had found, purely by accident, that drove her to the edge. The wet suction of his fingers thrusting in and out of her was unbearably erotic.

He kissed back up her neck, finding his way to her ear. "You are so wet. Did you like it, being on your knees for me?"

"Yes," she gasped, thrusting into his fingers and bringing him deeper. "Oh, Gabe. I want you so much."

How he loved her when she was wicked and wild.

He stayed that thought, banishing it from his mind. For love had no place in his life, no place in their union. Love only led to disaster and ruin. This bliss between them needed only desire. Physical joining. Mutual respect.

A cordial union. That was all he had to offer her.

He nipped her earlobe, and then he withdrew his fingers, slicking her juices on his rigid cock before aligning himself to her entrance. Mindlessly, he pressed. One thrust of his hips, and her body welcomed him. The angle and the grip of her surrounding him was enough to make his body flood with fire. The flames licked through him. Consumed him.

She cried out and his restraint snapped. He drove into her deeper, not stopping until he was fully seated. He held still by sheerest force of will, allowing her body to adjust to the different position.

"More," she said.

One word. His complete undoing.

He gave her what she wanted, drawing back and then plunging him deep inside her again and again. The harder he fucked her, the tighter and wetter she became. He was delirious with lust now. Drunk on it. Drunk on her.

He reared back so he could watch. Helena's body was on display for him, her bottom lush and full. He gripped her hips and pumped into her, his cock disappearing within her perfect pink folds before gliding out again, glistening with her dew.

"Do you like it when I fuck you, Helena?" he asked, the dams inside him bursting open.

He was awash in wickedness and sin. Later, he would worry over what he had said and done, the boundaries they had crossed this night. For now, all he wanted was to revel in this sensual onslaught.

"I love it," she said, breathless as she met him thrust for thrust. "I love the way you fuck me, Gabe. I love..."

She never finished what she had been about to say, because in the next instant, she convulsed on him, milking his cock as she spent. He could not keep himself from coming as well. On a guttural growl, Gabe lodged his cock deep one last time, filling her with his seed as she tremored around him and slumped against the tub.

The release was so powerful, it took Gabe a few moments to return to himself. When the delirium of his crisis faded, he realized he was still semihard inside her, his chest pressed to her sweat-slicked back. She had been about to tell him she loved him, he feared. But reckless fool that he was, instead of her words turning him cold, they had heightened his desire. And now, he wanted her again.

What the devil was the matter with him?

He had intended to keep his distance this evening, and yet he was turning into a raging satyr. He had to get out of this bathroom and return to the safe haven of his own chamber before he made love to her again.

He kissed her cheek and forced himself to withdraw from

the sweet haven of her body. Then he drew up his dressing gown, averting his gaze from the temptation she presented. "Thank you, my dear. I bid you good night."

As he hastened his escape, Gabe inwardly kicked himself in the arse.

What a prig he had sounded like.

He had never hated himself more.

CHAPTER 20

Only a villain would deny us our right.
—*From* Lady's Suffrage Society Times

he last person Helena expected to pay a call upon her was Lord Algernon Forsyte. The moment he entered the blue salon, dread squeezed her heart in its icy grasp. She knew instinctively that no good could come of his visit. Nor of the smug look on his countenance.

Still, she strove to settle her inner tumult and dipped into a curtsy to match his bow. "Lord Algernon, what a pleasure to see you again."

He took her hand in his, raising it to his lips for a kiss. "The pleasure is all mine, Lady Huntingdon. Where is Lord Huntingdon this lovely afternoon? It has been a few weeks since our paths have crossed."

"My husband is not at home," she managed, withdrawing her hand from his grasp as the urge to wipe her hand upon her skirts rose within her.

How had she ever contemplated ruining herself with his aid? Her desperation had been not just reckless, but foolish as well.

"A shame, that." Lord Algernon's gaze raked over her form in a bold and assessing fashion. "Fortunately, Huntingdon is not the one I wished to see today. You are, my dear countess."

More misgiving blossomed within her. She stepped away from him, deeming it prudent to increase the distance. His cologne was overwhelming, filling her with the urge to sneeze. There also lingered on the air a faint whiff of hair grease and spirits, mingling with tobacco and linen in need of a fine laundering. Did the man not realize covering himself in scent did nothing to cloak his lack of care in his appearance?

She cleared her throat to chase away the unpleasant odors. "Forgive me, Lord Algernon, but I fail to see a reason for you to call upon me."

He cocked his head at her, flashing a sly grin. "Can you not, my lady? Because I can think of many. Specifically, one thousand pounds' worth."

"One thousand pounds?" She stared at him, failing to understand.

"Yes, Lady Huntingdon, one thousand pounds." He raised a brow. "Recently, I came into a bit of misfortune, and I find myself in need of funds. Therefore, I am making calls upon all those indebted to me. You are one such person."

She stiffened. "I am hardly indebted to you, my lord."

"On the contrary, my lady. You arranged for an assignation with me, did you not?"

Helena refused to answer. For they both already knew she had.

"I think it is best if you leave now, Lord Algernon," she

told him frostily. "I owe you nothing. You shall have to collect your thousand pounds from someone else."

"I am afraid leaving would not be in my best interest." He moved toward her. "You are wrong to think you owe me nothing. It is thanks to me that you find yourself the Countess of Huntingdon. And what a clever jade you are, entrapping him into marriage when all London knows the earl was betrothed to Lady Beatrice first. Tell me, my lady, did you allow him to toss up your skirts at my bachelor residence, or did you go somewhere else for the honor?"

She would have slapped him for his impertinence were he nearer, the despicable cad. "If you will not leave, Lord Algernon, I shall have you thrown out."

"I do not think you will, my dear countess," he countered smoothly. "You see, there is something I have of yours, something which shall only be returned upon my receipt of the one thousand pounds."

Instantly, she thought of the necklace she had lost. "I will not be coerced into giving you funds in return for anything."

"Ah, I see your mind feverishly working," Lord Algernon said. "However, you may wish to rethink your opinion on the matter. The item in question is a pearl necklace with an emerald pendant. One you are known to wear frequently. I do not see you wearing it today. Could it be because you left it on the floor of my chamber?"

Her necklace. *Good heavens.* She had noticed it missing that day, but in the madness which had followed, it had fallen from her mind.

Her fingers sank into her silken skirts, crushing them. "Your possession of a necklace hardly means anything, Lord Algernon."

"Perhaps not to you, but I dare say it would mean a great deal to the gossips and the scandal mongers." His smile turned nasty. "Imagine the details which could circulate. Such shocking tales. I do not suppose your husband would be pleased if all England knew what a scheming harlot he has taken as his countess."

The thought of her plot to ruin herself being turned into fodder for the gossip mill made bile rise up her throat. As did the notion of the shame it would bring upon Gabe. They were newly married, and he placed such high importance upon his sense of honor and duty. They had only just begun to find a tentative truce. Scandal of the sort Lord Algernon threatened could have a devastating effect upon them both.

Still, she would not be strong-armed into doing this villain's bidding. "My husband is aware of the reason I was attempting to ruin my reputation. It was solely to avoid an unwanted betrothal and marriage."

"Do you suppose anyone will give a damn about the reasons, Lady Huntingdon?" Lord Algernon sneered. "I think not. They will be only too eager for fresh scandal. Imagine, if you will, the great Earl of Huntingdon's reason for hastily abandoning his betrothed and marrying you. I will happily tell everyone I had you first."

She recoiled at his last threat, for it was what she feared he had been intimating. "That would be a lie."

"Yes, but who has your necklace, my lady?" He raised a brow, victory in his voice. "You never should have been so reckless, attempting to ruin your reputation. If you had taken greater care, you would not find yourself in this position. However, you did. I need one thousand pounds to settle some gambling debts, and you need the return of your necklace. It seems an honest trade."

Nothing about the trade was honest, and they both knew it.

"I do not have one thousand pounds," she said, for it was

the truth. Her dowry was modest, and she did not have all the funds immediately at her disposal as Huntingdon had invested many of them with her blessing.

"Your husband has that and more," Lord Algernon countered.

Correctly, drat him, for Gabe's wealth was undeniable and well-known. And yet, she could not ask Gabe for money to pay for Lord Algernon's silence. Just when she felt as if they were making progress in their marriage, he withdrew. Their evenings were spent in passion and by day, they remained the same polite earl and countess who were virtual strangers to each other. She feared that broaching the topic would shatter what little Gabe was willing to share with her.

"He will not give you a thousand pounds," she said, knowing it was true.

Even if she went to Gabe with the request, he would be outraged. He would likely charge instantly to Lord Algernon's apartments, and she could only shudder to consider the consequences of such a meeting.

"No, he will not." Lord Algernon smiled again. "*You*, however, will, my dear countess. That is why I have sought you out. One thousand pounds in return for my lifelong silence and the necklace. Say nothing to your sainted earl of the matter. If you do, I will go to the gossip rags with my sordid tale, but I shall make it worse by letting everyone know Huntingdon wedded you after our *affaire* out of sympathy. Bring the funds to me tomorrow at two o'clock in the afternoon, or your secret will be shared with the world. And I dare say your husband will never forgive you for the shame you shall bring upon him."

Helena stared at him, stricken, fearing he could be right.

She had already forced Gabe into this marriage. If she ruined his reputation, she did not know what would happen to the progress they had made. The last few days had given her a glimmer of hope they could have a happy marriage in the future, and now, it seemed it would be ruthlessly snatched away.

Unless she did as the insidious man before her demanded.

Lord Algernon bowed again. "I shall leave you to think upon your choices, Lady Huntingdon. I trust you will reach the right one, and that you know the direction to my rooms."

With that parting shot, he stalked from the blue salon, taking all her incipient hopes with him.

* * *

Lord Algernon Forsyte was feeling quite pleased as he entered the carriage which had been awaiting him. The equipage was sleek and well-kept, the Moroccan leather squabs oiled and comfortable. Different than the conveyances in which he could ordinarily afford to travel, that much was true. Fortunately, Lady Beatrice Knightbridge hailed from a family flush in funds. It was about the only thing to recommend her aside from her bubbies.

Fat purses and fat bubbies.

Lord Algernon appreciated both, and not necessarily in that order. Well, he also appreciated brandy and gin, but that was to be expected. What he did not appreciate, however, was a frigid female. And Lady Beatrice was decidedly that. He did not think he had ever met a colder fish.

Further proof of his grim supposition was provided by the manner in which she stiffened and shoved him to the bench opposite hers when he attempted to seat himself at her side.

"Do not crowd me, you oaf," she snapped. "Your seat is over there."

Lord Algernon settled himself on the bench and raked her prim, buttoned-up form with a disdainful glare. "I thought you might at least give me a kiss after my efforts on your behalf today. One could say it is the least you could do. Instead, you are more swaddled than a babe."

His chief objection was that he could not see the only part of her that rendered her somewhat tolerable. Although the day was warm, later summer upon them, she had donned a drab gray walking gown fastened all the way to her throat with a pelisse gathered atop the unsightly affair.

"I would sooner set my lips upon an eel," she told him crisply as the carriage rocked into motion.

"I have an eel for you to kiss," he suggested lewdly, just to nettle her.

She blinked at him, his double entendre apparently lost upon her. "Of course a man like you would eat eels for his dinner. I ought not to be surprised."

Eels were easily and cheaply had, and he well understood her insult. He supposed he, in turn, should not be surprised she had not comprehended his. Of course, he had meant she ought to kiss his cock, and damn him if the notion of Lady Beatrice doing so did not make him harder than a fire poker, right then and there.

He inhaled deeply to chase away the lust pounding in his loins, for it would not, sadly, be satisfied by the prim lady opposite him. "One would think you more accommodating of a man who has just done everything you asked."

She inhaled slowly, then released the breath. "It is done, then?"

He nodded at her query, trying to stifle a sudden, unexpected surge of guilt. The devil of it was, he enjoyed Lady Helena Davenport—*er, Lady Huntingdon*. She was beautiful and tall, with legs a man could not help but imagine wrapped around his waist. If he had not been so bloody soused the night he had lost her in a hand of cards to Huntingdon, he would have enjoyed those damned legs.

And that rapturous bosom. Lady Huntingdon's breasts were truly outstanding. Like twin mounts of blancmange, he had no doubt, topped with the sweet cherries of her luscious nipples. A dessert course in feminine form. Why, he could have covered them in an effusion of his manly cream…

Damn, when was the last time he had fucked a decent pair of bubbies?

The pointed end of a leather boot connected with his shins, sending pain searing through him. He howled, rubbing the wounded leg and pinning Lady Beatrice with his most displeased glower. "What the devil is the matter with you, kicking a man who has just done your bidding?"

"I kicked you because you have yet to confirm you have indeed done my bidding," she said coldly. "I asked you if it was done, and your response was to stare at my person as if you were eying a feast laid before you."

Color tinted her cheekbones.

She was comely, Lady Beatrice. But he hated to tell her he had not been looking at her so much as he had been fantasizing about her rival, laid bare before him. Ah, if only he had not had the devil's own luck that night…

"It is done," he forced out instead of entertaining further lewd thoughts of the new Countess of Huntingdon, however well-deserved they might be. He needed to remind his cock that bedding Lady Huntingdon would not pay his gambling debts. But playing Lady Beatrice's games would.

The lady in question's eyes went wide, a cat-in-the-cream smile curving her lips. "Do you think she will come to your chambers as arranged?"

In truth, he could not be certain. He had blustered his

way through the interview with Lady Huntingdon, his bravado fortified by the gin Lady Beatrice had offered him on the ride to Wickley House. The countess had seemed suitably affected by his claims. However, whether or not she would appear with one thousand pounds on the morrow was anyone's guess.

"Of course she will," Algernon said smoothly. "She was quivering in her petticoats at the notion of being connected to me through the gossipmongers and the damage it might do to the earl."

Lady Beatrice nodded, her nostrils flaring. "That is most excellent news, my lord. Most excellent indeed. The rest of my plan shall proceed tomorrow then, as we discussed."

Algernon grinned. "It will as long as I have the funds you promised me, Lady Beatrice."

With a disapproving sniff, she reached into her reticule, extracting a bank note. "You will have half the monies today and half tomorrow, upon the full execution of my plan."

He plucked the bank note from her gloved fingers. "That is not what we discussed, my lady."

Her eyes narrowed. "I do not trust you, Lord Algernon. Until I have what I want, you shall not have what you desire either."

Half the funds he had demanded for his part in this farce she had concocted in her mad little mind was more than enough to settle his debts and leave him some to spare. Which meant Algernon was going to have an excellent night.

He tucked the note into his coat. "Fair enough, my lady. Just what is it you want tomorrow?"

Lady Beatrice's smile was cold and calculated. "Everything I deserve." She paused, her smile fading. "And everything Lady Helena Davenport deserves as well."

Algernon did not bother to remind her Lady Helena was the Countess of Huntingdon now. He had money in his pocket and the prospect of a decidedly jolly evening awaiting him.

He had every intention of getting properly drunk and then fucking the most luscious pair of bubbies to be found. And the tightest cunny, while he was at it.

CHAPTER 21

We strongly believe, based upon sound reasoning and the example
we have in the Territory of Wyoming in the United States, that,
contrary to the fierce-minded opponents of women's suffrage,
domestic discord will be avoided, rather than caused, by the
universal extension of the Parliamentary franchise.
—From Lady's Suffrage Society Times

Seated in the crimson drawing room that evening following dinner, Gabe watched Helena play the grand piano. The song was a mournful Chopin, and she played it with an elegant proficiency he could not help but to admire. Her dainty fingers traveled over the ivory without missing a single note.

In spite of his every intention to cast thoughts of Lady Beatrice from his mind, he could not help but to compare Helena's skill to that of his former betrothed. Along with her loveliness and passion, her talent at the piano far exceeded that of the woman he would have made his countess. More reason to wonder at his grandfather's plans. Had he been right in thinking Lady Beatrice would have made the ideal countess? Wrong to believe that love and passion had been the downfall of his parents' marriage?

More and more, the answer to those questions grew murky.

Gabe sipped his port as he allowed the music his wife was creating to wind around his senses, wrapping him in a pleasant state of calm. He and Helena had settled into a comfortable rhythm. Polite breakfasts, days spent apart, and nights together, when they could slake their mutual passions.

Still, he had taken note that something was different about Helena this evening.

Gabe could not quite determine what it was. However, it was there, hovering between them, almost as tangible as the golden curl which oft seemed to fall across her cheek. He found it most endearing, that curl.

In fact, he found *her* most endearing.

And enthralling.

Beautiful, too.

By God, he was falling beneath his wife's spell.

It was happening too quickly. They were moving too quickly. Had he learned nothing from his parents' destructive union?

Apparently not. Because ever since the fateful evening when he had vowed he would not share her bed, he had been bedding her at every opportunity. Not necessarily involving a bed. He had made love to her on the chaise longue in the library, against the wall of his study, on the carpeted floor of an anteroom, and once—though he had previously doubted the facility of such an action—in his carriage.

The unholy urge to bed her everywhere arose within him now, and not for the first time. Wickley House was rife with possibilities. The kitchens. The larder. The guest rooms. The emerald drawing room. The stairs. The portrait gallery. The mews. The gardens…

Damnation. This was doing nothing to ease the sudden tightness of his trousers.

He rose as the song came to a close and Helena stood, turning to face him.

"*Brava*, my dear," he said. "Listening to you play was a delight."

She sent him a small smile. "Thank you, my lord."

Again the notion struck him that there was something unusual about his wife this evening. She was more…solemn. Less vibrant, almost like a faded version of herself.

"Is something troubling you, Helena?"

She moved past him, crossing the Axminster to the wall where his sister's portrait hung. "If something was, why should it be your concern?"

He did not miss the edge to her voice, but he chose for the moment to ignore it. "You are my wife. Of course if you are troubled, it is my concern."

That emerald stare studied him. "It is because I am a duty to you?"

Yes and no. But he would fret over the *no* later.

He inclined his head. "I take all my duties seriously."

"And your honor and reputation," she observed.

"Yes. I do my utmost to live in the mold of my grandfather." He paused. "All too often, I fail."

Her lips tightened. "Because of me, you mean."

"Because of my weakness for you," he corrected.

"Your *weakness*." She said the word as if it were an epithet.

Obsession had been the obvious choice of word. He had ignored it. However, it seemed the word he had decided upon instead was no better. The expression upon his wife's lovely countenance was distinctly unenthused.

He attempted to explain. "I ought to have been strong

enough to resist the pull I have felt for you instead of allowing myself to become ensnared in your plotting to ruin yourself. It is my own failing."

"You consider our marriage a failing?" she asked next.

"I consider my conduct a failing." He moved toward her, attempting to close the chasm he had created between them with proximity. "Our marriage has proven pleasant. Do you not find it so?"

Better than pleasant, at least when they found each other in the darkest hours of night.

"I cannot say what I find it just yet. I fear you will resent me forever, Gabe." She cocked her head, studying him intently. "What shall happen if I do something to displease you? Or if I should cause you scandal?"

He stiffened, stopping just short of her, the claret-red of her silken skirts brushing his trousers. "Do you intend to cause me scandal?"

"Not if I can help it."

That was not the response he had been looking for, but he ought not to be surprised. She was the lady he had spent so much time chasing about London whilst she attempted to ruin herself. Her willingness to do so with any man she could cozen into her scheme returned to him, nettling. A woman with her passionate nature…

Shelbourne claimed she fancied herself in love with him.

Love begot nothing but hurt and devastation.

Love could so quickly fade and turn to enmity.

"I will not accept you taking lovers, Helena," he bit out.

She flinched as if he had struck her. "Is that what you think of me?"

"What am I to make of your own words?" He raked his fingers through his hair. "Why should you cause a scandal, if not by cuckolding me? I cannot think of any other means.

Most society marriages involve husband and wife turning a blind eye to each other's sins."

Her chin tipped upward in a familiar show of stubborn defiance. "Would Lady Beatrice have taken lovers?"

Damn it, how had they come to this impasse? One moment, he had been listening to her play, and the next they were at each other's throats.

"It hardly matters what she would have done," he growled. "She is not my wife. You are."

"Yes, but I am the wife you did not want, am I not?" she asked.

There was no good way to answer her question.

"I want you," he rasped, irritated with himself at the hoarseness in his own voice. "Let there be no question of that."

He wanted her endlessly. Every way he could have her. He desired her in a way he had not thought possible, and making love to her did nothing to quell the ache within him. Rather, it just made him long for her even more.

"You desire me." Her voice was cool. "That was never in question. Your wanting me as your wife, however, always has been."

He was a confused mass of emotions. Ever since he had kissed her for the first time, he had been tangled in knots. Knots which only grew tighter and more complex with each passing day. He had spent so much of his life fearing he would make the same mistakes as his parents had. Grandfather's maxims were so ingrained in him as to be a part of him, no different than a limb.

And yet, the woman before him vexed him.

She entranced him.

She brought him low.

"Is not desire enough for us to build our union upon?" he countered.

"You say nothing of love," Helena pointed out.

Ah, there they were. At the crux of the matter and the heart of all the problems his parents had faced in their disastrous marriage.

"Love is not the proper foundation for a marriage." Grandfather's words, touted so oft. Not his own.

But he believed in the truth of them.

Helena's eyes flashed with fire. "And what *do* you consider the proper foundation for a marriage, Gabe? Mayhap we should have discussed this before we wed, because I am beginning to suspect the two of us have vastly different opinions on the matter."

"Mutual respect," he answered easily. "Politeness. Treating each other with perfect courtesy."

Also Grandfather's suggestions. Excellent ones, Gabe thought.

Apparently, his wife, however, did not.

She shook her head. "But why not love?"

His response was instant. "Love is a dangerous emotion, quick to change. When it is destroyed, it cannot be repaired. Believe me on this. I witnessed the hell my parents' own union became. It ended with both them and my sister dead, my sister as a result of their selfish, reckless actions."

He hated the tremor in his voice when he mentioned Lisbeth. Hated even more the sudden fit which hit him at the reminder of what she had endured. His chest tightened. His vision grew dark around the edges. Breathing became a struggle. His heart pounded furiously against his chest.

He froze, giving in to his old demons once more.

* * *

Helena sensed the moment her husband's attack was imminent. His entire demeanor altered. He stiffened, and his eyes darkened from sky blue to navy, his pupils wide and obsidian.

She wondered again at the full story of what had happened to his sister. She had witnessed the reaction that came over him, and she knew what to expect by now. Regret and guilt washed over her in unison as she reached for him, cupping his cheeks and forcing him to meet her gaze.

"Look at me, Gabe. Breathe. I am here."

His skin was rough with the shadow of his whiskers and slick with an abrupt sheen of perspiration. He inhaled slowly, gazing at her as if he did not see her. He was somewhere else, though his physical body was present. It was as if he had descended into the hells of the past, where no one and nothing existed but his painful memories and the ghosts that haunted him.

She caressed his jaw. Soothingly ran her hands over his dark hair. "Talk to me, my love."

His breath wheezed. "Can't."

Fair enough. It would not do to push him too much. Mayhap she had already pushed him far too much this evening, driven by Lord Algernon's hateful visit and her own roiling fears over the decision she must make.

She did the next thing that felt natural in that moment, and she took her husband into her arms. She embraced him, pressing a kiss to his cheek, to his ear. "You are with me. You are safe. The past cannot hurt you now."

He shuddered, and then his arms wrapped around her, his grip so tight as to verge upon painful. But Helena did not care if she would find bruises on her waist by the morning light. If he needed to hold her as if he were a drowning man clinging to shore, she would stand here all night long.

He was so beloved to her.

She would do anything for him, anything to protect him, anything to make him happy and to chase his pain. Even if he did not want her love, even if he believed love was what had soured his parents' marriage, he could not change the way she felt about him. It was unchangeable. Eternal. Even if he never loved her back.

Was she a fool?

Mayhap.

He was a beautiful, flawed, hopelessly confounding man. But he was the man she loved, and she would stand by his side forever.

"Helena." He said her name reverently, as if it were a prayer.

As if he had not, minutes before, suggested he feared she would make a cuckold of him. The hurt from his words lingered, simmering just beneath the surface. But she would tend to it later. She would prove to him she was nothing like his parents. For now, he needed her far more than she needed to lick her wounds.

What had Gabe endured, what had he witnessed, to make him into the man he had become?

"Yes, my love." She ran her hands up and down his spine, caressing him, soothing him. "I am here. I will be here for you always, whenever you need me. This, I promise."

His heart, which had been racing in a tangible thud against her, seemed to calm. So, too, his breathing. He inhaled slowly, sharply, then exhaled, making the tendrils of hair that inevitably worked themselves free of her coiffure dance and tickle her cheek.

He shifted in her arms, pressing his lips to her skin. "Thank you, hellion. I...want to tell you about Lisbeth. About my sister."

It seemed too soon. He was still trembling in her arms,

and *oh* how her heart ached at this seemingly omnipotent man, brought so low.

"Hush," she whispered, still stroking his back. "You need not tell me anything. We shall have a seat on the settee, and I will ring for a tea tray or mayhap something stronger. Would you care for some Moselle? A whisky, perhaps?"

"You."

She was not certain if his terse response meant that he wanted her alone or if he was asking her to decide what she ought to ring for. In the end, Helena decided to guide her husband to the settee so they could sit down.

Slowly, haltingly, they traveled across the thick Axminster.

"Here we are, Gabe." She puffed out a breath, for though she was tall and though he had moved on his own, she had put a considerable effort into hauling him to the piece of furniture in question. "Have a seat."

"You as well."

Three words. Mayhap she could count it an improvement. A sign his attack was receding.

"Of course," she said agreeably, attempting to infuse her voice with calm and cheer. "You first, my love."

He lowered himself to the cushion, then gestured for her to do the same.

How he could appear imperious and demanding when he was not himself, she could not say. However, the Earl of Huntingdon was, indisputably, a law unto his own.

She seated herself at his side as he wished, so near their hips were aligned. She felt him keenly, even through her layers. He seared her everywhere their bodies connected. And she knew he always would. It was simply the way of it between them.

Her heart gave a pang anew at the difficult—nay, impossible—decision before her. Did she dare defy Lord Algernon and invite the possibility of scandal and lies into her life when Gabe had just told her himself that he would not tolerate scandal, that his honor and duty were paramount? Or did she betray her husband by going to Lord Algernon and paying him the funds he required for his silence?

It was a horrible choice, either way.

Given Gabe's state of mind this evening, she did not even dare broach the subject with him. What she needed to do now was to be as supportive and calming an influence as possible.

His hand shook her from her reveries. Their fingers tangled and held, there in her lap. His touch was warm and reassuring, his grip strong. All signs he was reemerging from the tunnel into which he disappeared in these rare moments.

She turned to him, searching his countenance and noting some of the life had returned to his handsome face. He was no longer the color of ash. "How are you feeling, darling?"

He licked his lips. "I am calming. Forgive me, Helena."

She would forgive him anything. "Of course. I cannot begin to imagine what might have happened to cause such a visceral response in you, but please know I am here at your side whenever you have need of me."

He squeezed her fingers. "Thank you."

She brought their entwined hands to her lips, pressing a kiss to the top of his. "You need not thank me. As your wife, it is my duty to see to your well-being."

"Duty," he repeated.

She searched his gaze, fearing another episode loomed since they had returned to a lone word. "Yes, duty. You seem quite familiar with the notion."

A faint smile flitted with the corners of his lips, another indication he was returning to himself. "A woman once told me that if I said the word *duty*, she would stomp on my foot."

And so she had. She was surprised he remembered that

day, that conversation in his carriage. It seemed as if it had transpired a lifetime ago now.

"Mayhap she was frustrated with your overbearing nature," she suggested sweetly, hoping to tease him and further ease his mood.

"I dare say she was." His eyes seemed to bore into hers as his faculties returned to him and he was once more the bold, strongly opinionated man she had come to know as her husband. "I am imperfect, by nature."

"As am I," she agreed readily. "I am sorry for telling Shelbourne what I did, sorry for forcing you to forego your future plans and marry me instead of your paragon Lady Beatrice. My actions were inexcusably selfish. I see that now. You had settled upon your course, and then I upended everything."

She had been thinking of herself when she had told her brother about what had happened between herself and Gabe. She had known the revelation would hurt the both of them. And yet, she had done so anyhow. To save herself. Because she had cared more about what she would endure as Lord Hamish White's bride than she had cared about what Gabe wanted.

More and more, she understood what she needed to do on the morrow. How she could make amends for her actions. She could not risk further scandal and upset for Gabe if she ignored Lord Algernon's warnings. She had gotten them into this infernal mess with her own reckless actions, and she alone could extricate them from it.

"I had settled upon my course, and I do not deny it," her husband said at her side, taking her by surprise with his smooth baritone. "However, I am pleased by our marriage. Just as you beg my forgiveness for your actions, I must apologize for my own behavior. I know I have not been the husband you expected; mayhap not even the husband you deserve. Helena, I...I want to tell you about my sister. About my parents."

It was her turn to squeeze his fingers. "Only if you wish it, Gabe. I will not force it out of you. I want to know, but the choice must be yours and yours alone. You do not owe me your secrets."

He nodded jerkily. "I am your husband, Helena. It is only right and fair that I tell you my story. My mother and father...they were a love match, both terribly young when they wed. It did not take long for their love to fester and turn into hatred. Father was a jealous man, and possessed of a mercurial nature. Mother was a bit wild. He sought to cage her, she rebelled. They each began taking lovers. My childhood was a tawdry map of furious fighting and volcanic loathing."

Her heart ached for him. "I am so sorry, Gabe."

"It is hardly an original tale of woe. Many children are born to parents who do not deserve them. I had it better than most, for I had my grandfather." He paused, running his hand along his jaw, his countenance taking on a faraway look as memories no doubt returned to him. "My sister Lisbeth and I spent most of our time with Grandfather and our governesses as children, whilst our parents went about their separate lives. We were close, though she was older than I. However, as we progressed in age, we spent more time apart."

Helena brought their entwined hands to her lips, pressing a kiss to the top of his. She knew what delving into the darkness of his past must be costing him. But she was also appreciative of the rare glimpse he was providing her to the man within. To the boy he had once been.

"My mother died when the cutter she was sailing in with one of her lovers sank," he continued. "Not long after, I went off to Eton. Lisbeth remained with Grandfather. But it pleased my father to force her to play the part of his hostess at various country house parties he hosted for all his cronies. At one of those parties, Lisbeth was raped."

Helena could not stifle her gasp of shock. Little wonder he grew so ill whenever thinking of his sister. She could not bear to think what Lisbeth must have endured. "You do not need to continue, Gabe."

"That is not where her story ends." His complexion was ashen once more, his jaw tense, tone grim. "As a result of her attack, she became with child. Not only had our father failed to protect her, he did not give a damn about what had happened to her other than the selfish fear it would bring him shame. When Lisbeth told me everything, I was sick. He intended to send her away, that she could birth the babe and he or she would be given to another family. In spite of what had befallen her, she did not want to lose her child. I went to our father on her behalf. He accused her of being just like our mother, calling Lisbeth a whore."

His voice shook with anger on the last note, his entire body stiff with fury.

She stroked his back, feeling terribly ineffectual. "I am so sorry. I cannot imagine what your sister must have suffered, and then to have her own father turn against her…"

"It was more than Lisbeth could endure." He bowed his head, struggling for words. "I promised her I would do everything in my power to keep her safe, but our father was her guardian. There was a clear limit to what I could do to aid her. I had planned to help her run away. I had secured a cottage for her in Shropshire, but our father discovered our plans and went into a rage. Lisbeth was terrified, and she… she hanged herself. I was the one to find her."

"Oh dear God, Gabe." She threw her arms around him again, holding him to her. "How awful that must have been for you."

He held her tightly, another shudder wracking his big body, and buried his face in her hair. "I will never forget that day, how helpless I felt, knowing I had failed her."

"You did not fail her." She drew back and cupped his beloved face. "You did everything you could for your sister. You could not have known she would take such drastic measures to escape your father's plan for her."

She could see, quite clearly now, that Gabe blamed himself for what had befallen Lisbeth. She could also see why duty was so important to him, why he hated his father, why he believed love was the enemy. Everything came together. She understood this man for the first time, completely. Her heart broke for him.

"I did not do enough, or she would still be here." His voice broke. "If I had been there for her when she needed me, she never would have been attacked. I begged her to tell me who was responsible, but she refused. Now, I will never know, and she will never have justice."

How truly helpless he must have felt at the entire situation. She knew him to be a loyal, strong, caring man. A man who bore the scars of the past upon his heart.

"I am sorry." She could not say it enough.

Not that words could do anything to ameliorate the pain within him or the sorrow at his loss. But that, and her love for him, was all she had to offer.

However, it was not her love that he wanted.

"I do not want your pity," he said hoarsely.

"And you do not have it." She searched his gaze, silently urging him to see what was before him. "All you have is me."

He pressed a kiss to each of her palms. "You are everything I want, Helena."

His words filled her heart with hope she feared would inevitably be dashed.

CHAPTER 22

We must never give up our fight until we emerge victorious.
—From Lady's Suffrage Society Times

*H*elena had formulated a battle plan.

Following breakfast that morning with Huntingdon—their usual polite affair—she arrived at the townhouse of Lady Jo Decker. The hour was unfashionably early, and it was rude for her to pay a call just now, but she was desperate.

Jo was expecting her, for she had sent word ahead.

They settled down over a tray of tea.

"Thank you for seeing me on such short notice," Helena said.

"It is my pleasure, dearest." Jo pinned her with a dark, searching gaze. "You know you are welcome here whenever. Is something the matter? You are looking rather Friday-faced."

Everything was the matter.

Where to begin?

She took a deep breath. "Do you recall Lord Algernon Forsyte?"

Jo's nose wrinkled in elegant distaste. "Dreadful man. Far too much hair grease."

Yes. What *had* Helena been thinking in going to his rooms that day?

She frowned. "An excellent description."

Jo's brows rose. "What of him?"

"Do you also recall my plan to achieve ruination so I might avoid marriage to the equally odious Lord Hamish?"

"Oh, dearest." Jo settled her teacup in its saucer. "Pray tell me you did not consider Lord Algernon as one of your options. I do believe you had only mentioned Dorset before."

"Lord Algernon was prior to Dorset." Helena sighed. "Both of those plots were foiled by Huntingdon, of course. But Lord Algernon is not as willing to forget my plan as Dorset appears to be."

"That dog." Jo sat up straighter. "What has he dared to do? If there is any way I may be of assistance, I would be more than happy to do so."

"He came to me yesterday and demanded one thousand pounds in exchange for his silence." She closed her eyes against a sudden onslaught of emotion. Yesterday had left her feeling battered and raw, in more ways than one. "Apparently, he has gambling debts to settle. He has threatened to reveal our connection to the gossipmongers if I refuse or approach Huntingdon with his demands. I am expected to meet with him this afternoon at two o'clock."

"But that is absurd! It would be your word against his, and all society knows Lord Algernon is a drunken, gambling reprobate. Why should anyone believe him over you?"

Helena took another deep breath, attempting to calm her nerves. "Because he has my pearl-and-emerald necklace. It would be sufficient proof—there is no other means by which Lord Algernon should find himself in possession of a piece of my jewelry. I must have inadvertently lost it when I went to his rooms for the assignation and Huntingdon was there instead."

"Do you truly believe he would dare?" Jo frowned, her expression hardening with anger on Helena's behalf.

"I fear he may." She paused, gathering her tumultuous thoughts. "And the fear of the damage it would inflict upon my husband if word of this scandal were to emerge... Oh, Jo. I do not know what to do but pay the one thousand pounds in exchange for my necklace."

"That is blackmail." Jo sounded outraged. "How dare he?"

"It is thoroughly rotten," she agreed. "But the fault is mine for associating myself with such a scoundrel. Not even my desperation is an apt excuse. I was being careless and imprudent, and now I must pay the price so that my husband does not."

"You are still hopelessly in love with Huntingdon, are you not?" Jo asked quietly, sympathy softening her features.

She thought of the husband she had come to know, the tender lover who kissed and caressed her so sweetly, who brought her to such unimagined heights of pleasure. The man who could not escape the demons of the past.

"I love him more now than I ever have," she confessed quietly. "Unfortunately for me, his parents' disastrous marriage before him has left him with the belief that love is an insupportable base for a marriage. I must keep my feelings a secret, lest he discover them and seek to put some distance between us."

Like going to Shropshire.

"Helena, that is perfectly dreadful for you. I am so sorry, my dear friend. What a merciless muddle you have on your hands."

She sighed. "That is one way of describing it, I suppose. Another is hopeless. How is your marriage with Mr. Decker, if I may ask? I long to cling to some hopeful news."

Jo's countenance once more changed, the softness turning into a look of such undeniable tenderness that Helena knew a pronounced pang of jealousy in response. "My marriage has become everything I hoped it would be and more. I find myself falling more in love with my husband with each passing day."

"And I have it on excellent authority that your husband feels the same way about you, *bijou*." The smooth drawl of Mr. Elijah Decker matched his flawless appearance as he prowled unannounced into the salon. "But do not stop extolling my virtues, I beg you. Carry on. I would dearly long to hear more."

Jo laughed, the smile she sent in her husband's direction filled with love. "What are you doing back from your office this morning? I did not expect you until later."

"I was missing my lovely wife, and as none of my business concerns were pressing, I decided to indulge in my whim." Mr. Decker dropped a reverent kiss upon Jo's brow and then turned to Helena, offering an effortless bow. "Lady Huntingdon, it is an unexpected pleasure to see you this morning."

Unexpected, yes. Helena's cheeks went warm as she realized she had unintentionally interrupted a mid-morning tryst between husband and wife. Mayhap thinking to embroil her friend in her foolishness had been a mistake.

"I was just leaving," she began, starting to rise.

"Nonsense," Mr. Decker said congenially.

"I refuse to allow you to go," Jo said in unison.

Helena blinked. "But my problems are mine and not yours. Moreover, I have no wish to intrude upon your day."

"Sit!" Jo ordered, then waved a hand at her husband. "You as well, darling. Helena needs our help."

Helena looked from Jo to Mr. Decker, the latter whom proceeded to obey his wife by obligingly sinking into a nearby settee. She gathered her courage and her original purpose in this visit.

Another deep breath, and then she plunged onward. "Mr. Decker, would you be able to loan me one thousand pounds? I am happy to repay you, with interest, on a schedule decided upon by you."

Mr. Decker eyed her, looking bemused. "Huntingdon is withholding funds from his new countess? I always thought him a prig, but never a miser."

Gabe *was* a bit of a prig, and she had thought so to herself on many occasions, but Helena nevertheless felt the need to defend her husband. "He is neither prig nor miser, Mr. Decker. I require the funds without his knowledge."

"Ah." Mr. Decker cocked his head, silent for what seemed an eternity but was likely no more than a few seconds as he considered her. "A loyal wife who nevertheless wishes to keep a secret from her husband. Intriguing."

"Helena is trying to protect Huntingdon," Jo added, before turning to Helena. "Decker will keep your secret, this I promise. However, the choice is yours if you wish to divulge the full truth. We will aid you in your cause either way."

Helena relayed the sordid tale of her attempts to escape her looming marriage to Lord Hamish White, her involvement with Lord Algernon Forsyte, her lost necklace, and Lord Algernon's subsequent demands.

When she finished, Mr. Decker narrowed his gaze upon her. "Why not involve your husband, my lady? Why come to me instead?"

"Because Lord Algernon threatened to proclaim his story far and wide if I do, and because I am seeking to avoid scandal and upset for Huntingdon in every way possible." Out of deference to her husband, Helena neglected to mention anything deeper concerning Gabe's past.

"Hmm." Mr. Decker tapped his chin, as if he were contemplating the matter further. "Why should Lord Algernon care if you tell Huntingdon he has demanded one thousand pounds of you, do you suppose?"

It was an excellent question, and one which had been troubling Helena herself. "I cannot think of a good reason, other than that he fears Huntingdon would refuse to give him the funds. Apparently, he possesses some pressing gambling debts that are being imminently called in."

"And yet, a gambler is, by his nature, a man who takes risks. Enjoys the thrill of them," Mr. Decker said. "It is the potential reward that drives him, but he also loves the game of bluffing. Why would he not bluff to Lord Huntingdon as well as to his wife?"

Helena frowned, considering Mr. Decker's query. "Would not bluffing to me create the same effect? Moreover, how can we be certain he is bluffing? My necklace has been missing since the night I went to his rooms."

"I think he is bluffing because I make it my business to know the men of the Upper Ten Thousand, and Lord Algernon is no stranger to me," Mr. Decker responded. "To call the man a bag of shite would be an insult to offal everywhere."

Helena grimaced. Jo made a sound of disapproval. "Decker."

"What?" He grinned at his wife. "Do you think any friend of yours could be offended by plain speech, *bijou*? I dare say not."

Mr. Decker had a sweet sobriquet for Jo. Envy speared her. Oh, to have that love, that devotion from her own husband.

Then again, Gabe did have a pet name for her, on the odd

occasion. Though she could not entirely be certain *hellion* was a term of endearment.

"I am not offended in the slightest," she hastened to reassure Jo and Mr. Decker both. "And I could not agree with your assessment of Lord Algernon more, Mr. Decker. Why do you suppose he would bluff about going to the scandal mongers with his story?"

Mr. Decker quirked a dark brow, and Helena had to admit he was a ridiculously handsome fellow. Charming as well. She could see the allure he had presented for her friend, and she was more than pleased to see the manner in which he treated Jo, the easiness between them. Even if it was what she so desperately wanted for herself with her own husband.

"Call it a hunch, Lady Huntingdon. I wish to do some reconnaissance on the matter, but I will loan you the thousand pounds for your afternoon meeting with the arse, as you wish."

His easy acquiescence had her on edge, nonetheless. "What manner of reconnaissance, Mr. Decker?"

"Leave that to me, my dear. I must insist it, as a stipulation of my loan, if you will." He flashed her a rake's grin. "I shall have a man deliver your funds by noon. But now, if you do not mind terribly, my dear Lady Huntingdon, there is a matter of grave import that I must imminently discuss with my lovely wife."

Helena thought she knew what manner of *discussion* he required.

Jo's pretty flush confirmed her suspicion. "Decker," she chastised without heat. "You are incorrigible."

He turned his charm upon his wife. "Always, my love. Have I neglected to mention I brought your favorite strawberry cream ice?"

Her color heightened. "You certainly could have mentioned it sooner."

As husband and wife became lost in each other's eyes, Helena took her cue to leave.

She rose from her seat, shaking out her skirts. "Thank you for the tea and company, and for your willingness to offer me aid. I cannot express enough gratitude to either of you."

"Anything for you, any time you ask, Helena," Jo vowed. "I cannot forsake a fellow sister of the Lady's Suffrage Society, nor a friend as dear as you."

Mr. Decker winked. "And make no mistake about it, I will be more than happy in the knowledge that the Earl of Huntingdon shall owe me a favor."

* * *

Gabe tried to suppress his mounting irritation as the hulking Scotsman who had directed him to the small anteroom in the offices of Mr. Elijah Decker finally returned. He had spent nothing short of the last quarter hour pacing the floorboards, and his patience was not just thin; it was thoroughly decimated.

"A tart?" asked the Scotsman.

Gabe blinked at him, certain he had misheard. "I beg your pardon?"

"Ye have the look of someone in need of sweets, m'lord," the man elaborated. "Would ye care for a tart? Mayhap a wee pudding?"

Was the man daft?

"Do you offer the dessert course to every caller of Mr. Decker's?" he demanded, quite rudely, he was aware. "Or am I alone in the dubious honor?"

But ever since his conversation with Helena the evening

before, he had been on edge. The combination of his worry over whatever had been troubling her and the revelations he had made to her had been gnawing at him. He did not possess the requisite calm to entertain the whims of a cheeky, flame-haired giant.

"Dinna fash yerself," said the Scotsman. "My dear, puir mother, saints preserve her, always said that when a man looks as if he could spit nails, ye ought tae offer him a balance."

Huntingdon stared at the Scotsman. "*Have* you any tarts?"

The man grinned. "Nay."

"Pudding, then?"

The Scotsman shook his head. "Nor puddings."

Gabe ground his jaw, exasperation mingling with impatience. "If you are in possession of neither tarts nor puddings, why offer them, sir?"

"The name is Macfie, yer lordship," the giant corrected gently, "and I dinnae blame ye for forgetting. 'Tis nae a terribly memorable name for a Scotsman, is it?"

"You neglected to answer my question, Mr. Macfie," he said acidly, wondering once more at the reason for his summons.

He was a member of Mr. Decker's club, but their paths had not often crossed. Yet the missive the man had sent to him had suggested he required an imminent meeting. Only for Gabe to cool his heels whilst being bedeviled by the man's Scottish beast.

Macfie nodded, as if Gabe's ire was only to be expected. "In truth, yer lordship, Mr. Decker is unexpectedly detained with a matter of grave import, and I am attempting tae distract ye until he is ready for ye. I was intending tae offer cream ice next."

Gabe was saved from having to respond when the door clicked open to reveal Mr. Elijah Decker.

"Thank you, Macfie, for entertaining Lord Huntingdon whilst I was otherwise occupied," he said easily. "Please make certain that Lady Jo makes her way safely to the carriage, won't you? She ought to be leaving my office in just a moment."

"Aye, Mr. Decker." The Scotsman bowed and disappeared, the door closing discreetly behind him.

Mr. Decker's last words revealed to Gabe the nature of his host's distraction.

"I ought to have known it was a female causing your distraction," he said coolly, taunting his host with the reminder of his reputation as a rakehell.

"You may want to play nice, Huntingdon," drawled Mr. Decker. "My wife is aiding you in a most important endeavor."

"Your wife," Gabe repeated. "Aiding me how?"

Decker grinned. "She is making a delivery to *your* wife."

He remained nonplussed. "Do not you have servants for such things, Decker?"

"Not with a matter this delicate, no." Decker's grin faded. "Would you care to take a seat in my office or here?"

"This will suffice." Along with his patience, his ability to be polite was also waning. "Are you going to tell me the reason for my presence here, or are you going to continue being coy?"

"Calm thyself, Huntingdon." Decker gestured to the pair of leather chairs in the corner of the room. "If you cannot be civil, I will force you to sit through another half hour with Macfie. Have a seat."

Gabe reluctantly sat. "Happy now, Decker?"

His host folded his tall frame into the chair opposite him. "I dare say I could be happier. However, this shall have to do for now, no?"

Gabe resisted the urge to growl. "You are enjoying this too bloody much."

Decker's grin returned. "You did have the temerity to flirt with my wife once at a dinner party before we were married. Forgive me if watching you squirm is cause for enjoyment."

Had he? Gabe could not recall. Lady Jo Decker was a lovely woman, short, dark-haired, and quiet. He favored tall, golden-haired, and reckless.

"My apologies for any flirtation, Decker. Now out with it, if you please."

His host studied him, drawing out the moment. "Very well. The delivery my wife is making to yours consists of a pearl-and-emerald necklace she lost."

Gabe knew the piece of jewelry Decker spoke of—the strands of pearls Helena often wore kissing her throat, adorned with the emerald pendant that matched her eyes. "I was not aware Lady Huntingdon was missing it. Did she lose it at a Lady's Suffrage Society meeting?"

"Indeed not. She lost it at the rooms of Lord Algernon Forsyte, and the maggot was holding it over her head, using it as leverage for blackmail."

Rage shot through him, and immediately thereafter, a hundred different questions followed. "How did you come to be involved in this matter when my wife failed to mention it to me? How in heaven's name did Lady Jo come to be in possession of the necklace if Lord Algernon had it? Why am I in the dark about all this when you are not?"

"Because your wife came to my wife and I this morning seeking our help," Decker explained. "Said maggot threatened to spread damning rumors about your wife, using the necklace as proof, if she breathed a word of it to you. He also demanded one thousand pounds, which Lady Huntingdon requested to loan from me, in payment."

Gabe was going to kill the bastard.

He started to rise from his chair.

"Do not go running off to slay the spineless weasel just yet, if you please." Decker stopped him. "This story is far from over."

Grimly, Gabe forced himself to heed his host's decree. "I shudder to think what more there could be, and I still fully intend to rip his arms from his body and bludgeon him with them. But do go on."

"Perfectly reasonable." Decker nodded. "Now, then. I sent some of my acquaintances to pay Lord Algernon a call. These acquaintances of mine are a bit...rough and ragged, one might say. Our maggot was no match. I also threatened to see him banished from my club and from every gambling den worth a damn. You would be amazed at the effect of a few meaty fists and the prospect of never again depleting his family coffers in style. He was only too pleased to return the necklace, forego the one thousand pounds he demanded, and provide the reason behind his sudden campaign to discredit you and Lady Huntingdon. Or rather, I should say the person behind his campaign."

Gabe's mind was swirling with the ramifications of everything Decker had just revealed. The last sentence in particular.

"Who would dare to go to him and put him up to this?" he gritted, clenching the arms of his chair in twin iron grips. "And why? What was to be gained?"

"According to our maggot, the person responsible is your former betrothed," Decker said. "Lady Beatrice Knightbridge did not take kindly to your jilting, I am afraid. Lord Algernon had been suffering recent losses at the tables to the point his father the marquess was threatening to cut him off. In an effort to pay his debts, he sought out Lady Beatrice with the necklace. The two formed a plan. Our maggot was to receive the one thousand pounds from Lady Huntingdon and a matching amount from Lady Beatrice."

A sick feeling twisted in Gabe's gut at the revelations, understanding dawning. "They were planning to make it seem as if my wife and Lord Algernon were having an *affaire*, were they not?"

Decker inclined his head. "An anonymous note was to be sent to you, and when you arrived, Lord Algernon would have made certain you were witness to a spectacle. Lady Beatrice, meanwhile, was to have been watching all unfold from an unmarked carriage across the street."

Anger and disgust warred for supremacy within him. His hands shook. "If that bastard had dared to force my wife…"

He could not finish his sentence. The thought was too awful to even contemplate.

"I do not blame you for your rage," Decker said quietly. "If I were in your place, I would not stop until I destroyed the people responsible."

Lady Beatrice, his perfect, composed fiancée. The bride Grandfather had selected for him, had attempted to hurt Helena. And not just hurt her, but worse. She would have had Lord Algernon force his attentions upon Helena. Bile rose in his throat as bitter memories of the crime perpetrated upon Lisbeth renewed themselves. Gabe burned with fury.

"Thank you for your intervention," he managed. "I am indebted to you."

"Think nothing of it, Huntingdon. Our wives are friends, and Lord Algernon was overdue for a sound drubbing."

Though Decker was nonchalant, Gabe heartily appreciated the actions the man and his wife had taken on behalf of both himself and Helena. *Good God*, to think of what may have occurred. And all because the incomparable Lady Beatrice Knightbridge was a conscienceless witch.

Gabe stood. "Nonetheless, I will be more than happy to

return the favor to you however I may. Lady Huntingdon and I would be honored if you and Lady Jo were to join us for dinner one evening soon."

Decker stood. "I am sure it would be our pleasure to be your guests."

He bowed. "But first, Lord Algernon and Lady Beatrice must face their reckonings from me."

He was going to trounce Lord Algernon Forsyte, and he was going to make certain Lady Beatrice would never again hurt Helena.

No one dared to threaten his woman, *damn it*.

"Of course," Decker said. "I completely understand, Huntingdon. When you love a woman, you will crawl through the fires of hell on broken glass for her. And when someone tries to hurt her, you are going to bloody well destroy them."

His host's words gave Gabe pause.

When you love a woman.

"I am not in love with my wife, Decker," he bit out. "I respect her. Admire her. But love has no place in a marriage that is going to weather the storms of life. I have no wish to indulge such fanciful notions."

Decker had the effrontery to laugh. "Oh, Huntingdon, you dense shite. You cannot decide not to fall in love with someone. Love is not a choice. Love is a force. And at this moment, you have the distinct look of a man who is hopelessly, helplessly mired deep within its clutches. Whether you like it or not."

"I do not like it, nor do I want it in my life or in my marriage," he denied coolly. "Love leads to disaster and hatred and bitter enmity."

"Trust me on something, Huntingdon. The best decision I ever made was to embrace life with my wife, to accept her love for me, and to give her my heart in return." Decker paused, quirking a brow. "Accept your fate. Thank me later."

Accept his fate? Nonsense. Gabe was not in love with Helena.

Or was he?

He had never shared the truth of what had happened to Lisbeth with anyone other than Grandfather. Nor had he ever longed for a woman the way he burned for Helena. He spent every hour he was apart from her telling himself it was for the best and counting down the minutes until he would have her back in his arms.

"I am not in love," he said, with far less assurance than he would have preferred. "I am in lust. Obsessed, perhaps. Not in love."

"Is she all you can think about?" Decker asked, his tone knowing.

Yes.

"That is none of your affair, Decker," he growled.

"You have never been happier than you are now, have you?" the blighter pressed.

Gabe searched inside himself. No, he had not. And there was only one reason for the vast feeling of contentment he had been steeping in ever since making Helena his countess.

The woman herself.

He cleared his throat. "I have always been happy."

Liar.

Decker's grin told him he was not fooling either of them with his response. "Love only leads to disaster when you *allow* it to, Huntingdon. Take my word for it."

"Good day, Mr. Decker," he bit out pointedly, having had enough of this unwanted discussion.

"Give Forsyte a black eye for me, won't you?" Decker asked.

Yes, he bloody well would.

But as he made good on his escape, he acknowledged inwardly that there was one inescapable fact he could not flee. He had somehow—against his will and against every one of Grandfather's maxims—fallen in love with his wife. What in the hell was he going to do about that?

"Tell her you love her, Huntingdon," Decker called after him, as if Gabe had requested his advice.

He did not need Elijah Decker's counsel on the matter, confound it.

Gabe thought of the look of undisguised adoration and happiness on the man's face as he had spoken of his own marriage. Then again, mayhap he did.

CHAPTER 23

The difference between right and wrong cannot be argued. The division is clear. The time to act, now.
—*From* Lady's Suffrage Society Times

*H*elena took great pleasure in the expression of shock upon the ordinarily placid countenance of her nemesis. It was apparent that Lady Beatrice Knightbridge had not been anticipating her call.

Excellent.

"My lady," said Lady Beatrice in a stilted tone, recovering sufficiently from her surprise to dip into an elegant curtsy.

"Lady Beatrice," she returned, grateful when her voice did not even betray a hint of a tremor. She refused to allow the other woman to see how shaken the incident with Lord Algernon had left her.

Or to give any indication of the fury burning within her soul.

The woman before her had conspired to hurt her,

mayhap even to destroy her marriage. Fortunately for Helena, she had friends she could trust, friends who had helped her to unravel Lady Beatrice's sick plan. Friends who had also enabled her to dismantle it.

There only remained the *pièce de résistance*.

"Do you care to sit, my lady?" Lady Beatrice queried, her complexion quite pale, her bright-blue eyes wide and laden with worry.

"Thank you." Helena seated herself on a chintz settee.

The other woman sat on a chair opposite her, looking distinctly uncomfortable at the prospect of a tête-à-tête. Silence reigned, with Helena's reluctant hostess making no indication she was about to attempt idle conversation or a lessening of the tension.

Helena decided to take charge. "You may be wondering why I am calling upon you, Lady Beatrice."

Lady Beatrice's lips tightened. "I will admit to some curiosity on my behalf, Lady Huntingdon."

She did not miss the bitterness in the other woman's voice when she referred to Helena by her title. "Let us be candid then, shall we? I find no need to prolong this visit."

"Please do proceed," Lady Beatrice urged coolly.

"Of course." Helena paused, trying her best to calm the raging emotions churning through her. "Mayhap we should begin with a common acquaintance of ours, though I truly wish my path had never crossed with his."

Lady Beatrice's nostrils flared. "You would dare to disparage Lord Huntingdon, your husband, to me, his betrothed? And so soon after you have wed. Have you no shame?"

Helena would have smiled at her hostess' supposition were she not so thoroughly outraged. "I would never dare to disparage his lordship to anyone, least of all his *former* betrothed. You are mistaken, Lady Beatrice. The mutual acquaintance I refer to is, regrettably, Lord Algernon Forsyte."

Lady Beatrice's sharp intake of breath gave away her guilt even as she attempted to lie. "Lord Algernon Forsyte is most certainly not one of my acquaintances. The man is a scoundrel and a rogue with a reputation that precedes him. I would never lower myself to consort with a man of his ilk."

"How odd, then, that Lord Algernon was only too quick to share a tale concerning your collusion with him in an attempt to make it look as if I were betraying Lord Huntingdon," she countered.

Her hostess stiffened. "I will not subject myself to your vicious lies, Lady Huntingdon. If this is all you have come here for, I am afraid it is truly best for you to go."

"It is not *all* I have come here for," Helena said, smiling as the momentum of their visit changed in favor of her. "I have also come here to let you know that any future attempts at interference in my marriage by you—or anyone acting at your behest—will be dealt with swiftly and ruthlessly. I am showing you mercy on this occasion, Lady Beatrice. But do not fool yourself into believing I will not strike back if you ever dare to do something like this again."

"You are a lunatic, madam," Lady Beatrice charged, her voice shrill. "I would never lower myself to intervene in your marriage. You are beneath me. You are not worthy of Huntingdon. He could have had me at his side, and instead he had to settle for a woman who threw herself into the arms of every man in London, no better than a lightskirt."

Helena flinched at the vitriol in the other woman's tone, but still, she refused to be defeated. "Better me than a woman who would bribe a man to rape someone she perceived as an opponent."

"I never bribed that disgusting scoundrel to rape you! I paid him to make it *look* as if you were lovers."

Lady Beatrice's denial was so loud, it echoed in the silence of the salon. She clapped a hand over her mouth, as if belatedly realizing the confession she had made with her denial.

The vindication sweeping over Helena was bittersweet. "Just as I thought. You admit to offering Lord Algernon money in exchange for his blackmailing of me. What was the plan, Lady Beatrice? I was to give him the thousand pounds and in exchange, he would pin me to the floor and force his attentions upon me until my husband arrived?"

The notion of Lady Beatrice's scheming made Helena's blood boil. After Jo had returned to her with her necklace and the tale Decker's men had wrung from Lord Algernon, Helena had been struck numb. The terrible thought of another man forcing himself upon her, coupled with Gabe bearing witness, had been too much to bear. After his heartrending revelation about what had happened to his sister, the news had sent Helena running to the water closet to cast up her accounts.

Lady Beatrice was staring at her with a stricken expression, saying nothing in her own defense. Mayhap because her behavior had been indefensible. Helena could only hope the other woman knew it.

"Have you nothing to say, Lady Beatrice?" she prodded, her tone biting. "No more false denials?"

"Lord Algernon came to me with the idea," Lady Beatrice gritted. "The fault for what happened is yours, and yours alone. If you had not been conducting yourself in such despicable, amoral fashion, none of this would have happened. But instead, you were flitting about London, lifting your skirts for anyone in trousers. Huntingdon was attempting to save your reputation because he is a gentleman, and in the end, you caught him in your web like any spider. I never stood a chance against someone like you."

Helena rose to her full, commanding height. "You are correct in that assessment, Lady Beatrice. You never did stand a chance against me, and if you ever again attempt to interfere in my marriage, you will discover all the reasons why."

Lady Beatrice rose, but she was far more petite, reaching no higher than Helena's shoulder. "Are you threatening me?"

Helena stepped nearer, her gaze trained upon the other woman, never so much as blinking. "I am not threatening you, my dear. I am *promising* you. Keep your distance from myself and Lord Huntingdon from this moment forward. You can desire to hurt me all you like, but I will not allow you to hurt him. If I ever hear even the tiniest speck of a rumor that you are attempting to hurt us again, I will come for you. And I will not be nearly as understanding as I was on this occasion. Consider this your first and only chance, my lady. There shall not be another."

"How dare you presume to speak to me thus? Who do you think you are?" Lady Beatrice demanded.

Helena smiled. "I am the Countess of Huntingdon. Never forget it."

On that note, she turned and began taking her leave before recalling she had failed to play her final trump card. She waited until she had nearly reached the door to the salon before spinning about and facing Lady Beatrice for what she could only hope proved the last time.

"Oh, and my lady? One more thing before I take my leave. Lord Algernon may be a disreputable scoundrel and an abysmal gambler, but he is also quite sly. You left him with a parting gift when you last met, and I have in my possession a handkerchief embroidered with your initials, complete with a delicate little rose in the corner. Roses are your favorite flower, are they not? If you ever dare to try anything like this again, I will not hesitate to return the *mouchoir* to Lord

Algernon so that he may use it as evidence to anyone and everyone in London that Lady Beatrice Knightbridge shared a bed with him."

"You would not do something so despicable!" Lady Beatrice gasped.

Helena laughed. "When it comes to protecting the man I love and my marriage, I would do anything. Do not test me, my lady, or you shall be sorely disappointed. I bid you good day."

* * *

The last person Gabe expected to cross paths with on the pavements outside Lady Beatrice's father's townhome was his wife. But there was no denying it—just as he was striding up the cement, she was sailing down it. They met halfway.

Her vibrant eyes went wide, her hand flying to the base of her throat, until she realized it was he before her on the path. "Gabe!"

"Helena." He bowed formally, his guts still churning with the horrible revelations Elijah Decker had made, his knuckles throbbing with the aftereffects of his call upon Lord Algernon. The pain had been worth every bit of the satisfaction of watching his fist connect with that bastard's jaw, however. "I did not expect to find you here."

"Nor I you." Her hand lowered, revealing the creamy elegance of her throat. "What are you doing here?"

Was any woman's neck as delectable as hers? Gabe could not summon an image of one to his mind. The day was gloomy, the skies gray with the ominous portent of rain, and yet she shone like a beacon.

He recalled her query and swallowed, trying to gain

control over his tumultuous thoughts. "I met with Lady Jo's husband, Mr. Decker. He had a great deal to say, all of which was disturbingly enlightening. The only course of action seemed to be to confront Lady Beatrice and let her father know the deviousness and treachery his daughter has been about."

That was putting it mildly.

But Gabe could not face the full implications of Lady Beatrice's plans for Helena. Not if he wished to continue functioning. Not if he wanted to confront his former betrothed and make her pay for what she had been plotting to do to Helena.

"I just met with Lady Beatrice myself," Helena said softly. "I do not think an interview with her on your part is necessary, though if you deem it such, I shan't offer any opposition."

Her graciousness in this, as in every matter of their marriage thus far, could not be denied. He had been searching for the perfect countess, the wife who would never betray or disappoint or hurt him. The wife who would be loyal and true. And all along, he had been looking for her in the wrong place. He had seen her in the wrong woman.

Because as he gazed upon Helena, Countess of Huntingdon, this magnificent lady he had married, he knew with sudden, undeniable clarity, that the woman who was the perfect wife for him in every way was the one he had wed.

Grandfather had been wrong, and breaking his vow to wed Lady Beatrice had been the best decision Gabe had ever made. A sudden rush of peace traveled over him, profound and sweeping.

He had to swallow against a knot of emotion rising in his throat. "I am sorry, Helena. So damned sorry."

For more than he could say.

"I am not nearly as concerned for myself as I am for you

and what it would have meant for you had their plotting come to fruition." Helena's gaze upon him was unbearably tender. "And I am sorry for ever aligning myself with such a hopeless blackguard. If I had not arranged for that assignation, I never would have lost my necklace."

He reached out, grazing his fingers over that stubborn chin of hers. "But then, you would have never wed me, and I, for one, am heartily glad you did."

Her lips parted. "You are?"

He could kick himself anew for being a cad. "I am."

There was no mistaking the sadness in her eyes. "But I am nothing like the woman you would have married before I came along and ruined your plans."

"Thank God for that," he said with great feeling. "What did you say to Lady Beatrice? I want to be certain she will never cause further problems for you. I had intended to see her father, to inform him of everything his daughter has been about."

Helena smiled. "I told her about a handkerchief now in my possession, one embroidered with her initials and with her favorite flower, which her co-conspirator managed to filch from her. I warned her that if she ever attempts to interfere in our marriage or cause trouble for us, I will use the handkerchief against her in the same manner she would have used my necklace against me."

He ought to have known she could handle herself. She was the smartest, bravest woman he knew.

"When Decker's ruffians met with Lord Algernon, they managed to get him to surrender the necklace *and* the handkerchief?" he asked, impressed, though he knew he ought not to be surprised.

Mr. Elijah Decker was a man of cunning and grit, and he had built his empire upon both. Gabe was once more grateful Helena possessed such good friends. But here was a reminder of the fact that she had not come to him, her husband. Instead, she had sought the aid of others.

"They did," Helena confirmed, grinning. "Lady Beatrice was not impressed with the notion of her actions spreading all over London. I do believe her days of meddling and consorting with Lord Algernon are decidedly over."

"They had better be, or she will answer to me," he growled, a protective surge for his beautiful wife hitting him.

Helena clasped his hand, holding it to her cheek. "Thank you for wanting to defend me."

"You need not thank me for that, Helena." He frowned at her. "I also paid a call upon Lord Algernon, and I can assure you he will never trouble you again without fear of further retribution. I am your husband, and shielding you from all harm is my duty."

The moment the word left his lips, he regretted it, but it was too late.

Helena released his hand and took a step away from him. "Of course. Shall we travel home separately, my lord? I left in such a hurry that I neglected to ask that my carriage be brought round."

He hated the distance she had put between them. Hated too the conflicting emotions inside himself. But there was one thing he knew for certain—he was not about to send his wife home in a separate carriage.

"We shall go together in the brougham." He offered her his arm. "I will see that the other carriage is notified."

Helena placed her hand on his elbow, and they made their way to the waiting conveyance.

CHAPTER 24

There can be no true happiness until our objective is achieved.
—*From* Lady's Suffrage Society Times

Silence pervaded as the brougham rumbled through the London streets, taking Helena and Gabe to Wickley House. Her husband's posture was stiff, his jaw tense, as if something weighed heavily upon him. She knew the feeling.

Finally, Helena could bear no more of the quiet, so she broke it. "Did you mean what you said?"

His arresting gaze seared her. He was so beautiful, her heart hurt.

"I meant everything I said, Helena. And far more."

She swallowed. "You are truly pleased to have me as your wife?"

"More than I can properly convey in words." He held out a hand to her. "Come here."

The only place for her to go was his lap.

So Helena went, settling herself gingerly upon his broad thighs, no easy feat given the encumbrances of her skirts and tournure. "I shall crush you."

"Hush." He removed his gloves and then cupped her face. "You are light as a bird, and I cannot bear to have you sitting on the other side of this bloody carriage when you could be right here, where you belong."

Where she belonged? *Yes. Oh, yes.* She liked the sound of that.

Helena plucked the hat from his head, placing it on the bench at his side, before positioning her hands on his broad shoulders. As always, his warmth and strength seemed to sear her palms. The love she had been carrying for him all this time surged. She could not keep it to herself any longer. But how to tell him, when he believed love was the source of anguish and ruin?

Her heart gave a pang.

"Thank you for dashing off to see Lady Beatrice on my behalf," she said, instead of saying those three terrifying words just yet.

His deep-blue gaze searched hers. "Helena, I will always defend you. As your husband, it is my—"

She pressed a finger to his lips, silencing him. "Pray do not say *duty* again. I do not want to be your obligation, Gabe."

He kissed her finger, then plucked it away from his lips so he could continue speaking unimpeded. "I was going to say that as your husband, it is my honor to defend you. I will do anything and everything in my power to protect you and keep you from harm, always. That is my solemn vow to you."

He would defend and protect her, but would he ever love her? *Could* he ever love her? Helena did not dare to hope. Her love could be enough for the both of them.

"I can defend and protect myself," she told him in lieu of making any dangerous confessions.

"I have no doubt of that." There was a note of pride in his voice that settled into the deepest recesses of her heart. "You are the most daring, brave, strong woman I know. But I am here for you, always. You need never take on the world alone or seek the aid of others instead of me. I am yours."

Hers.

She liked the sound of that as well. Indeed, she had spent years longing for him, wishing, hoping.

"Mine," she repeated, scarcely trusting the word or the implications behind it. Scarcely believing the Earl of Huntingdon could possibly be hers and hers alone. "Truly, Gabe?"

He caught her wrist in a grip that was firm yet gentle and flattened her hand over his heart. Beneath the layers of his clothing, his heart hammered a steady, reassuring *thud-thud-thud*.

"Yours," he said again. "Forever yours, Helena. Only yours."

She froze, staring at him. Surely he could not mean what her foolish heart hoped to hear? Gabe was not telling her *his heart* was hers.

Or was he?

"But you wanted to marry Lady Beatrice," she protested shakily. "I forced you into marrying me."

"No one could have forced me to marry you, darling." He caressed her cheek, the expression on his handsome face filled with a new tenderness. "I *wanted* to marry you. At the time, I was too stubborn to see it for myself. I was also blinded by my past and a promise I never should have made."

She could not look away. He had called her *darling*. He had said he had wanted to marry *her*, Helena Davenport. Not Lady Beatrice Knightbridge, the paragon.

"But I lied to Shelbourne," she reminded him.

"You were desperate," he countered, "and I was an idiot."

Tears stung her eyes. "You have never been an idiot."

"Yes, I have." He caressed a path of fire down her throat and slid his hand around to cup her nape. "I was too stupid to realize the perfect wife for me was the one I was chasing all over London. The one I couldn't seem to stop touching or kissing or yearning for. The one who found her way into my heart."

Did he just say what she thought he had said?

His *heart*? *Thump, thump, thump* it went beneath her splayed palm. Hers joined, meeting it beat for beat. The time to tell him had arrived. It was now, here, this moment.

This man. This man she had loved for so long.

She took a deep breath. "Gabe, there is something I must tell you."

He caressed her nape, that same expression of profound affection upon his countenance, making her weak, giving her hope. "It is not that you are going to flee for Shropshire without me, is it?"

She smiled at his jest. "No, of course not. If I am ever off to Shropshire, I promise to bring you with me, my lord."

"Nor is it that you regret marrying an oafish prig?" His tone was teasing, but his expression was serious, his eyes intent upon her.

Did he truly hold himself in such low regard? How could he not see he was everything she had ever wanted, the only man for whom she had ever longed?

Helena pursed her lips. "Fortunately, I escaped the fate of marrying an oafish prig by ruining myself so that I would not have to spend the rest of my life tied to Lord Hamish."

"I should have thrown you over my shoulder after your first attempt at ruination and married you then." He leaned forward, bringing their lips deliciously near and yet refraining from kissing her as she so desperately wanted him to do. "It would have spared us both a good deal of trouble and hurt. I ought to have made love to you in this carriage and bound you to me forever."

His words, coupled with his nearness, the warm flow of his breath over her lips, his scent surrounding her, his heart beating beneath her palm, his heat searing her, all combined to make the flesh between her thighs throb. She wanted him there. Wanted him again and again. Wanted to straddle his hips, release him from his trousers, and sink down upon his cock. Wanted him to erase the awfulness of the past two days. To banish the specter of what could have happened.

"Perhaps you should rectify that error in judgment and make love to me now," she dared.

He brushed his lower lip tantalizingly over hers in the most decadent half kiss. "Tell me first."

Her ability to think had been impacted. "Tell you?"

He rubbed their lower lips again. "You said you had something to tell me." And then he punctuated his reminder by kissing the upper bow of her lips.

Oh. So she had. But first, she never wanted this kiss to end.

He deepened the kiss, his heart beating faster now. She kissed him back with all the desire and love she felt for him, trying to show him with actions what she had yet to admit in words.

I love you.

I love you.

I love you.

He nipped her lower lip. "I know you do."

Had she made her confession aloud? Helena jerked her head back, tearing her mouth from his. "I beg your pardon?"

He held her gaze, unwavering. "I know you love me."

She noted the other half of that particular equation was absent. He had not told her he returned her love. The hope which had been building inside her, gathering air and buoyancy like an ascension balloon, went abruptly flat.

It sank all the way to her toes and then fell out of the carriage entirely, to become macerated on the roadway beneath the carriage wheels. What had she expected? A great soliloquy? An earnest declaration from a man who believed marriage should be loveless in order for it to succeed?

Stupid Helena. When will you learn your lesson? The Earl of Huntingdon will never, ever love you.

She swallowed down the lump rising in her throat, willing the tears that threatened her vision to dissipate before she humiliated herself even further. "How do you know?"

Had she somehow given her secret away before now? Had she whispered her love for him in her sleep? There had been the time she had almost revealed her feelings to him when they had made love, but she had stopped herself in time, had she not?

"Shelbourne told me," he admitted. "Do not be angry with him, darling. He told me to aid our union, I suspect, not to cause you any embarrassment."

Embarrassment? Her cheeks were positively aflame. How humiliating. She was going to box her brother's ears for this. She was going to dump all his bawdy books into the nearest water closet. She was going to...

Drat it, Helena. Plot your revenge later. This is important.

"When did he tell you?" she asked, needing to know for the sake of her own pride.

Good Lord, had he always known? Since before they had wed? Humiliation churned through her. How long had he been aware of her pathetic feelings for him without entertaining even the slightest inkling of love for her? And after they had shared so much of themselves with each other, all those endless nights of passion?

"Since I met with him to calm the waters of our friendship," Gabe admitted.

"Since almost the beginning of our marriage," she translated, her mind working out the timing for itself. "You mean to say you knew I loved you all this time?"

"Yes."

One word from those sensual lips of his. Curse him, why did he have to be so dratted handsome? It made holding on to her irritation dreadfully difficult. Nigh impossible, really.

"And yet you felt nothing?" she prodded, needing to know the answer.

"I felt everything." He pressed a kiss to the corner of her lips, the gesture at once sweet and thrilling. "I was terrified of what you made me feel, and I was doing all that was within my power to hold tight to my restraint. To keep you from burrowing so deep into my heart there would be no removing you, regardless of the dangers you presented me."

Helena frowned. "You make me sound as if I am an invasive creature stealing into your garden rather than your wife."

He grinned at her, making new heat flare to life. "Never an invasive creature. I was merely not prepared to accept what you did to me. What you *do* to me, hellion."

What did this mean? Stupid, fruitless hope was at it once more, trying to rise like a loaf of bread no one would ever slide into the oven. Useless, these feelings. Foolish for her to entertain them. She seized upon the one thing she could, settling for taking him to task.

"I ought to take umbrage at your continued use of that sobriquet," she told him, nettled with herself for the shakiness in her voice.

"Helena, sweet." His other hand cupped her cheek, his thumb traveling over her cheekbone with painstaking affection. "You are a hellion. *My* hellion. And I love you for it."

She stilled. Her hand remained over his heart, and it was pounding now with furious insistence. So was hers. Once more, words fled her mind. Her lips parted. Sound was reluctant to emerge.

So she breathed in this moment, the carriage swaying around them, her settled in Gabe's lap, his strong hands upon her with such caring, his sky-blue eyes devouring her, his lips so near to hers. This was a moment she would never forget, a moment she had scarcely dared to dream could exist.

"You...love..." Oh, blast. There were the tears, blurring her vision and gathering on her lashes.

She blinked furiously to clear them, but it only sent them rolling down her cheeks in fat trails.

"*You*, Helena," he finished for her. "I love you. Completely and utterly, in every way, more deeply than I could have fathomed possible."

"But you do not believe a marriage ought to involve love," she could not help but to protest, even as part of her was inwardly shouting at her to keep her concerns and fears to herself. To settle instead for his avowal. For his words of love to be enough.

And yet, she loved him too much to accept any half measures. She had to know the truth, to be certain of it and him as well. She had to believe his love was true and strong, and that he would not seek to banish it in a moment of fear.

"My parents were in love once, and their marriage toppled like a poorly stacked wall of bricks without mortar. I was raised in the shadow of that failed union, and my grandfather taught me to believe that love was the reason for its demise." Gabe paused, seeming to collect his thoughts. "I have spent so long believing that what I needed was a loveless union based upon mutual respect, a bloodless society marriage such as my grandparents enjoyed. So long believing love was the reason for all my parents' woes and for all the devastation that came after."

His admission was raw, and her heart ached for him anew. "What changed for you?"

If anything?

But she kept the last question to herself, too terrified to ask it.

"*You* changed," he said, taking her by surprise. "You changed *me*, Helena. I have been in love with you for years, and for years, I have been fighting the feelings, tamping them down, dismissing them. But I realized that I am fighting a losing battle, a battle I no longer want to win. I surrender, hellion. To you. To love. To *us*."

Us, he had said.

Yes, oh yes. She liked the sound of that very much. Her husband was exceeding her every hope and it was too good to be true. Had he just officially surrendered?

To her?

She grinned at him. "I was not aware this was a war between us."

"Mayhap a war of my own making." He grimaced. "A war of the past and the present, of old ghosts and new."

Helena shook her head. "I do not want to go to battle with you, Gabe. I just want to love you. I have always wanted to love you, from the first I saw you."

"God, woman." He pressed his forehead to hers, closing his eyes and inhaling deeply. "You undo me. You complete me."

This was what she wanted to hear. What she had spent years dreaming she would hear. From these lips. Helena could not wait a moment more. She lowered her head and captured his mouth with hers.

* * *

Helena's lips were on his, moving in a sweetly possessive kiss. He tugged her head lower, deepening the pressure, devouring her as best as he could. She was intoxicating. Delicious. Everything he had always wanted and everything he had been warned against.

And yet, she was his wife.

She had done all she could today to protect him. For him, she would have placed herself in a position of potentially great danger. Just the thought of Lord Algernon Forsyte ever so much as laying a finger upon her was enough to make Gabe haul her closer, crushing her against him. He kissed her as if he could forever claim her with his lips.

Because he intended to. There was no more fighting the way he felt for her. What was the sense in pretending he was not hopelessly, helplessly in his wife's thrall? He was. He had been at her mercy for longer than he had even realized.

He loved her.

That was the strange sensation he had not been able to shake, ever since the day their paths had first crossed, on that long-ago country house weekend when he had accompanied his old school chum on the hunt. He had found a spirited young lady with golden hair, emerald eyes, and a flashing, quick wit.

She had been what he had wanted, all this time. And for so long, he had resisted.

As he slid his tongue into her mouth and deepened the kiss, he mourned all the time he had wasted. What he had once been convinced was the correct path for him to trod had been proven, beyond a doubt, to be a farce today. The woman Grandfather had deemed to be a perfect countess— the same woman who had encouraged Gabe to take a mistress rather than bed her—had conspired against Helena. He could not bear to think of what she could have endured as a result.

It was too much.

He needed his wife. He needed Helena, of the white-blonde hair and the enchanting freckles on her dainty nose and the tiniest gap between her front teeth and the lips that knew just how to kiss his, the body that was meant for his, the heart that beat to the same rhythm.

The woman who loved him.

He had held the knowledge of Helena's feelings deep within himself for so long, terrified of what it meant. Afraid to embrace it as he longed to do. But here and now, in this moment, with the woman he loved in his lap and her mouth on his, he could celebrate both her love and his.

They would not be bound by the constraints of the past. He knew that now. Rather, they would be shaped by the hopes of the future. Their future.

Together.

A rapping on the carriage alerted him, belatedly, to the fact that they had rolled to a stop. Reluctantly, Gabe tore his mouth from Helena's. A glance out the window confirmed they had reached Wickley House. But what was happening between them was far from over. Rather, they had just begun.

He kissed the corners of her lips and then the tip of her nose for good measure. "We have arrived at home. Shall we continue this conversation in privacy?"

"If by privacy, you are suggesting we go inside and head straight to one of our chambers, I wholeheartedly approve," she said.

He kissed her again. "My God, what did I ever do to be so fortunate as to have you as my wife?"

"You attended a country house party when I was sixteen

and made me fall in love with you," she said breathlessly, and then sealed their lips in another kiss.

When it ended, he allowed his head to drop back against the squabs, studying her, this wild, wonderful woman he had wed. "You remember?"

Her smile was secrets and seduction and Helena. He felt it in his cock.

"I remember everything," she told him. "From the moment I first saw you. You were wearing tweed. You had the bluest eyes I had ever seen. I thought them more glorious than the sky and the ocean combined. I still do."

Her revelation stole his breath. Made him feel like a green lad. He wanted inside her. Immediately.

Gabe clenched his jaw against a swift tide of desire. Now was neither the time nor the place. He would not fuck his wife in a carriage parked just outside their home as their staff listened on, suspecting every act in which they were engaged. No, indeed. He was going to do this the proper way. He was aiming to make up for everything he had missed, all this time.

Dozens of pretty phrases and flowery words swirled in his mind, clamoring for his tongue. In the end, he was lost to anything but Helena herself. His wife, his countess, his love. He had fought her for so long. But he intended to heal them both.

"Into the house," he told her, kissing her again swiftly. "Now."

"That sounds like an excellent plan," she told him, kissing him once more before sliding from his lap.

For what was perhaps the first time in her life, his hellion had obeyed without a hint of protest. Nary a stubborn tip of her chin nor a cutting remark. It would seem he knew the way to tame her.

They disembarked, and Gabe cast propriety to the devil

and took her up in his arms. Ignoring the astonished stares of the servants who quickly averted their gazes, he proceeded to carry his countess down the front walk, through the entry hall, and up two sets of stairs. She giggled and buried her face in his neck as they went.

By the time they reached his chamber, they were both breathless and grinning at each other like a pair of lovesick fools. He settled her on her feet and elbowed the door closed at his back.

"What do you suppose the servants will think of us?" she asked, grinning as if she did not give a damn.

Likely, she did not, and that was one of the qualities he loved about her best. It was also one of the qualities which had terrified him. She was unpredictable and wild, his Helena. But she was also sweet and good and kind. She loved him without reason. Had loved him all this time.

As he stood here with her, he knew, unequivocally, that love was not the path to ruin and disaster. Rather, it was the road to the future. His future. Their future. To happiness.

"I suppose they will think I have gone mad over my wonderful, beautiful, perfect wife," he told her, shrugging out of his coat.

Her full, pink lips parted. "I am far from perfect, and hardly wonderful or beautiful."

Gabe pulled at his necktie next. "You are the perfect wife for me, and you are the most beautiful woman I have ever known. As for the question of whether or not you are wonderful, the word hardly does you justice, but it will have to suit for now. My mind is having a difficult time managing fluent speech when all my body wants is you beneath me."

Charming color tinged her cheekbones. "Oh."

Her fingers went to the accommodating line of buttons bisecting the front of her bodice. One by one, she plucked them from their moorings as he tossed his waistcoat to the floor. His shirt was next, and then he toed off his shoes and strode for Helena, unable to last another second without his hands upon her.

"Yes, *oh*." His lips settled over hers.

Together, they shucked her bodice, and then he found the tapes on her skirts, undoing them and the hidden button as he slid his tongue inside her mouth. Her petticoats and bustle went next, followed by her corset and drawers. Helena's knowing fingers brushed over the fall of his trousers, unerringly finding his cockstand and palming him through the fabric.

Need surged, drawing his ballocks tight. He growled into the kiss, deepening it, wanting her so badly he ached. It was not enough. He wanted no barriers between them. He wanted skin on skin.

The next few moments were a blur of kissing, touching, and disrobing. They made their way to the bed together. Helena lay on her back, Gabe between her thighs. He took a moment to bask in the glory of her beneath him, all soft, smooth curves and delicious womanly flesh, her legs parted to reveal the pink folds of her sex.

"I love you, Helena." He could not keep the words to himself as he began raining kisses all over her body, worshiping her as she deserved. "I love you so bloody much." He kissed her knee, her thigh, all the way to her hip bone. He kissed the velvety curve of her belly. She shifted beneath him, arching, seeking.

He knew what she wanted. The air was perfumed with the decadent scent of her desire, musky and floral. His cock twitched and his mouth watered. He had to have her on his tongue. Caressing her hips, he pressed another kiss on the swell of her mound, just above the tempting bud of her clitoris.

"Gabe." She writhed beneath him with her protest.

She was getting desperate for him.

Good. He wanted her out of her mind with desire.

"Go on." He kissed her again, then grinned up at her. "Tell me what you want, darling."

"You know what I want." She was breathless, her verdant eyes glazed with desire.

"Mmm." He ran his lips over the skin of her inner right thigh, gently nibbling there. "I am afraid I don't unless you tell me, hellion."

"Wicked man," she said without heat. "I want your tongue on me."

He kissed her left inner thigh, then glanced his tongue over her flesh. "Like this?"

"No." She lifted her hips impatiently. "You know where."

He did know where, but he enjoyed watching her frustration. It was so erotic, the sight of her overwhelmed with desire, spread before him, all his. His cock was harder than marble. At last, he decided he could not prolong the torture for either of them any longer.

He dipped his head and ran his tongue along her pearl.

Her low moan was all the reward he needed. The taste of her was sweeter than sugar-laced tea. And he wanted more. He flicked over her in rapid strokes that had her bucking against him. Then he sucked hard, worrying the sensitive bundle of flesh with his teeth as he sank a finger inside her dripping channel.

She gripped him tightly. Silken, wet heat bathed his finger. He added another, stretching her, working her into a frenzy as he continued suckling her clitoris. She clutched his hair, grinding her cunny into his face, and he knew she was close. He fucked her with his fingers, in and out, faster, harder, deeper, flicking his tongue over her nub.

Helena came, clenching on him as she shuddered and thrust beneath him. Another surge of wetness coated him, and he withdrew from her as the last of her spasms rippled through her, replacing his fingers with his tongue. He lapped up her spend, thrusting his tongue into her, claiming her in every way he could. He had never been so overwhelmed with the urge to possess her as he was now.

Love did not make them weaker. Love made them stronger.

Gabe kissed his way back up her body then. How glorious she looked, sated and flushed, golden tendrils of her hair coming undone from her careful coiffure. He could spend all day drinking in the sight of her, except for the uncomfortably rigid state of his cock. But now that he had the taste of her on his tongue and had experienced the sensual bliss of her coming on his fingers, he was not going to last much longer.

When he reached her breasts, he sucked first one hard nipple, then the other. Her hands flitted over his shoulders. The quiet hum of her satisfaction was not lost on him. He bit her nipple lightly and reached between them to part her slick folds and toy with her clitoris once more.

"Gabe," she moaned.

Damnation, but he loved the sound of his name in her husky contralto as he was pleasuring her. He licked a circle around her nipple. "Yes, love?"

"I need you inside me."

If he did not take care, he would spend into the bed linens like a callow youth.

He suckled her other nipple, coating his thumb and forefinger in her dew before gliding it through her folds and then slicking it over his ready cock. The urge to claim her could not be denied. He kissed his way to her collarbone, then found her cheek. Her ear.

"I love you, hellion," he whispered.

He dragged his cockhead through her folds, finding her pearl.

"I love you, my beautiful man." Her nails raked down his back all the way to his arse. "Now make love to me."

"With pleasure." He kissed down her jaw, all the way to her lips, as he aligned himself to her entrance.

One thrust and he was seated deep inside her. Her cunny was hot and tight, and somehow, and though they had made love many times before, there was something different about this time. Something wilder, fiercer, stronger. The intensity built at the base of his spine and radiated outward, almost overwhelming him.

She felt so good wrapped around him, her dripping cunny clamped on his cock, her soft, feminine body beneath his. The scent of her desire swirled through the air, mingling with the perfume of bergamot and citrus. His every sense was more heightened than it had ever been. He kissed her hard, his tongue gliding into her mouth, and he had no doubt she could taste herself on his lips.

Her arms locked around his neck, and she made an erotic little mewl of pleasure as he began a steady rhythm. Although Gabe had intended to be gentle, to make love to her sweetly, slowly, the moment he started thrusting, he could not stop. He drove himself into her again and again while he teased her pearl with his thumb. Her cunny tightened on a sudden series of spasms.

He was going to lose control and spend.

But curse it, this was too quick. He wanted to make it last.

Gabe withdrew, his heart pounding, his prick throbbing. Helena made a sound of protest, but he drowned it out with another kiss as he rolled to his back, bringing her with him so that she was astride him. He wanted her to take her pleasure. To control the pace. He wanted her to ride him until she came all over his cock and then he wanted to fill her with his seed.

Her palms flattened on his chest. More of her hair had slipped free of the pins, sending curls cascading down her shoulders, a few errant strands over the full swells of her breasts.

"I saw this in one of the naughty books," she said approvingly.

The minx.

God, he loved this woman.

"It is called riding St. George," she added for good measure.

His cock throbbed. To the devil with the past. He had everything he needed right here. Why had he ever imagined, even for a moment, that he could settle for a frigid, proper bride? How wrong he had been.

How right for him Helena was.

"Yes," he managed, taking her hand in his and wrapping it around his cock. "Put me inside you and take your pleasure as you like, darling. This way, you are in control."

She stroked him, then rubbed her thumb over the tip of him where a pearly drop of his mettle was already leaking from the slit. "Oh, I like the notion of being the one in control. Very much so."

He had known she would.

Helena punctuated her pronouncement by sinking down on his cock, taking his full length. *Pure bliss.* She was still soaked, her grip on him tighter than ever. He anchored her with a hand on her waist and used the other to toy with her nipples as she moved, riding him. She made a throaty sound of satisfaction.

With great effort, he restrained himself, allowing her to maintain power. He tweaked her nipple and she tightened on him. Emboldened, he lifted his head and caught a nipple in his mouth, dragging on it while she rode him. For good measure, he reached to the place where their bodies joined and found her clitoris. He rubbed his thumb over her in firm circles as he licked and sucked her breasts.

It did not take long for the stimulations to have their intended effect upon her. She sank down on him hard and came with a cry, her cunny tightening on his cock with almost painful pleasure. And then, he was coming too, his hips thrusting toward hers as he emptied himself inside her. The bliss was so intense that little black stars peppered his vision as he spent.

They rolled as one, landing on their sides, their bodies still joined, arms and limbs entwined, hearts beating furiously. He studied her for a long moment, taking in her lovely face, from the bewitching trail of freckles on her nose to her kiss-swollen mouth. A fresh rush of love washed over him as he gazed at her.

"I love you, Helena." Having embraced the truth of his feelings, he could not seem to say the words enough.

"And I love you."

Grandfather's favorite maxim returned to him suddenly.

A man without honor is a man who has nothing.

In truth, he had been wrong about that. There was one necessary change.

A man without love *is a man who has nothing.*

Gabe had never been more certain of the veracity of that statement than he was now. He pulled his wife to him for a lingering kiss that turned into another. And another. And then another.

Because this Earl of Huntingdon had *everything*.

EPILOGUE

Together, we can accomplish anything we wish.
—*From* Lady's Suffrage Society Times

"*I* officially declare myself the most besotted man in London."

"And why is that, my love?" Helena attempted to get up from the chaise longue as her husband approached: tall, handsome, long-legged, and dressed to perfection. No earl had a right to look so sinfully good.

"Do not rise on my account," he said swiftly, hastening his pace so that his strides ate up the Axminster separating them. "I know how much your feet and back have been aching recently."

On a sigh, Helena settled once more into the stack of pillows her lady's maid had helpfully arranged behind her. "If you insist, I shall remain right here. Now, do tell me why you are the most besotted man. That does seem a rather extensive claim to make. How can you be certain, and with whom are you besotted?"

He grinned, lowering himself to the cushion at her side, and held up a box that had been wrapped with a neatly tied satin ribbon of emerald green. "I am besotted with you, of course. And as for the boldness of my claim, I can assure you of its veracity. No other man could possibly love his wife as much as I love you."

He was adorable.

She scrunched up her nose. "What about a man and his mistress? Mayhap another man, somewhere in this vast city, loves his mistress just a speck more."

"Impossible." He kissed her nose. "I have proof."

She raised a brow. "Oh?"

How she loved to see this lighter side of him. He seemed so carefree these days, and it was a welcome change. As they had settled into their marriage and grown together, the walls of the past had been dismantled, stone by stone, until at last, none remained. He had not suffered any of his attacks in recent months, and he was finally healing, at long last.

He held the box toward her. "I brought you a present, hellion."

"A present for me?" She smiled at him. "It was gift enough to learn that Lady Beatrice Knightbridge has married Lord Hamish White this morning."

"They deserve each other," Gabe said simply.

Truer words had never been spoken.

Helena reached for the box. "They do indeed. Now, what can you possibly have for me?"

"Open it and you shall see."

Was she mistaken, or was there the slightest hint of a flush tingeing his sharp cheekbones? Curious, that.

Helena plucked at the ribbon, undoing the bow, and then lifted the lid. Inside, wrapped in tissue, was the latest edition of the bawdy book series she had thieved from Shelbourne's collection.

Wicked heat flared to life within her. She may be heavy with child, but staying off one's swollen feet had benefits. Namely, spending more time in bed with one's delicious husband.

"You bought me filth!" she crowed, her heart seeming to swell inside her breast at the gesture.

His color deepened. "It is not filth."

"That is what you called it once," she reminded him.

"Saucy minx. Mayhap I was overly harsh about it once upon a time."

"I have thoroughly corrupted you," she declared. "First you have fallen in love, and now you are buying me bawdy books. You *are* the most besotted man in London."

He smiled back at her, giving Helena a look of undisguised love. "You see? I told you so."

"Will you come to bed and read it to me?" she asked, batting her lashes at him in exaggerated fashion.

He kissed her long and deep. "You make me despicably randy, hellion."

She slid her hand up his thigh and confirmed that she did, indeed, have such an effect upon him. "There is only one cure for that, my love."

He caressed her swollen belly over the *robe de chambre* she wore. There were definite benefits to being so near to her lying in, she had discovered. No one complained if she lounged about all day wearing scarcely any garments, least of all her husband.

"In addition to being the most besotted man in London, I am also the most fortunate," he said, his voice low and tender. "You look like a goddess, carrying our babe."

She was sure she did not, but he could tell her so all he liked.

Helena linked her arms around Gabe's neck. "I can think of a way to make you even more fortunate."

He grinned. "God, I love you."

"I love you more," she said, and then she pulled his lips down upon hers.

The End.

* * *

Dear Reader,

Thank you for reading Helena and Gabe's story! I hope you enjoyed this third book in my *Notorious Ladies of London* series and that Helena and Gabe's path to happily ever after touched your heart and left you smiling. I love writing my notorious ladies, and I thank you for spending your precious time reading them!

Please consider leaving an honest review of *Lady Reckless*. Reviews are greatly appreciated! If you'd like to keep up to date with my latest releases and series news, sign up for my newsletter here or follow me on Amazon or BookBub. Join my reader's group on Facebook for bonus content, early excerpts, giveaways, and more.

If you'd like a preview of *Lady Wicked*, Book Four in the Notorious Ladies of London series, featuring Lady Julianna Somerset and Sidney, Lord Shelbourne (plus a huge secret, lots of angst, and plenty of steam), do read on.

Until next time,

Scarlett

AUTHOR'S NOTE ON HISTORICAL ACCURACY

As always, I've done my best to provide you with a read that's as entertaining and historically accurate as possible. Lady Jo Decker's outrage after reading a letter to the editor in *The Times* is based upon an edition from June 10, 1884, which featured similar letters to the editor arguing against woman's suffrage.

My inspiration for the *Lady's Suffrage Society Times* came from *The Women's Penny Paper*, which was edited by Henrietta B. Muller using the *nom de plume* Helen B. Temple, and from the *Women's Suffrage Journal*, edited by Lydia E. Becker. I used archived copies of these nineteenth century British journals as inspiration for the chapter epigraphs and Helena and her fellow members of the Lady's Suffrage Society.

And now, on to that preview...

PREVIEW OF LADY WICKED

NOTORIOUS LADIES OF LONDON
BOOK FOUR

*O*ne reckless moment was all it required for Lady Julianna Somerset to lose her innocence to her best friend's brother. But when he broke her heart, she fled London to heal her wounded pride. A desperate change in circumstance has forced her to return. And in a cruel twist of fate, the man who ruined her may be the only one who can save her.

Sidney, Lord Shelbourne has always wanted one woman at his side and in his bed. The only problem? She refused his marriage proposal and disappeared from his life. He's resigned himself to a life of duty when her arrival in London rekindles old, dangerous flames.

Sidney has not forgiven Julianna for spurning him or for the shocking secret she has been keeping. Now that she needs his aid, he has a plan. Revenge will be his, and so will she. But Julianna is determined to protect herself against the handsome lord she never stopped desiring. This time, she has vowed *she* will be the one to force *his* surrender.

Chapter One

1885

She had returned to London.

He had celebrated this decidedly unhappy event by drowning himself in Sauternes at the Black Souls Club. But the wine had done nothing to quell either the ire or the ardor which had been threatening to consume him since the moment he had discovered they once more shared the same shores.

Shelbourne's carriage conveyed him over the London streets beneath the cloak of darkness. The jangling of tack, the familiar scent of the well-oiled squabs, and the sound of the wheels rumbling on the road did nothing to distract him. Still, there was no comfort to be found in either the lateness of the hour or the commonplace encroachments upon his senses.

Damn her.

Nothing could keep her from his thoughts. Nothing could abate the knowledge that Lady Juliana Somerset had come back to England.

The vehicle came to a halt at last in the mews behind his townhome. Cagney House was one of the lesser holdings of his father, the Marquess of Northampton. But as Viscount Shelbourne and the heir to the marquisate, it was his London home. A place of respite from his father's tyrannical insistence Shelbourne marry and secure the line.

Marriage would happen soon enough.

Lady Hermione Carmichael was as uninspiring as a piece of buttered toast, with hair the color of a murky puddle and the personality of a plate of biscuits. Her face was plain, her voice was quiet, and she would never refuse him when he asked for her hand in marriage.

Unlike *her*.

But he would not think of *her* now, curse her to the devil. On a growl, he leapt from his carriage and stalked into a pelting wall of rain, much to the consternation of his groom, who called out some nonsense about an umbrella.

"Fuck the umbrella," he called over his shoulder with a dismissive wave of his hand.

Mayhap dousing himself in rain would prove the diversion he required.

"But sir," came the protest, along with scurrying boots.

Shelbourne did not bother to turn. "If you follow me with that contraption, I'll shove it up your arse and then open it."

The footsteps stopped.

Excellent.

He was in a grim mood, and he had no wish to be fussed over by well-intentioned servants. He had every expectation of settling in the library, calling for a bottle, and continuing down the path of destruction he had begun earlier this evening. Or had it been afternoon?

Who the devil cared?

What he needed was more wine, and he needed it now. If he spent the day with his head hung over a chamber pot, at least he would not be thinking of the flame-haired temptress who had given him her innocence and then laughed at his offer of marriage.

Shelbourne made his way into the main hall, dripping water as he went. His butler hastened toward him, looking as if he had just caught a mischief of rats in the larder.

"What can it be, Wentworth?" he demanded, irritated by the thought of any domestic squabble that would dare to stand between him and his mission of getting so soused he would forget her name.

Hell, he may as well get so tap-hackled he forgot his own name as well.

Wentworth bowed. "Lord Shelbourne, there is a visitor who has been awaiting you for the last several hours. I have repeatedly informed her you are not at home, and that the hour is late, but she refuses to leave. She claims to be a lady, or I would have had her removed well before now."

A visitor? At this time of night? Christ, it was likely half past two in the morning.

It could not be Charlotte. Although she had begged him to visit her this evening, he had known he would only be thinking of Julianna while bedding his mistress. It was no mistake he had chosen a stunning redheaded actress as his current paramour. He would sooner eat a pail of nails than allow himself to imagine he was fucking Julianna.

Mayhap he would have to get thoroughly drunk before he visited Charlotte next.

Or find a replacement.

One with hair as black as his heart.

"I do not want to be troubled, Wentworth," he snapped, shaking himself from his reveries. "Send her on her way and see to it that a bottle of Sauternes is delivered to the library, won't you?"

"Of course, my lord." Wentworth bowed. "I would be more than happy to do so."

"Oh, and Wentworth?" he called belatedly. "Mayhap some towels as well. I am a bit…wet."

Without awaiting a response, Shelbourne trudged down the hall to the library, leaving a veritable river in his wake. Once within the familiar, shelf-lined walls, he discarded his wet coat, tugged open his necktie, and flicked open the buttons of his waistcoat. His pocket watch would live to see another day.

A consultation of it revealed he was either more inebriated than he had supposed, or he was sorely in need of spectacles.

"Fuck," he swore, and tossed the elegant gold timepiece to the floor atop his sodden coat.

He paced the library while he waited for his bottle, his soaked shoes making interminable squishing sounds that had him toeing them off and hastening toward the door. Where the devil was Wentworth with his wine?

He was almost to the threshold when the clack of approaching footfalls in the hall alerted him to the presence of someone else. Someone who was decidedly not Wentworth. Someone who was wearing a lady's heeled boots, and who walked with purpose.

"Madam! I beg of you, please stop or we shall have no recourse but to bodily remove you from his lordship's home."

The breathless, frustrated male voice calling after the owner of the boots was undeniably his butler's.

"I will not go without speaking to Lord Shelbourne first," countered a feminine voice he knew too well.

Except, there was something about it that sounded... different. A change in the accents. They were less clipped and precise, more drawled and drawn out. But there was no mistaking it otherwise. He had never heard another quite like it, throaty and yet innocent, husky and melodious.

Once upon a time, he'd experienced the singular pleasure of hearing that voice moan his name. But that had been when he had been deep inside her, when he had thought it an undisputed fact that they would be married.

Rage soared through him. He stormed toward the library door with purposeful strides, reaching the threshold just as she came barreling into him. They collided, the impact sending him staggering backward.

Into a bloody table, as it happened.

One moment, he was on his feet, and the next, he was on

his back, staring up at the intricate plasterwork on the ceiling. Only, he could not truly see the delineations. The ceiling was deuced blurry.

His arse and his head were sore.

So, too, his pride.

The combination of which was only made worse when the loveliest face he had ever beheld hovered over him. *Good God.* His first sight of her in two years, and she was sideways, presiding over him like some sort of avenging deity.

She was no deity, however.

If anything, Lady Julianna Somerset was a witch.

"Shelbourne," she said, as if his name produced a bad taste in her mouth.

And mayhap it did, because Christ knew hers did in his.

"My lady," he gritted, clenching his jaw.

"Madam, come this way, if you please," said Wentworth then, reaching for Lady Julianna, his sideways face a mask of concern. "Your lordship, are you injured?"

Was he injured?

Ha!

The sudden urge to laugh hit him.

He clutched his heart. "Mortally wounded."

"My lord?" The butler's brows raised to his hairline.

"'Tis a joke, Wentworth. Get me the goddamn Sauternes, if you please. One glass. The *lady* will not be staying."

At his mocking emphasis on the word lady, Julianna's lush lips tightened.

Damn her thrice to hell and back. How had she gotten more alluring since he had seen her last? Were her bubbies larger? Her eyes bluer? Her hair more vibrant? Skin creamier?

He did *not* fucking care.

"Are you certain, Lord Shelbourne?" Wentworth pressed.

"Utterly." He sat up, rubbing the back of his head. "Get out, Wentworth."

His butler bowed and made haste on his retreat.

Shelbourne turned to his most unwanted—and despised —guest. "What the bloody hell are you doing in my house, Lady Julianna?"

She sniffed the air. "Are you drunk, my lord?"

"Not as drunk as I am about to be," he said cheerily, rising to his considerable height. All the better to tower over her. One thing had not changed. Julianna was still deuced petite, the top of her head not even reaching his shoulders. He refused to think about the way her body had fit with his. "You did not answer my question. Why are you here?"

Her tongue darted over the lush fullness of her lower lip. "I need to speak with you."

He threw back his head and gave in to the mad urge for laughter, which had been flirting with him ever since his tumble to the floor. He laughed. And laughed. And laughed some more.

When he was finished, he took a deep, calming breath, and held her gaze. "How amusing you are. Unfortunately, for you, I do not give a damn what you need."

"Lord Shelbourne," she began.

"Get out, Julianna," he bit out atop anything else she would have said, all pretenses gone. "Now. Before I do something we will both regret."

Want more? Get *Lady Wicked* here!

MORE BY SCARLETT SCOTT

Complete Book List

HISTORICAL ROMANCE

Heart's Temptation

A Mad Passion (Book One)

Rebel Love (Book Two)

Reckless Need (Book Three)

Sweet Scandal (Book Four)

Restless Rake (Book Five)

Darling Duke (Book Six)

The Night Before Scandal (Book Seven)

Wicked Husbands

Her Errant Earl (Book One)

Her Lovestruck Lord (Book Two)

Her Reformed Rake (Book Three)

Her Deceptive Duke (Book Four)

Her Missing Marquess (Book Five)

Her Virtuous Viscount (Book Six)

League of Dukes

Nobody's Duke (Book One)

Heartless Duke (Book Two)

Dangerous Duke (Book Three)

Shameless Duke (Book Four)

Scandalous Duke (Book Five)

ABOUT THE AUTHOR

USA Today and Amazon bestselling author Scarlett Scott writes steamy Victorian and Regency romance with strong, intelligent heroines and sexy alpha heroes. She lives in Pennsylvania and Maryland with her Canadian husband, adorable identical twins, and one TV-loving dog.

A self-professed literary junkie and nerd, she loves reading anything, but especially romance novels, poetry, and Middle English verse. Catch up with her on her website www.scarlettscottauthor.com. Hearing from readers never fails to make her day.

Scarlett's complete book list and information about upcoming releases can be found at www.scarlettscottauthor.com.

Connect with Scarlett! You can find her here:
Join Scarlett Scott's reader's group on Facebook for early excerpts, giveaways, and a whole lot of fun!
Sign up for her newsletter here.
Follow Scarlett on Amazon
Follow Scarlett on BookBub
www.instagram.com/scarlettscottauthor
www.twitter.com/scarscoromance
www.pinterest.com/scarlettscott
www.facebook.com/AuthorScarlettScott

Printed in Great Britain
by Amazon